HAWAIIAN SHADOWS

BOOK THREE: LOKAHI

Edie Claire

For all the Oahu locals who have seen me wandering
around carrying bird-watching binoculars and a notebook
and wearing my hair in a braid with a visor perched on my
head looking like a total loser tourist person —
and who have nevertheless managed to smile,
or at least politely ignore me.

Thank you for sharing your home.

Lokahi:
A Hawaiian word meaning
"harmony" or "unity."

chapter one

Author's Note: This is the third book in a series. I promise you'll enjoy all the books much, much more if you read them in order. So if you can, please start with *Book One: Wraith*, even if it means you have to return this one first. I promise you'll be glad you made the effort!

My exhausted muscles screamed in protest as I pulled myself out of the water at the shallow end of the community pool, dragged my feet across what little grass still survived on the lawn by this point in August, and collapsed on top of my beach towel.

"You go, girl!" my friend Lacey hooted from her perch on the lifeguard's chair. "Are we shooting for the Olympic trials now, or what?"

"Next year, maybe," a cheerful male voice rang out. Zane was smiling down at me, his wet blond curls glinting in the sun and his green eyes laughing. He gave his head a shake and sprayed me with water droplets.

"Nice try," I moaned. "But I am never moving again."

He dropped down onto his own towel with a chuckle. "You're doing great, Kali. I'm proud of you."

"Thanks," I said dryly, feeling my muscles twitch like I was being slowly electrocuted. It's not like I was in bad shape. I was seventeen and I'd been dancing since I was six. I was limber. I was flexible. I was fit. But doing sixty thousand laps in four different strokes could take it out of a person. Particularly when they'd only just learned to swim two months ago.

"I'm pretty wiped myself, actually," Zane admitted,

although he wasn't even breathing hard. "I've still got a long way to go."

"Only because your goals for yourself are insane!" I protested between pants. Only five months had passed since he'd nearly bled to death in a car accident, and he knew perfectly well that you didn't bounce back from massive internal injury and a prolonged coma overnight. His doctors had warned him that it could take a year for him to fully regain his strength. He was already progressing way ahead of schedule, but nothing short of his former peak-condition, eighteen-year-old body was good enough for him. "You're too hard on yourself," I repeated for the fortieth time.

And you're too hard on me, I thought but didn't say. I knew I shouldn't say it. He'd helped me get over my fear of drowning and taught me how to swim after every other swimming instructor on the planet had long since given up. Of course, it helped that he was drop-dead gorgeous, not to mention the fact that splashing around in the water with your boyfriend was a whole lot more fun than being a kid taking lessons from some random dude at the Y. Still, to give Zane credit, he *was* a really good teacher. It's just that once he'd gotten it into his head that we should go surfing together on the shores of Oahu, he'd turned into the personal fitness trainer from hell.

Unfortunately for my aching muscles, I was madly in love with him anyway.

I turned sideways on my towel. It took effort.

"You said that whenever I hit Goal #8 we could spend a whole afternoon on the beach and then eat dinner at La Ola," I reminded him. "And that we wouldn't have to swim laps the whole next week."

He turned his head toward mine with a smirk. "Dream on. I agreed to the beach and La Ola, no more."

I sighed. "It was worth a shot. Next week *is* the last week of summer, you know."

I cringed to hear the words out loud. They were so darned *sad*. Not that I wasn't looking forward to starting my senior year at Frederick High School in Honolulu. I was. And technically, once Zane moved into the dorms at the University of Hawaii he would be living closer to me than he did right now. But still, I didn't want summer to end. These precious weeks of vacation with Zane had been far too amazing. Too fun-filled. Too warm. Too cuddly. Too blissfully carefree.

Way, way too short.

With my only job being to fix up the family's house in Honolulu and Zane's taking the summer off altogether to recuperate, we'd had a heavenly amount of time to spend together, even if he did live all the way out on the North Shore. Half the time that I'd been pulling up carpet, wiping away grime, and repainting walls he'd been by my side helping me, even though he refused any pay himself. In my free time we'd swum at the pool, toured the island, or just relaxed on the beaches near his place, catching up on a lifetime of dumb stuff from our childhoods, puzzling out how to solve the world's problems, and feeling our way through the whole "relationship" thing one lazy, dreamy day at a time.

Now we had only one more week. Then it was back to English Lit and Calculus.

Ugh.

Zane threw me a sexy smile that showed his dimples — the smile that still got to me every time. My tall, boyish figure and unruly crown of dark brown curls might not be society's idea of female perfection, but when he looked at me like that, I couldn't help but feel beautiful. "Don't look so down," he chastised. "Senior year is a happy thing, remember? I'm the one who should be depressed. I'm the one who has to leave the North Shore just when the surf starts pumping!"

"I know," I admitted. "I shouldn't be so bummed. I'm not even sure why I am, really. I do like school. I think it's just that the summer's been so great, and also that..." my words trailed off as bittersweet memories swamped my brain. *Last day of summer.* Back in Wyoming my best friends Kylee and Tara and I had always celebrated in style just like the last day of school, with a little bit of craziness, a lot of laughs, and extreme amounts of junk food. I missed them both terribly.

"You miss Kylee and Tara, don't you?" Zane asked. "Even more when you think about starting school again?"

I smiled at him. "You are creepy perceptive for a guy, you know that?"

He shrugged and lay back flat on his towel. "It's a gift."

I propped myself up on an elbow. "It better not be *that* kind of gift!" I teased. "You and I are gifted enough already, thank you very much. I do *not* want you reading my mind."

He looked at me out of the corner of his eye, then closed both his lids against the sun. There was something in his expression that rang an alarm bell in my brain. He looked almost halfway... *guilty.*

"Zane?" I asked sharply. "You can't read my mind. Can you?"

His eyes flew open. "Of course not."

We stared at each other a moment.

He was definitely hiding something.

Crap!

My heart began to pound. Ever since Zane's near-death experience in March, he'd been able to see ghosts.

Four of them, that we knew of. A guy in his rehab hospital in California, my grandmother Kalia, a former neighbor woman here in Honolulu, and then just last month the ghost of an Australian tourist girl in Haleiwa. He'd been able to help all of them in one way or another, which made his gift maddeningly more useful than either of mine. I could see shadows of the past — explained to me as "residue from bursts of intense emotional energy" — and I could feel the emotions of everyone around me, both the living and the shadow people, too. But the first had made for a freakish childhood and the second would have driven me insane had Kylee's grandmother not taught me a way to shield myself. My "gifts" were a mixed blessing, at best, but at least I had more experience in dealing with them. Despite the fact that Zane had actually been through an out-of-body experience himself, the idea of bumping into another lost soul in the middle of an ordinary day still freaked him out. If he did feel something else going on, something even more weird, he might not want to admit it. Even to himself.

The more I thought about it, the more suspicious I got. Every day, all summer long, I had felt my own abilities increasing. I could see more and feel more, but I also got better at blocking things out. Gifts like mine, I had been told, blossomed with maturity. They also drew strength from the intensity of a person's emotions. And there was no question that every day I spent with Zane, I was falling more deeply in love with him.

Did he feel the same way about me? And if he did, was something else going on with him? Something new?

The idea was as exciting as it was terrifying. Because, now that I thought about it, I *had* noticed that his mind seemed to be wandering more often lately. I would look at him, and his thoughts would be elsewhere, and I would have to get his attention. When I asked what he was thinking about, he never gave a real answer.

Then again, everyone did that sometimes. Was I making something out of nothing?

Lacey cried out suddenly, startling me. I sat up and looked toward where she sat on her lifeguard's chair, but it was clear that no one was drowning. She didn't look distressed; she looked giddy with happiness. I followed her eyes as she glanced toward the pool's front gate. Then I exhaled with annoyance.

"Rebound guy's back," I mumbled to Zane.

"Austin!" Lacey called, twisting in her chair to wave at the tall, lean blond-headed guy who waited outside the entrance. "I'm on break in two minutes! Hang on!"

"Don't count on it, Lace," I grumbled under my breath.

I've never been the meddling type. Really, I haven't. But watching Lacey, who had just gotten her heart broken at the beginning of the summer by a faithless longtime boyfriend, fawn over such an obvious player was seriously painful.

"He bailed on her three times last week, you know," I whispered to Zane bitterly. "*Three times!*" Lacey had been "dating" Austin half the summer now, which as far as I could tell meant that whenever he was actually with her, he treated her like she was his girlfriend. The problem was that when he wasn't with her, he might or might not answer texts and he completely ignored phone calls. They would talk in vague terms about getting together in the future, but when it came to making actual plans, he would get cagey. Whenever Lace did pin him down to doing anything it was usually only a couple hours beforehand, and even then, half the time he would cancel at the last minute for stupid reasons or no reason at all. What made me crazy was that whenever he actually did show, Lacey acted like he was doing her a favor.

The guy was cute, there was no question about that. And he could act very sweet. But I hated the way he treated her and I hated even more the fact that she put up with it.

"She should know better!" I continued to bemoan. "Particularly after what happened with Ty. Can't she see that he's just not that into her? She's going to get herself hurt again."

Zane cracked open an eye and looked at me, but made no comment.

"What does that look mean?"

He smirked. "Can't you read my mind?"

"You know I can't!"

"It means," he said mildly, "matchmaking never works. Let it go, Kali."

"Let what go?"

He threw me another look, and this time I suppose I could read his mind. He knew there was another reason why Lacey's infatuation with rebound guy got under my skin. She was supposed to be with somebody else. She and our mutual friend Matt were perfect for each other. Unfortunately, neither one of them seemed aware of this obvious truth. So what if I was anxious to... well, help fate along?

"I have no idea what you're talking about," I replied with a smirk of my own.

One of the lifeguards stepped up to relieve Lacey and she jumped down out of the chair. Lace was short and slightly on the plump side with naturally blond hair and friendly blue eyes. The smile she flashed at Austin lit up her whole face, and as she practically skipped off toward the pool gates, she looked dazzlingly pretty.

No, Lacey! I secretly begged her. *You're too good for him!*

She kept going anyway. Austin met her with a showy hug followed by a PG-13 kiss, and I turned my head away and flopped flat on my towel again.

"Just give me five more minutes to catch my breath, okay?" I said to Zane. "Then how about we go to Turtle Bay and do some snorkeling? We could walk north up the beach, too, toward the bird sanctuary. I like it up there. It's practically deserted... so peaceful."

Zane made no response that I could hear, which I decided to take as agreement. His eyes were closed, and I closed mine also, and we both lay still, soaking up the sun. The moment was surprisingly restful. The pool wasn't nearly as loud and chaotic as it had been at the beginning of the summer. The littlest kids were still coming, but most of the older crowd had already bored of the summer routine and gone back to staring at screens all day. Personally, if it weren't for missing Tara and Kylee, I wouldn't care if I never saw a screen again.

I walked my fingers across the grass between us and onto Zane's beach towel. My hand brushed his, and the amazing sensation of warmth and happiness that I'd become used to now — but still loved to feel every time we touched — spread up my arm and put a smile on my face. *Oh, yeah.* Who needed screens? The real world suited me just fine.

My fingers curled around his. But he did not hold my hand back. His own fingers were limp.

Was he asleep? I propped myself up on an elbow and looked at him. His eyes were closed. His head was tilted slightly away from me. "Zane?"

He made no response. My heart skipped a beat. I sat up, put a hand on his shoulder, and shook him gently.

His head wobbled a bit, but his eyes didn't open.

I totally panicked.

"Zane!" I cried. I patted his cheek, but he made no response. I pried open his lids, and one beautiful eye stared back at me. Blank. Unseeing. I jiggled him by the shoulder again. He was warm. He was breathing. What was wrong with him?

My body went cold as ice. All at once it was as though this whole, magical summer had never happened, as though every incredible minute of it had been nothing but a dream. I was back in that long-term care home in Nebraska, looking at a Zane who was sickly pale and comatose and barely alive, and I didn't know if I had gotten to him in time, if he was too far gone already, if he would ever wake up again...

"Zane!" I pleaded at a near-scream, my voice frantic as I put both my hands on his shoulders and shook him again, hard.

"What?" he cried out gruffly, pulling himself up onto his elbows with a jerk. "Kali, what is wrong with you?"

I let go of his shoulders, then sank slowly back on my heels. My whole body trembled. If I didn't love the guy so much, I would definitely kill him.

"What's wrong with *me?*" I sputtered. "You were... like, in a daze or something. I couldn't wake you up!"

He stared back at me with confusion. After a few seconds, his expression turned grim. Then he looked at me apologetically. "I scared you, didn't I?"

I nodded. There wasn't much point in denying it. My breath was coming in ragged gulps.

"I'm sorry," he said sincerely, sitting up. "Why don't we head on out to the beach?"

My heart fell. I wanted a hug. I needed a hug. But it didn't look like I was going to get one. Zane had always insisted that the intensity of the physical vibe between us was way beyond natural, and because of that, I guess, he was always a little guarded. But over the summer I thought we'd managed to work that out. He knew when I wanted to be held, and he could handle that now. He could handle kissing me, too — as long as I didn't push it when he needed to back off. But right now, we were clearly out of sync again.

He stood and pulled up his towel.

I rose on my own still-shaky legs and did the same. We dried off and slipped back in our clothes and shoes, and I kept trying to catch his gaze, but couldn't. He was intentionally avoiding my eyes. "Ready?" he asked finally, looking off toward the parking lot as he dangled his keys in his hand.

There was definitely something wrong with him. "Those don't work in my car," I reminded.

He looked down at his keys with a dazed expression, then dropped them back in a pocket. "Oh, right. What I meant to say was, 'I'm ready. Let's roll!'"

His attempt at a smile was beyond pathetic.

I frowned at him. "I've seen better acting in those commercials where a car dealer just stands there screaming at the camera."

Zane frowned back at me. His mother had been a professional actress, and ordinarily he was very talented himself. I knew my jab would get to him, and I felt bad about that, but I was determined to make him look me in the eyes, which he did without thinking. And the instant our gazes connected, my body felt like ice again.

He wasn't upset with me.

He was afraid.

chapter 2

"All right," I said firmly, sitting down on a fallen tree trunk where the sand met the scrubby woods several minutes' walk north of Turtle Bay. I patted the empty spot on the log beside me. There was a shadow surfer stretched out on the beach by my feet, who I ignored. "I'm not driving now, so you don't have to worry about me flipping out and killing us both. And there's nobody else around to overhear. So, *talk* to me, Zane."

He sat down, the look on his face somewhat embarrassed. He wrapped an arm around my shoulders and gave me a friendly squeeze, which felt heavenly. "It's not that big a deal, really. I'm sorry if I scared you before. I guess I just zoned out for a minute."

"Not buying," I replied.

He sighed and dropped his arm. The temperature around me fell ten degrees, and I quickly reached back, grabbed his hand, and put it around my shoulders again.

He looked at me oddly.

"I keep telling you," I explained. "Every time you do that, it's like giving a toddler an ice cream cone, letting him take one bite, and then stealing it away again."

He chuckled and pulled me closer. "Sorry."

"Apology accepted," I said with a smile, snuggling in. "Now, I mean it. *Talk.*"

He looked out over the ocean. It was a classic late summer day. The sky was mostly blue, but with patches of low clouds scudding by in quick succession. The air was warm and the breeze mild. The surf was nearly flat, but little lines of waves still rolled onto the beach, transforming into spray as they crashed into the twisted coils of black lava rock that lined this stretch of the North Shore. The frothy seawater swirled lazily in the shallow tide pools, some escaping back into the ocean, the rest sinking deeper into the coarse brown sand.

"I don't know what to say," Zane remarked quietly.

"Tell me what you're afraid of," I pleaded.

He procrastinated for another long, agonizing moment. "I'm not sure," he said finally. "But something weird is definitely happening to me. Something I don't understand. It has to do with my imagination and... seeing things in my head."

"What kind of things?" I asked, keeping my tone matter-of-fact. I knew from personal experience that the absolute last thing he needed was to worry about whether *I* thought he was losing his mind or making it all up — or both. I didn't doubt him in the slightest, and rationally he should know that. But as cool as Zane had always been with my abilities, he still couldn't seem to wrap his head around his own.

"I'd guess you'd call them hallucinations," he said miserably.

"I would not," I disagreed. "Hallucinations are when your brain plays tricks on you. Chemicals misfire and show you things that aren't really there. That's not what's happening when I see the shadows. It's not what happens when you see ghosts, either. What makes you think that's what's happening to you now?"

He dropped his arm again and stood up.

Drat.

"It's not that I see things out *there*... in the scene in front of me," he tried to explain. "What's been happening is that, sometimes, when I close my eyes and I'm kind of... you know, drifting? Then another scene will pop into my head. Like a dream, but clearer. Just as clear as this beach looks to me right now. I can look at it and look into it and see everything in it. I can even sort of move around it, just by thinking about where else I'd like to go. But it's not like I'm actually walking around, touching things. All I can do is see it, like a vision. But I can't control anything about it, and then I wake back up or somebody gets my attention and it's just gone."

A gust of wind tossed Zane's blond curls about his face. I hated to see him so troubled. There was very little that got him down, and I suspected that as strange as what he'd admitted was, it probably wouldn't sound that scary to most people. But most people didn't understand. They didn't know what it was like to lose control of your own brain, to have no idea what was happening in your head, to honestly worry about whether the wellspring of your private mind, the part of you that nobody else could see, was supernatural... or pathological.

I couldn't stand it. I stood up, wrapped my arms around his waist, and buried my head in his shoulder. *Bliss.*

"There's nothing wrong with you, Zane," I assured him. "At least, nothing that isn't also wrong with me. You know we're weird. Both of us. Especially both of us together."

I raised my head and gave him a knowing smile.

He returned it.

I'd never had a boyfriend before, so as far as how his touch made me feel, I had nothing to compare it to. He'd never had a steady girlfriend either, but when he insisted that the effect I had on him was above and beyond normal teenage chemistry, I believed him. The nature of our effects on each other differed a little, although exactly how, we had trouble describing. But the chemistry thing and the bizarre abilities thing were definitely intertwined.

My abilities had grown stronger after I met him. Both our abilities grew stronger the closer we became.

"You think it's some... 'gift?'" he asked cautiously.

I nodded.

"But what?" he questioned. "What's the point? It's not like the shadows or the ghosts. The things I've seen are just... well, *boring*. Nothing even happens!"

"That doesn't mean anything."

"But how can you be sure?" he countered, frustrated. "It's so different from the other things. How do I know it's not some funky side effect of the concussion? Or the blood loss? Or some other physical problem? There's no other way to make sense of it!"

My mind flashed on a memory of the glazed look he'd had in his eyes back at the pool, and my pulse began to pound again. Could he be right? Could it be a seizure? He had just swum laps. He was tired. But you don't snap out of a seizure just because someone yells at you. And you don't have lucid visions of boring, ordinary real places, either.

No. Zane was perfectly healthy. He was fine.

He was developing some new ability — I was sure of it. We hadn't actually exchanged the big "L" words yet, but he certainly acted like he cared, and if what he felt for me was anywhere near as strong as what I felt for him...

That magic word. *If.*

I preferred to think positively.

"The shadows made no sense to me for most of my life," I reminded. "Whatever this new ability of yours is, it might not be fully developed yet."

He pulled away enough to face me squarely. "You're really not worried that it's *not* an ability?"

I smiled at him. "Not for a second. So cut out the dramatics and deal, okay?" I took his hand, swung us both around to where we were facing up the beach again, and started walking. "Let's analyze what we've got so far. What 'scenes' have you seen, exactly?"

His eyes twinkled at me a moment, his expression tender. Then he leaned over and kissed me on the cheek.

Triple bliss.

"When it first started happening," he began as we walked, "it was just flashes. Random stretches of beach. Most often at night. I tried to talk myself out of worrying about it because I'm always thinking about the beach. But even then, I knew it was different. The images were just too clear, too real. Too three-dimensional. Then gradually, they started lasting longer. I had one where I was looking at the inside of the Foodland. Do you believe that? I mean, *why?* And then, there were a lot of times I saw..." He hesitated. "Well, your house."

I stopped walking. "*My* house? What about my house? Am I in it?"

"No, no," he laughed. "It's just, like, rooms in your house. Empty rooms."

"Which rooms?"

He smirked. "Well, yours, mainly."

I exhaled roughly.

"Well, you asked!" He laughed again. He swung my hand and pulled me until we were walking again. "I don't try to do it. It's just that sometimes, when I'm thinking of you, I'll start to see an image of your room. *Not* you, just your room. But only a flash. A couple seconds, maybe." His expression turned sober again. "What could that possibly mean?"

I considered the question, but came up blank. The idea of his having visions of my room was almost as disturbing as his reading my mind. "When you zoned out at the pool earlier," I asked. "What were you thinking of then?"

He looked around where we were walking. "Actually, I was thinking of here," he answered. "You said we should come here, and I thought that sounded nice. The next thing I knew, I was looking at it."

I arched an eyebrow at him. Now we were getting somewhere. "Exactly where along here? You mean this whole beach, or this exact spot?"

He considered a moment, looking forward and back. "Well, I don't... I mean, we don't come here often enough that I have all the landmarks memorized."

"Of course you don't," I said, stopping again. "Which is why, if you do remember specifics, we'll know it's not just a memory — or a hallucination. What *do* you remember?"

Zane concentrated for a second. He looked up the beach a few yards to where a log of driftwood lay roughly perpendicular to the surf. "I remember seeing that," he answered, pointing. "A little boy in red swim trunks jumped over it. He was running ahead of his parents, and he jumped over it one way and then the other, and then they caught up with him and he ran on."

I blinked at him, surprised. "I thought you didn't see people. Only empty scenes."

He seemed surprised himself. "Oh, right. Well, I guess I see people sometimes. Not people I know or anything. Just background people."

I chuckled. "*Background* people?"

"I guess that sounds stupid, doesn't it? It's just that I'm not really watching them. They're just... there."

I stared at his confused expression another moment, then walked towards the log. There was no one else visible right now either up or down the beach. There weren't any little footprints in the sand around the log, but that was no surprise, as it was high tide now and the water was regularly lapping over the whole area. "Well," I said speculatively, "I guess we can rule out your having visions of your own future, anyway. There's no little boy in red trunks here now."

Zane looked relieved. "I don't want to see the future," he said thoughtfully. "Not unless I could change it, anyway. That would be awful."

I started to point out that just because he hadn't seen his own future didn't mean he hadn't seen *the* future, but I decided not to go there. "Well, it's close to high tide now. Was it high tide when you saw this log before?"

His forehead creased with thought. "It would have to be. Close to it, anyway. Waves were definitely hitting where the boy was jumping, and his parents were walking in the dry sand, and there was just a narrow strip of it up the beach, like now."

"What else did you see?" I pressed.

"I moved on around that bend," he continued, pointing ahead to where the shore jutted out, then cut away again. "I could see a long way from the other side, and there were no other people around. It looked so calm and peaceful... I started to really enjoy myself. But then there was something annoying... Oh! The bottle. Somebody had stuck a water bottle on the end of a branch. It annoyed me that I couldn't throw it away. And then... And then you yelled at me and nearly shook my head off."

I ignored the jibe. I was a woman on a mission. I walked on around the bend and looked up the beach. There was a shadow couple walking toward us, holding hands. But Zane couldn't see them. There was only one living person in sight, a man far ahead of us standing knee-deep in the water who appeared to be fishing. "Did you see him before?" I asked.

Zane shook his head. Then his eyes moved to the tree line, and his pace quickened. This stretch of the beach was rugged, covered with rocks and debris that were difficult to walk over, and by the time he slowed down enough for me to catch up with him, my already abused leg muscles were complaining again.

He stopped walking and made a sharp intake of breath.

"What is it?" I asked worriedly.

He gestured upwards with his chin. I raised my eyes to see an empty blue plastic water bottle sticking off the end of a dead tree branch.

Wow.

I smiled at him. "See there!" I said proudly. "Delayed effect of concussion, indeed."

Zane reached up, pulled down the branch at a lower point, and pulled off the offending recyclable. "Well," he said, not altogether steadily, "at least I can get it down now."

I gave him a hug around the shoulders. "What you saw was real, Zane! This proves it." I laughed to myself. "Someone else might argue that you must have seen that bottle before, even if you didn't consciously remember it. But we both know there's no way, because if you *ever* saw it, it wouldn't still be here!"

"True," he agreed. "So... am I seeing the past, or what? It can't be the future."

I kept holding him. I would hold him all day if I could get away with it. "Well, we really don't know for sure. It's been more than two hours ago now that you saw what you saw."

He threw me a nervous look. "It is just past high tide, isn't it?"

I nodded. Near high tide, the water level rose and dropped more gradually, so the window of time during which the boy could have jumped over the log into a wave could be broad. The events he saw *could* have happened after he envisioned them, but before we got here. He could have been watching them in real time. Or it could have all happened a month ago.

"We'll figure it out," I assured. "And if it has a purpose, we'll figure that out, too." I fixed him with a fake stern look. "Just don't go all geeked-out superhero on me this time, all right?"

He smirked.

I loved that he was a good guy who liked helping people. But his desire to help ghosts in need — particularly that whiny Australian girl — could get inconvenient. Zane seemed to feel that if he'd been given a gift, he *had* to use it, and it was a responsibility he took very seriously. But in my humble girlfriend's opinion, there was such a thing as going overboard.

The idea of being able to tell the future was distressing to him, and I understood why. If there was one thing Zane hated, it was feeling helpless. He didn't even remember the time he'd spent as a wraith, but I knew he remembered the frustration of it. I could see it in his eyes just now, when he talked about wanting to get the water bottle but not being able to grasp it. Being able to *see* the future, but having no power to affect it, would be hell on earth for him.

On the other hand, if he *could* affect it, I would most likely never see my boyfriend again. Lacey and I would spend all our Friday nights together binge-watching mindless television while chugging diet shakes and sending texts no one answered.

I shuddered at the thought.

Zane crunched the bottle in his hand, stuffed it in a pocket, and hugged me back. "Hey, I am what I am," he replied, his usual healthy ego apparently still intact. "There's no telling how many damsels in distress I can save with this new and fabulous ability to find trash on deserted stretches of beach."

I sucked in a breath and said nothing. He was kidding, of course. He was always kidding. But I wasn't. Whatever this new ability of his turned out to be, his putting it to good use like the kind-hearted guy he was would almost certainly involve both distress and damsels. It was a good thing I wasn't the insecure type.

Really, I wasn't.

He stepped away from our hug, but kept hold of my hand and led me back down the beach the way we had come. "Let's get to that snorkeling. We can work up a good appetite for your reward dinner."

My stomach rumbled. I'd been starving for an hour already. Swimming laps always made me ravenous. "I get dessert too, right?" I bargained. "I think I've earned it."

He stopped walking and looked at me. His eyes sparkled affectionately, and he gave me one of his most knee-weakening smiles. Then he reached out one hand, brushed my wild black curls behind one ear, and kissed me.

chapter 3

Zane seemed lost in thought again as we walked across the crowded parking lot of the shopping plaza in the North Shore town of Haleiwa. It was early enough that we should still be able to get a table at the popular Mexican restaurant, but the tourist business at the adjoining shops was brisk, and nearly every parking spot was taken. We strolled past the art gallery, various clothing and beach supply stores, specialty snack shops, and a realty outfit toward the bright red-painted doors of *La Ola*.

"I hope Matt's working tonight," I mused. "I guess it's pretty likely. He seems to be working every chance he gets now. Lacey said she hasn't seen him in a month."

"He's here," Zane murmured, looking down at his feet.

I tried to catch his eyes, but he seemed fascinated with the ground in front of him. "How do you know?" I asked.

He looked up at me and blinked uncertainly. "What?"

I stopped walking. "I asked how you know that Matt is working tonight."

His eyes flickered with distress. "Did I say that?"

Whoa. Could it really happen that subconsciously? "Zane," I asked pointedly. "Were you having a vision just now?"

He considered a moment, then took a deep breath and started walking again. "Maybe. I... well, yeah. I guess so. I was thinking about *La Ola* and I imagined Matt working inside. It was... just a flash. Nothing earthshattering."

He sounded thoroughly annoyed with himself.

I frowned. An attitude adjustment was definitely in order, here. And where exactly was the happy-go-lucky surfer wraith who kept insisting that *my* seeing dead people everywhere was the greatest thing *ever?*

He reached out to grasp the metal pepper-shaped door handle, but I stopped him with a hand on his wrist. "Wait. What kind of shirt was Matt wearing?"

His green eyes studied me warily as he thought about it. "Like, a red polo shirt. I think."

I nodded and offered a smile of encouragement.

He smiled weakly back.

We entered the restaurant and were seated by a familiar hostess who confirmed that my future classmate at Frederick High was indeed on duty. She led us to a prime booth in his assigned section, and within seconds the football/water polo player appeared, toting the obligatory basket of tortilla chips, bowl of salsa, and two ice waters. On recognizing us, his handsome baby face lit up into a smile, and his friendly voice boomed. "Hey, guys! What's up? Haven't seen you two in a while. You haven't been cheating on me over at Dos Amigos, have you?"

I chuckled. Zane faked a smile.

Matt was wearing a bright red polo shirt.

"Never!" I protested. "Really. How could you even think that? The way they put rice inside their enchiladas? Please."

"Yeah," he teased back, serving his wares and then tucking the empty tray under his arm. "I thought you had better taste."

"We do," I agreed. "We're just poor, that's all. Been having a lot of picnics from Foodland."

"I hear that." Matt cast a glance at Zane, who was being uncharacteristically quiet. "You okay, dude?" Matt punched him in the shoulder with his order pad. "You look like you just saw a ghost, man."

I choked back a laugh, gracelessly spitting out a sip of

ice water. *Awesomely smooth, Kali.*

Zane threw me a glare.

"Oo-kay," Matt said humorously, looking from one of us to the other. "Story behind that. Too bad I've gotta work. What do you guys want to drink? Are you ready to order?"

I asked Matt for his always-sage advice on the menu, and by the time I made up my mind, Zane seemed to have recovered his usual good humor. "Surprise me," he told Matt. "Bring out whatever looks good."

Matt gave him a smirk and a fist bump. "Will do."

When we were alone again, I reached across the table and took Zane's hands in mine. "Since you're obviously going to obsess over this until we figure it out, why don't we just figure it out? I propose a test."

He arched his eyebrows at me. "Didn't we just do that?"

I shook my head. "We know it's real. But what are you seeing exactly? What brings it on, and how can you control it?" I smiled encouragingly at him. "Trust me. Control is everything."

He pulled one hand away just long enough to feed himself a chip. Then he fed me one. "Okay," he said when we'd finished crunching. "What do you suggest?"

I glanced around the restaurant. "Let's keep it simple, to start with. Let's see if you can imagine what's happening in the kitchen, right on the other side of that wall."

I gestured with our joined hands, and Zane looked toward the swinging saloon doors that led behind the bar area. We could hear voices and clinking dishes, and it seemed as though steam was wafting out the opening and into the room. Zane stared at the door for several moments, but then he shook his head.

"I've never been in the kitchen," he said.

"Does that matter?"

"Don't know. Maybe. All I know is I'm getting zilch."

I considered. "Interesting."

Matt's tall, solidly built form burst through the doors carrying a tray with a lemonade and an iced tea. He crossed over to us in a few strides and set the drinks down with a flourish. "How's Lace, by the way?" he asked. "I haven't seen her in ages."

"We just saw her and Austin at the pool earlier," I reported.

Matt's face fell. "Oh? They still going out?"

"Unfortunately."

Zane bumped my foot with his toe.

"Why do you say that?" Matt asked, looking genuinely concerned.

I shrugged. "I don't think he makes her very happy," I said honestly, giving Zane a stubborn nudge back. "But then, she didn't ask me."

"Oh," Matt said flatly. He stood awkwardly for a moment, staring at our bowl of chips. "Um... you guys need anything else right now?"

"No, we're good," Zane said quickly.

Matt's expression returned to normal. "Cool. Food'll be up soon."

He turned and headed back to the kitchen. "Don't start," I said to Zane. "There is a method to my madness."

He shook his head at me and dipped a chip.

"Lacey will thank me eventually," I insisted, dunking a chip of my own.

Zane quirked an eyebrow but said nothing else, and for a few minutes we concentrated on emptying the chip basket. Then I reached out and took hold of his hands again.

"Let's try having you imagine someplace you're more

familiar with. Like my house," I suggested. "Just sit back, relax, and concentrate on something specific. Like maybe my lanai?"

Zane settled more comfortably in his seat, although he couldn't really sit back without letting go of my hands. He closed his eyes and was still for a while, but then he shook his head and exhaled with frustration. "It's not working," he said. "When I try to think about your lanai I just think about you, and I know you're here with me, so I think about here instead."

"What if you relax instead of concentrating?" I suggested. "It seems to be more of an unconscious mind thing, after all."

He closed his eyes and let his shoulders slump, and I began to caress the backs of his hands with my thumbs.

His eyes flew open.

"Did you get an image?" I asked excitedly.

"Oh, I'm getting images all right," he said wryly. "But when you do that, they're *not* of your lanai."

I pulled back my hands. "Sorry."

He grinned at me. "No problem." He crossed his arms over his chest, leaned back against the seat of the booth, and stretched his feet out under the table. "All right," he reported again. "I'm relaxing. What am I supposed to think about? Besides you and your bedroom, maybe?"

"Um... yeah," I agreed. "How about outside the restaurant? You've certainly been there. Try to picture where we parked the car. Look around and find me a chicken."

He laughed. "A chicken?"

"Yes," I demanded playfully. "Start at the car, and then scout all around it until you come to a regulation, wild Hawaiian chicken. They're always out there; it's bound to happen. Then tell me exactly where it is and what it looks like, and I'll go outside and see if it's there."

He cracked open one eye and smiled at me. "You're a genius."

"Old news," I quipped. "Get busy."

His posture relaxed gradually, and he remained still for several minutes, during which I emptied the chip basket of any broken bits big enough to hold between two fingers and dip into the salsa. Then I sunk even lower and shamelessly scraped the paper liner for any crumbs that would stick to my fingers. Geez, I was starving!

A scream, a shout, and a loud crash of metal assaulted my ears. I jumped up in my seat, banging my thighs on the table. I looked out the window of the restaurant toward the sound but I couldn't see anything; the windows were colored glass. I heard a sudden thud and a scuffle and glanced toward Zane. He hadn't reacted to the sound when I did, but now he was out of the booth and running toward the door.

"Wait!" I called frantically, following him.

We joined the hostess and several other patrons rushing to the parking lot. Not far from where I'd parked my dad's car, a shiny new sedan had completely crumpled its trunk by running backwards into the rear of a parked minivan. As we approached, two obviously drunk middle-aged women were standing outside of the offending car, helping to pull a third occupant out of the rear compartment from in between the front seats. Apparently, both rear doors were jammed. None of the three well-dressed, heavily accessorized women appeared to be injured. In fact, they were laughing their heads off. "Don't wo-worry!" one of them yelled loudly to the gathering crowd, her speech slurred with drink. "It's a rr-rental!"

The other women hooted with laughter again.

"Are you insane?" a man yelled angrily, approaching

them from the direction of the minivan. "You almost hit my son!" He gestured emphatically towards a woman standing just to the side of the damaged van. She was holding a baby about a year old. The baby was crying. So was she. A stroller lay sideways on the ground beside her.

"You absolutely did!" another woman accused. "I saw the whole thing! And every one of you's drunk!"

"I called 911 already!"

"So did I!"

"Nobody let 'em go anywhere till the cops get here!"

"Ha! They can barely walk!"

The heavily accessorized women stopped laughing.

I breathed a sigh of relief that no one seemed to be hurt. But when I looked up at Zane, my anxiety level shot back up. He was far too tanned to go pale, but if his stiff posture and unsteady lower jaw were any indication, the guy was practically in shock.

"Come on, Zane," I said gently, taking his hand and attempting to pull him away. "Nobody's hurt, thank goodness."

The drunk women stumbled to a nearby picnic table, where they settled without protest, looking suitably grim. The baby's cries gradually subsided. At last Zane walked away with me, but instead of going back into the restaurant he veered off just outside the door and stopped to lean against a tree trunk. He ran a hand through his curls and blew out a breath.

"Are you okay?" I asked worriedly.

He shook his head. "I *saw* it, Kali," he whispered. "I saw the whole thing."

I stepped closer to him and steeled myself. "Tell me."

"It's... It's obviously real-time," he said raggedly. "I thought about your car, and the parking lot, and as soon as I relaxed enough to let my mind drift, there it was. Like a whole other world. Bright as day, crystal clear, right there in front of my face. It was so weird... I knew I was supposed to be doing something specific, but I couldn't remember what. And I had the feeling that if I thought about it too hard, I would wake up and I'd lose the scene. How bizarre is that? So I... I never even looked for a chicken. I was just moving aimlessly around the parking lot, and then I heard those women laughing and I saw them get in the car and I had the most horrible feeling."

There was a quaver in his voice — so slight most people wouldn't hear it. But to me it rang out loud as a foghorn. I moved closer to his side. "Zane," I said firmly. "Never mind. I understand what happened. Don't do this to yourself."

"The parking lot was so busy," he continued, speaking so low I could barely hear him. "There were people everywhere. I wanted someone to notice the women, to stop them, but no one did. They got in and started the car and pulled out, and I felt myself... well, it was like I was inside the car with them. And I could see that the driver wasn't shifting out of reverse. I could see her foot move to the accelerator anyway."

"*Zane*," I tried again. "That's enough. I get it. You don't have to—"

"Then I moved out of the car and I could see the woman and the stroller and the baby," he continued, his green eyes awash with horror. "I could see the car moving right towards them, the mother reaching down with the baby in her arms. She was just about to buckle the baby in, and the car kept coming—"

"And the father shouted!" I interrupted desperately. "And the mother heard and no one was hurt. That's all that matters."

His tortured eyes met mine. "I couldn't *do* anything,

Kali. I couldn't yell, I couldn't scream. Couldn't shift the gear into drive, couldn't shove the stroller out of the way. *Nothing.*"

I breathed out slowly. Experiencing that kind of helplessness had to feel like a knife twisting in his gut. I remembered the anguish he'd felt as a wraith — I remembered it better than he did. But at some level, the pain of that past must still haunt him.

"Come back inside," I ordered, taking his arm. "I know that was a terrible thing to watch, but there was no harm done. This *is* a gift. We just have to figure out how to control it. Then I'm sure you can put these... visions of yours to good use."

I tugged on his arm and he followed me like a zombie. We returned to our booth to find our dinners waiting for us. "There you are," Matt greeted. "I told the manager you wouldn't dine and dash. I said, 'Hey, man — did you see how hungry they looked? No way would they bolt *before* the entrees.'"

"Sorry, Matt," I said sincerely. "The accident kind of rattled us. But no one got hurt."

"Yeah, I heard," he replied. He threw a curious look at Zane, who was clearly out of sorts again, but this time Matt made no comment. He merely gestured to the steaming food and retreated. "Enjoy!"

We ate in silence for several minutes. Despite the shock of everything that had happened and my concern over Zane's somber mood, I still managed to be ravenously hungry, and it was all I could do not to put my mouth level with my plate and use my fork like a backhoe. Thankfully, after a much slower start, Zane's appetite picked up. By the time he finished off his last bite of rice, I was relieved to see that he almost seemed back to normal.

"You're right, you know," he said, breaking the long

silence. "I've got a lot of nerve feeling sorry for myself. And I've for sure got no business complaining to you, after all you've been through thinking your own gifts were a curse." He offered me a smile and drummed his hands on the tabletop. "There *must* be something good that can come from this... 'special sight' of mine."

I smiled back at him, exhaling with relief. He was going to be okay. "Of course there is," I assured. "Think about it. You can be in one place and see another place in *real time*. How cool is that?"

"Just think," he offered cheerfully, "If I want, I can tell you whether there's a roach crawling across your bedroom ceiling *right now*."

I made a face. "Gee. Thanks."

His eyes sparkled with mischief. "And maybe later, I can see how well that new grout we put along the base of your shower is holding up!"

"Don't even think about it," I said heavily, frowning at him. "That creepy invisible stuff was bad enough when you were a wraith!"

"Yeah, but I can't remember any of it!" he protested innocently.

I growled at him. The supernatural spying thing really had been annoying. "You *told* me you didn't snoop!" I reminded.

He smirked at me. "Oh, well, I'm sure I didn't, then."

I groaned out loud. I hadn't thought about this wrinkle. So he could see anywhere he was familiar with? In real time? And he'd already seen my house?

Crap.

I held his eyes. "I *trust* you, you know," I said pointedly.

He looked back at me a moment, his green eyes dancing with amusement. Then he turned away from me with a sigh. "You would have to put it that way, wouldn't you?"

Matt returned to the table, pulling out his order pad with a flourish. "So, Svenson," he said to Zane. "You springing for the lady's dessert, or what?"

"Yes," I said sharply, thinking of my aching muscles and remembering that I had been looking forward to a long, soaking bath tonight. How could I enjoy it now?

"Yes," I declared again. "He is *definitely* buying dessert."

chapter 4

"So where's Zane?" Lacey asked me as I pulled myself out of the pool the next day, huffing and puffing with exhaustion again. She was surprised that I would come out and swim laps alone, and frankly, so was I. With no drill sergeant barking at me, I could have gotten out of it. But exercise was addictive, and besides, Zane wouldn't take me out surfing in the open ocean until he was convinced I was a strong enough swimmer.

"He's doing something in town today," I panted. "But he's supposed to meet me pretty soon." I collapsed onto my towel and looked up at Lace, who was on a break. Usually she disappeared into the clubhouse, but today she threw her towel on the grass and sat down beside me. She looked tired. And more than a little sad.

"What's Austin up to?" I returned, then felt guilty. I hadn't meant to kick her when she was down.

She sighed. "I don't know. He was supposed to come out today, but now he's not answering my texts. I hate it when guys do that." She gazed out over the pool, probably by sheer force of habit. Then, seeming to realize her mistake, she turned and rotated to where she couldn't see the water at all. "But all guys do it," she continued, catching my eyes with a plea. "Don't they?"

Well, now I was stuck. But I wasn't going to lie to her. "I don't know about all guys," I answered softly. "But Zane doesn't ignore my texts, no."

Lacey lifted her eyebrows skeptically. "Come on. He may be perfect *looking*, but I know he's not perfect *perfect*. Are you saying he's never stood you up for anything?"

"Of course he's not perfect," I retorted, subconsciously covering the bruise over the knuckles of my right hand. It looked like I had hit somebody in the jaw. In reality, I had rammed my hand into the corner of the soap shelf last night while trying to take a shower with the lights off. "But no, he's never promised to be somewhere and then left me waiting, either."

Lacey looked at me with annoyance. "Never? Really?"

"Really," I replied. Then I decided to go for it. "What makes you think all guys pull that kind of stuff?"

She shrugged. Then she looked wistful and fell silent.

I really, *really* wanted to say, "You know, I bet Matt would never do something like that." But I controlled myself.

"I think some guys are just naturally more considerate than others," I said instead. "I mean, not just with girlfriends, but in general."

My phone made the sound of a rooster crowing. I pulled it out of my bag to see a text from Zane.

> Sorry. Something else came up in town. Can we meet later at your house? Like 5ish?

My heart fell. I was disappointed we couldn't spend the afternoon together. But under the circumstances, his timing couldn't be worse. I answered him with a quick "K."

"Bad news?" Lacey asked, showing no glee, but clearly having to work at it.

"He can't make it till later," I reported, tucking the phone back in my bag. *But at least he let me know*, I left unsaid.

Zane never had told me exactly what he was doing today. Which bugged me... a little. Not that he was obligated to report his every movement. Neither one of us were the creepy controlling type. But we generally *did* know what each other was up to, just because we were close, and we talked a lot. When he said he couldn't make it for laps today, he'd been vague about why he was coming into town, and I didn't ask him to explain because I specifically didn't want to be the creepy controlling type.

But that didn't mean I didn't wonder.

"I wish I didn't have to work till closing again," Lacey said sadly. "You and I haven't hung out in forever. But with Lea quitting early, if Debra keeps going AWOL I'll be working, like, nonstop till school starts."

"Bummer," I agreed, disheartened. I had been about to ask her when she got off work today. As wonderful as it had been spending so much time with Zane over the summer, I'd had pretty lousy luck meeting up with anyone else I knew. I saw Matt because he worked on the North Shore, and I saw Lacey because she worked at the pool, but I hadn't run into any of their other friends I'd met at the dance at Frederick High over my spring break. Everyone seemed to be so busy that even Matt and Lacey didn't see each other, much less have time to reintroduce me to the rest of their crowd. I had expected as much, and was glad to be able to start my senior year with at least a few familiar faces. But still, I did miss having girlfriends around. And this time of year especially, it made the pang of missing Tara and Kylee all the more intense.

"So much for 'the lazy days of summer,'" Lacey said with a sigh, mirroring my thoughts. "Whoever said that obviously did *not* have parents who expected them to pay for half their own clothes."

A whistle blew.

"Back to the grind," Lacey declared as she stood. "Well, hey. At least I get a killer tan out of it, right? Helps with the highlights, too." She threw me a smile and a wink and bounced back to work.

I smiled back at her. Lace had had a tough summer, but she wasn't one to feel sorry for herself. Kylee and Tara would like her. Another pang hit my gut, and I tried unsuccessfully to squelch it.

The three of us had pretended, before I left Wyoming, that Tara and Kylee would come to visit me in Hawaii. We talked about how they would meet all my friends here, especially Zane, whom they had yet to lay eyes on. But deep down, we all knew it would never happen. Airfare was close to a thousand dollars each, and none of us had any money to spare with senior year coming up and college looming. I would be lucky to get myself back to Cheyenne before they graduated. I would be happy to see them anywhere, of course, but it was tough not to be sad when I thought about how much they would love Oahu. It was hard to share what I was doing and seeing without it sounding like bragging. And besides, how could they ever really understand just from texts and pics? I wanted so much for Tara to breathe in the smell of the ocean and the flowers for herself. And Kylee would love to feel the wind in her hair and the salty spray on her cheeks.

I sighed again. Then I told myself to stop sighing. Hadn't I just been thinking how nice it was that Lacey didn't feel sorry for herself?

Deal with it, Kali.

I tried to think more pleasant thoughts. I rested another few moments, catching my breath while mindlessly surveying the pool grounds for its usual complement of shadow people, none of whom were particularly interesting. Then I packed up my things and headed slowly home. I walked into the house to find my mother the technical writer busily typing away in her cordoned-off "speak to me and you die" corner of the main room. My father wasn't home; he was at work at Hickam Air Force Base, as usual. I climbed the narrow steps to the open half second story that was my bedroom and opened the door that led to my lanai.

"Lanai" was a grandiose term for it — really, it was a flat spot on the roof of the first floor surrounded by a cheap iron railing. And if you looked down, the view of cluttered yards and privacy fences and barbecue grills and kids toys and lawn tools and junk was perhaps less than inspiring. But if you looked straight across or up, you saw sharp emerald peaks glistening with dew or mist or rain, stretching upward into blue sky or gray fog or white puffy clouds as the hour and the winds dictated. Always colorful, always changing, always dramatic, always full of life. My lanai was my happy place.

I sank into one of my folding lawn chairs, slumped down, and gazed up at my mountains. Out of the corner of my eye, I saw the little shadow boy scramble over the railing and out onto the roof again, and I couldn't help but smile. The first time I had seen him, the image had disturbed me, and I had turned my eyes away. I was afraid that he was one of the shadows whose energy had been burned into time at one of his darkest moments — when he had looked into the face of death. But once I'd gotten a better handle on my empathic capabilities, I'd realized the little imp was actually having the time of his life. He didn't return to the lanai once he crawled out of sight over the peak of the roof, so I would never know how he got down, or how badly he got yelled at, or... truth be told, if he ever got down safely at all. I only know that, for him, those few seconds in time were pure, unadulterated bliss.

My phone vibrated and I jumped to look at the text, only to find that it was worthless spam. My shoulders sagged. First thing this morning, I'd had a nicely nostalgic conversation with both Kylee and Tara, but since then they'd both clammed up on me. Neither one had answered all day, in fact, which was weird. I backed up the thread and looked to see if I had said anything stupid or offensive. I didn't see anything. Maybe they'd gone swimming or out for a drive beyond signal country. Or something.

I sat for a few more minutes, feeling lonely and trying not to, and then I forced myself to snap out of it and accomplish something. I set about the task of planning for the new school year, including looking at last year's supply inventory and then trying to guess what I'd need for that all-important first day, as opposed to what I should put off buying until the teachers asked for it. Usually I enjoyed the process, but this time there wasn't as much to go through, and I wound up inventorying my clothes as well, which got depressing fast because a summer of sun and sand had not been kind to any of the new things I'd bought since moving. So much for the bank account.

The hours began to drag. The day was hot and the house was way too quiet. I kept checking my phone to make sure the battery wasn't dead. There was an unusual lack of wind outside, which made my bedroom feel like a sauna. It seemed to take forever for five o'clock to roll around.

And then it was five-fifteen.

I stared at my phone for the forty-eighth time. *Nothing.*

I gave in. I guess I was no better than one of those creepy-controlling girlfriends after all, because I really couldn't stand it anymore. "Ish" meant fifteen minutes, give or take. Right? I fired off a text. What *was* Zane doing today, anyway?

You still coming to my house?

No answer. The minutes ticked by. I walked downstairs into the living room. My mother had finished working and was doing something in the kitchen. "What's up, Kali?" she called.

"Zane's coming over," I answered. "Can I ask him to stay for dinner?"

"Sure," she called back. "When is he coming?"

I glanced down at my silent phone again, and my spirits sank. "Half an hour ago," I said flatly. I walked out the front door and leaned back against it. He must be on his way, driving. I wasn't anxious. Not really. He wouldn't just ignore me — I knew that. But then I started worrying about the whole "zone out" thing. We'd never considered whether his new ability could actually be dangerous to him as a driver...

I got anxious.

By 5:43 pm my heart was racing, my shirt was stuck to my back, and I had paced a trail of trampled grass across the lawn. *Where was he?*

When at last I saw his beat-up sedan turn down the street, I almost collapsed from relief. As the car rolled slowly up to the curb, I turned and did my best to calm down before he saw me.

As soon as he parked I headed out towards him, but he jumped out quickly and met me in the middle of the yard. "Sorry I'm late," he said cheerfully.

I threw myself onto his chest and stole the bear hug I so desperately needed.

He wrapped his arms around me and was quiet for a moment. When at last I drew back, he looked at me carefully. "Are you all right?" he asked.

How embarrassing. "Um... yeah," I lied. "I just... Well,

it occurred to me that it might be dangerous... to drive around by yourself not knowing when a vision might come."

He blinked back at me. He hadn't thought of that, either, obviously. "I guess you have a point," he admitted. "But I'm sure I'll be fine as long as I'm concentrating. I'm sorry you were worried. I would have texted, but..." His eyes twinkled at me oddly.

He seemed in rather too good a mood, for the circumstances.

"But what?"

"I have a surprise for you," he taunted. "In the house."

"In *my* house?" I said skeptically. "I just came from there!"

He shrugged and pulled me toward my front door. "Come check it out."

I followed him, baffled. My house wasn't the kind of place where you could hide something, unless it was the size of a hairpin. Most houses in Honolulu were small, and we affectionately referred to ours as "the cottage." We stepped into the main room, which served as living room, family room, hall, den, etc., and I looked around aimlessly. My mother wasn't visible, although I could hear her making noise in the kitchen around the corner.

"Upstairs," Zane instructed.

I shot him a quizzical look. There was no way he'd hidden anything in my room. I had just gone through the entire thing! But he clearly had something up his sleeve, and whatever it was, he was excited about it. So, upstairs I went.

When we reached the top of the stairs, he gestured to the lanai. "Wow, it's hot up here today," he noted.

"You think?" I teased, leading him outside.

I expected him to sweep me up in his arms and kiss

me. Or something. But all he did was sit down in one of the lawn chairs. "So, what did you do all afternoon?" he asked casually, a grin playing around his lips.

I groaned. "Zane Svenson! What are you up to?"

He looked back at me with wounded innocence.

I told you he was a really good actor.

"Me?" he defended easily. "All I did was ask what you've been doing all day. What's wrong with that?"

I was about to wring his neck when his phone buzzed. He glanced down at it and then quickly shut it off. "It's hot up here. Let's go back downstairs." He rose and held open the door to my room. "After you," he said courteously, all smiles.

I heard some noise downstairs. I didn't know what I was hearing exactly, but I was pretty sure it was human. I had a sudden, disturbing vision of Zane hiring some world-renowned ocean safety instructor to come chain blocks to my feet or make me swim with tires on my back. Zane would think that was fabulous.

Crap.

I might as well get this over with.

I shot Zane an anxious, pitiful look and forced my feet down the stairs. I made the tight turn in the bend and hopped down into the main room with feigned enthusiasm.

Kylee and Tara smiled back at me. "SURPRISE!!!"

Their screeches nearly brought the roof down — particularly when mine got added to them. If they hadn't both rushed me at once, my knees would have given out, taking me straight down to the carpet. We screamed and group-hugged for I don't know how long, but when we all came up for air, Zane, my mother, and my father (when did *he* get home?) were all standing there watching us with silly grins on their faces.

"How did you—" I babbled to no one in particular, "and did they, and how—" I looked over at my grinning father, assuming they had arrived with him.

Colonel Thompson took a half step back and raised his palms in the air. "Don't look at me," he chuckled. "I got here just in time for the screaming."

Kylee and Tara looked at each other and wiped tears of laughter from their eyes. Kylee took a step towards me and leaned into my ear, fresh tears already replacing the ones she'd just cleared away. "Zane did it," she whispered. "He bought tickets for both of us!"

I pulled away from her enough to get a clear view of Zane, who stood several feet away from me, smiling almost shyly now.

He shrugged.

My heart melted.

"But you, how did—" I mumbled incoherently.

"Zane arranged everything," my mother confirmed. "The rest of us were just innocent bystanders."

"You *knew?*" I protested, looking at my parents. They were both terrible at keeping secrets! How blind had I been?

Zane laughed. "Well of course they knew. I couldn't invite two people to stay at their house for a week without asking them, could I?"

I sucked in a breath and turned back to my friends again. "A week? You're staying a whole week?"

They nodded.

More hugging and screaming followed. I was so happy I couldn't stand it, but not so happy that I failed to notice Zane slipping out the front door. I made a quick apology to Kylee and Tara, detached myself, and followed him.

"Oh, no you don't," I ordered, catching him just outside. "Come here." I threw my arms around his neck and held him as tightly as I dared. I wanted to kiss him too, actually, but as crazy in love as I felt right now I was afraid that if I did, we might cause another tsunami.

"You," I told him fervently as I hugged him, "are the most amazing boyfriend ever. Thank you! How did you know the one thing that could make me so happy, when I'm already the luckiest, happiest person alive? I don't deserve it!" I drew back and looked at him. His green eyes were shining, and I could see my own happiness more than reflected in them. "I don't deserve *you*," I said softly.

He raised a hand to my temple and brushed a shock of curls behind my ear, then traced a finger lazily along my cheekbone. "Well," he replied in that irresistibly sexy, husky whisper of his, "everyone needs a goal, I guess."

I threw back my head with a groan. "You are terrible!"

"You just said I was amazing!" he protested. "Some people are *so* indecisive."

"You are amazingly terrible," I corrected. And then I did break down and kiss him. But only briefly, because you could see where we were standing from the far end of the front window, and Kylee had no shame. "And terribly amazing," I finished in a whisper as I pulled away.

"Hold that thought," he said with a smile, moving towards his car.

"You're not leaving already, are you?" I asked, surprised. Surely my mom was planning a welcome dinner for everybody? She had already said I could invite him.

"And miss your mom's cinnamon chili? Never," he explained with a grin. "I just thought I'd grab their stuff out of the trunk." He pulled his keys out of his pocket and extended the remote.

I stepped after him to help. His keys fell to the ground.

His eyes went wide and his body froze with horror.

chapter 5

I stared where Zane was staring. There was nothing on the car. There was nothing under or around the car. No fleeing footsteps. No shadows. I rolled back the defenses I usually kept in place so I could pick up any stray emotions in the area, and a burst of raw hostility hit me like a sucker punch to the gut.

"Geez," I muttered out loud, shoring up my defenses again. I turned to Zane and took hold of his arm. He quickly gripped my hand in return, and I was glad to see that he had recovered from his initial shock. Nevertheless, his eyes stayed glued to his car.

"I'm assuming there's a ghost there," I said unnecessarily.

"Oh, yeah," he confirmed dryly.

"I also get the feeling it's not too happy with us."

Zane shook his head. "Um... no. No, you could definitely say that."

"What is it doing, exactly?"

"Well, he's kind of floating over the back of my car. Crouching and floating. With his arms crossed over his chest. That's when he's not making a fist and pounding it into his other hand. The rest of the time he's just glaring at me."

"Ouch," I sympathized. "What era?"

Zane looked pained. "Hard to say... he's just wearing these grungy cut-offs... could be any time since, like, the sixties, maybe? He's a surfer. Local guy. Built like a truck. He's the kind of guy who'd show up in your nightmares if you dropped in on his wave. If you lived long enough to have nightmares, that is. Why's he mad at me?"

"Don't take it personally," I assured. "He's a ghost. He's dead. He doesn't even know you."

"But what if I *did* drop in on his wave?" Zane insisted nervously.

"Will you stop?" I demanded. "If some guy like him died surfing on the North Shore in the last three months wouldn't you know about it?"

Zane considered. "I guess so." He kept on staring. "He's just so... determined. He wants me to stay away."

"Away from what? Your own car?"

"He's fading," Zane reported. "And he's angry about that, too." He stepped back a few paces, pulling me with him. "Chill, dude!" He raised his palms in the air passively. Then, a moment later, he looked around us and relaxed. "He's gone."

"What was he doing? I mean, there at the end?" I asked anxiously. We had never encountered a hostile ghost before, and I didn't like it. Hostile living people were bad enough. Whether they were better or worse as ghosts was an open question.

Zane's eyes studied mine a second, then darted away. "You don't want to know," he answered, which came dangerously close to reading my mind again.

"Okay, time's up!" Tara proclaimed, banging through the front door with Kylee at her heels. Tara was tall, slender, blond, and very pretty, but she managed to hide almost all of the above behind cheap glasses, a perpetual ponytail, and clothes borrowed from her brothers. "We gave you enough time for a thank-you kiss," she announced, but the least we can do is carry our own bags inside. Kylee's weighs, like, eighty pounds."

"It was fifty-nine!" Kylee protested. "And it's important stuff! Well worth the surcharge, I'll have you know." Kylee was a good foot shorter than her travel companion and considerably curvier. She had glossy black hair and light brown skin from the Vietnamese side of her family, as well as sparkling dark eyes and a sunny smile.

Seeing the two of them make their way up the yard had me bouncing on my toes with happiness all over again. How the heck had Zane been able to afford two tickets? I knew he had inherited money from his father, but he always watched what he spent. To get me a gift like this was insanely extravagant of him, and we needed to talk about that. But now was obviously not the time.

"You should have seen the grief we had getting Tara packed," Kylee bemoaned. "I pretty much forced her to go buy a new suitcase that was plane-worthy. First she wanted to take this tiny beat-up roller thing that fit two shirts and wouldn't have made it to the far end of the conveyor belt in Denver—"

"It was fine," Tara protested. "It was just a little small is all."

"And then she was going to bring this totally disgusting green duffel thing her great-grandfather brought back from World War II or something—"

"My dad got it for scout camp!"

"But it was big enough to hold a tent and ugly as sin besides," Kylee continued, "and I told her no way was I walking around an airport with her if she was lugging that thing. So finally we went out and she bought, like, the cheapest, most generic-looking black roller on the market that looks exactly like eighty percent of the bags on the planet."

"It's functional," Tara concluded. "Hey, Zane, can you pop the back open?"

"Sure," he agreed, hitting the remote on the keys he had only just managed to pluck out of the grass. I grinned at him, and he winked back at me. Kylee had been standing on them for a while, making an awkward explanation appear unavoidable, but at the last moment she had stepped to the side, and she and Tara were too busy arguing to pay attention to Zane's swooping save.

We all moved closer as the trunk popped up an inch. Tara pulled it up and started to lean in, then stopped abruptly.

All four of us let out a simultaneous groan and backed away from the car.

"Eewwww!!" Kylee squealed. "What *is* that? What died in there?"

Zane braved a step closer and looked inside his trunk. "Nothing's in here but your suitcases!" he defended. "And I just cleaned it out, I swear!"

"But they didn't smell like that before!" Kylee argued.

Tara stepped up by Zane. "Well, they have been baking in the heat a while," she conceded. "And we don't know what they smelled like when they came off the plane. All we did at the airport was wheel them outside and throw them in, after all."

"No!" Kylee cried, covering her mouth and nose with her hands. "What if something *did* crawl in one of them and die! My bikini! It fit like, *so* perfectly! I can't stand it!"

"Tragic a loss as that would be," Tara said sarcastically, reaching a hand in the trunk and prodding the suitcases around, "it doesn't smell like something dead to me."

"What does it smell like?" I asked her, feeling a little nauseated. I had smelled bad stuff before, but this... this *reeked*. It was like body odor, but worse. It was like a locker room for incontinent chimpanzees. It was—

"It smells like my brothers," Tara finished. "Specifically, like that time when Devin and Jory forgot to bring their middle school gym clothes home all year, and then they put them in a plastic bag with their sneakers the last day of school and Devin brought them home and threw the bag into the laundry room and it landed between the dryer and the wall, and then a couple weeks later I wondered why the room smelled so bad and I reached my hand down—"

"We get the picture!" Kylee interrupted desperately. "But our clothes are all clean!"

I took a step closer and looked into the trunk myself. The smell was still horrid, but at least with the trunk open it was dissipating a bit. Kylee's giant, flowered suitcase looked pristine, as expected. Tara's much smaller black one looked brand new. It was indeed about as generic a suitcase as one could buy, but at least Tara had spiffed it up with a colorful ribbon tied to the handle.

"Maybe they kept bad company in the cargo hold?" I suggested. "All we can do is get them out and see if everything in them is all right. *Before* we take them up to my room. Okay?"

Tara shrugged and reached in to grab her bag, but Kylee merely shrank from hers. Zane lifted it out himself and closed the trunk again.

"Nice touch," I teased Tara, pointing to her ribbon. The rainbow pattern in shades of purple and pink was pretty, but it was hardly Tara's style.

She rolled her eyes at me. "I did *not* pick that out. Kylee stuck that on."

"And a lucky thing for you I thought of it," Kylee said without looking at us. She was staring at her own bag as if afraid it would explode. "If I hadn't put something identifiable on it, you'd be wearing some strange dude's pjs all week instead of that sexy new one-piece."

"You want me to open yours for you?" Zane asked Kylee. His voice was polite, but I could tell he was trying hard not to laugh. The girl looked terrified of her own clothing.

"Um," Tara interrupted, carrying her own bag a few paces to the side with a grimace. "That may not be necessary. I'm pretty sure I've got the culprit."

Kylee darted forward to sniff her own suitcase. "Oh!" she said gratefully, dropping down to practically hug the thing. "Mine's not that bad!"

"Ugghh!" Tara exclaimed, getting another whiff of her own. "I don't get it! There's nothing in here but clean clothes!" With a grimace, she extended an arm as far as possible to reach for the zipper.

"*TARA!*" Kylee practically screamed, now pointing at her friend's black bag with an accusing finger. "That is a *rainbow!*"

We all looked at Kylee as if she'd lost her mind.

"Your ribbon was *PINK ZEBRA!*" she screeched louder, jumping up and down for emphasis.

Tara blinked dumbly for a moment. Then she swore under her breath and looked back at her bag. "Seriously?"

"I *told* you that!" Kylee exclaimed, still jumping up and down. "You *saw* me tie it on!"

"Yeah," Tara replied sheepishly. "But I wasn't paying any attention. I mean, how many suitcases have ribbons tied on their handles?"

Kylee collapsed on the grass with a groan.

I squelched my own desire to laugh. Tara was one of the smartest people I knew, but she had never flown on an airplane before. And the art of baggage handling did have its subtleties.

"I guess I should have checked the tag," Tara admitted. "But Zane got there just before the bags came, and—" she threw me a sheepish look. "Well, we were both a little... distracted."

I smiled knowingly back at her. "Entirely understandable."

Tara looked at the identification card that was contained in a plastic sleeve on the side of the suitcase. "Blank," she reported. "This one's brand new. Just like mine."

"On the handle by the ribbon," I pointed out. "Check out the sticker with the barcode. There should be a name on there somewhere."

Tara looked at the strip of sticker tape. "It says 'Jones, Tim.'"

"Well, somebody needs to tell Mr. Tim Jones to fill out his identification card," Kylee proclaimed with annoyance. "Not to mention doing his dirty laundry before he packs! Or at least not throwing in wet stuff to rot on the runway. Sheesh!"

"Well, at least we don't have to open it to solve the mystery," Zane said reasonably, taking the bag from Tara and walking it down to the carport. "We can leave it here for now."

"But," Tara fretted, "where does this leave *my* suitcase?"

"It's probably still at the airport," I answered. "We'll call the airline and see. I can drive us down after dinner, and we'll swap them out. Maybe we can see some of the city while we're at it!"

Tara smiled at me sadly. "I'm really sorry, Kali. I didn't mean to screw up everyone's plans for our first night here."

"What plans?" I argued cheerfully. "Who had plans?"

Zane brought Kylee's bag down from the street next and carried it into the house for her. "Thanks!" she said, beaming at him as she followed him inside. "Come on, Tar," she called over her shoulder, "I'll help you call the airlines. We might as well get it straightened out now."

Once we were all back inside, I directed Kylee and Tara to the landline and then stepped to Zane's side. "You'll see the city with us, won't you?" I asked hopefully.

His green eyes twinkled at me even as he shook his head. "Sorry. I was thinking of taking off right after dinner."

"But why?" I asked, disappointed. I knew he'd spent time with Kylee and Tara already, but I wasn't there to see the grand unveiling, which seemed a bit of a cheat. Besides, I had missed him today.

"Look, Kali," he said evenly. "No offense or anything. But you guys have 'reuning' to do. And with girls, that means squealing and shrieking and stuff. I'd really rather you got that out of your systems without me."

I threw my shoulders back with mock outrage. "We do *not*—"

He dipped his chin and threw me a look.

I smirked. "Well, okay. Maybe a little. It's possible."

"Two bowls of cinnamon chili," he promised. "Maybe three, if your dad leaves me enough. Then I'm out of here."

I conceded by giving him another quick kiss as my dad rounded the corner to announce that dinner was ready. The Colonel had just opened his mouth to speak when Kylee started screeching at the baggage claim agent over the telephone and Tara tackled her trying to pry away the handset. The Colonel let out a ridiculously loud whistle instead, which caused Tara to drop butt-first onto the floor and Kylee to accidentally hang up. Both girls froze in place and stared at him.

My dad smiled pleasantly. "Soup's on!"

Kylee and Tara collected themselves immediately, threw embarrassed looks at me, and followed him docilely into the kitchen.

"Are they scared of him?" Zane asked in a whisper.

"Terrified," I replied with a giggle. Then I turned and hugged him. "I am so happy to have them here. I've missed them so much. You have no idea how much this means to me."

"I think I might," he said softly.

I looked up at him. "You shouldn't have done it, though. Really. It must have cost a fortune. You can't have that much money. I know you're moving into the dorms. And it's not like you're driving around in a Porsche or anything..."

He shook his head dismissively. "Just because I don't waste money on stuff I don't care about doesn't mean I don't have it, Kali. I told you, I *want* to live in the dorms, just like any other college freshman. I never really got to be just any other high schooler. I'm kind of looking forward to being normal. As for a Porsche, what would I do with it besides get sand all over the upholstery and scrape up the paint job loading my board?"

"I guess I see your point."

"What I really wanted," he continued with a grin, "was to give you what *you* really wanted for Christmas."

"It's nowhere near Christmas!"

"Yeah, but I couldn't bring Tara and Kylee here *at* Christmas — their break was pretty short and everyone has family stuff anyway. And so I started thinking that maybe you'd be happier if they met your friends here and saw your school now, before you even started senior year. Then all along, they'd know what you were talking about, you know?"

My heart melted all over again. He knew me so well.

My dad whistled again. From three feet away.

"Yeah, Dad!" I replied, rubbing my ear. "Got that!"

He smirked at both of us and retreated. I supposed his timing was appropriate, because I was totally about to kiss Zane again, and I had totally forgotten where we were and how many people were waiting for us right around the corner.

"You figured exactly right," I whispered to Zane as we moved. "And you're right about the other thing, too."

He lifted an eyebrow curiously.

I grinned. "There *will* be squealing."

chapter 6

There was squealing. Enough of it to make me hoarse long before the sun set. But there was no trip back to the Honolulu airport and no suitcase for Tara. Several more calls to the baggage claim desk revealed that (1) Tara's bag had been delivered to the airport, (2) Tara's bag was not currently at the airport, (3) no one working for the airline had any idea where Tara's bag was, (4) no passenger named Tim Jones had reported a missing bag, and (5) the airline did not seem to believe that any of the above were their problem.

Thank goodness, Tara was not hugely upset about it. All of her true valuables had been in the backpack she'd carried onboard the plane, and since she and I were almost the same size, it wasn't like she'd have nothing to wear all week. The loss of the new one-piece swimsuit she and Kylee had apparently spent hours picking out seemed much more distressing to Kylee.

So instead of driving and sightseeing, we spent the entire evening outside on the kitchen deck doing nothing but talking, laughing, and catching up while the hours flew by and the moon rose. Only in the wee hours of the morning, when the air upstairs was cooler and Kylee and Tara were finally settled onto air mattresses on the floor of my room, did I finally get around to asking the question I'd been dying to ask them all night.

"So tell me what happened when you first saw Zane," I prompted. "What did he say? What did you think?"

My friends exchanged a look. "You know what we thought," Kylee said with a smirk. "We almost dropped dead, that's what we thought. *Damn*, Kali. I know you sent pictures, but..."

"We seriously considered never talking to you again," Tara teased. "But hey, you did get us to Hawaii. Indirectly."

I tried to control my delight. Kind of. "I still can't believe he brought you here," I gushed. "He is *so* sweet!"

Kylee and Tara exchanged another glance. "Shall we kill her now?" Tara asked.

Kylee shook her head. "Not yet. After the visit."

I laughed out loud and jumped out of bed to give each of them another hug. "I don't care what you say," I replied. "I know you're happy for me. Thanks for that."

"What you should thank us for is keeping his secret," Kylee said. "Do you have any idea how many times I almost spilled it? I've been, like, jumping out of my skin for weeks now!"

"So have I," Tara admitted. "My entire family's been ready to throw me out in the street, they're so sick of hearing about Hawaii!"

I laughed. "They'll get even sicker of hearing about it after you get back home! Oh, we've got so much to do this week! We'll do the city and Waikiki and I'll show you my school. We'll drive up Tantalus and around Diamondhead and go see the blowhole. We'll watch the windsurfers at Kailua Bay and we'll drive up the whole windward side and check out La'ie Point. And then there's the North Shore... we could spend days just hanging out on the beaches!"

Kylee sat up. "I want to meet surfers. Gorgeous, young, unattached ones."

"Are any of them smart?" Tara added.

"Zane is," I said.

They rolled their eyes with a groan. "Do not make us

kill you sooner than planned," Tara warned gravely.

"What about your swimsuit?" Kylee said to her, back on the familiar track of woe. "We *cannot* go to the beach until we get you a new one just as sexy!"

"Maybe we should look in Tim Jones' suitcase?" Tara teased. "Maybe he's got some trunks I could wear."

Kylee made a barfing sound. "If the airline doesn't call back soon about that thing, we really should just throw it out. I mean, if Tim Jones doesn't want it, what are we supposed to do with it? It's going to stink up your parents' car just by sitting out there next to it!"

"We could always—"

Tara's next words were cut off as Kylee let out a bloodcurdling scream and bounced off her mattress and onto my bed so forcibly she knocked me into the wall. *"Get out! Get out! Get out!"* she yelled. She looked around frantically, seized my laptop from my nightstand, stood up on the shaky mattress and wielded the heavy device over her head. *"Get away from her! Get out!"*

"Kylee, what is *wrong* with you!" Tara demanded, jumping to her feet.

Kylee's gaze shifted from the wall behind Tara to Tara herself. Her chest heaved with ragged breaths, and her eyes were wide with fear. But as she looked back and forth between Tara and the wall, she slowly lowered the laptop.

Hostility.

My empathic defenses weren't as good without Zane around.

I stood up on my mattress beside Kylee, hoping the bedframe wouldn't break. I gently removed the laptop from her hands. "What you're seeing isn't real," I told her. "It can't hurt us."

My dad appeared at the top of the stairs as alert and ready as a one-man SWAT team. "What's going on up here?" he boomed.

Kylee collapsed where she stood. I sat down on my bed beside her and set the laptop aside. "We're fine, Dad," I assured. "Kylee just had a really bad... like a nightmare. I'm sorry. She wasn't faking; she was honestly terrified. But she's okay now."

"Thank God," my mother murmured, pushing past my dad and into the room. "For God's sake, Mitch, put that gun away."

After a few seconds' more surveillance, my dad and his service pistol — which my mother never allowed him to keep loaded in the house — disappeared again.

My mom opened my door and stepped out on the lanai. Dogs were barking everywhere. She turned on the light outside. "It's all right," she called after a moment. "Everyone's fine. My daughter's friend just had a nightmare! Thanks!"

Just barely, over all the other noise, I heard Zane's rooster ringtone. No doubt my ears were attuned to it. I reached over and pulled my phone off its charger and into my lap. A text from him glowed on the screen.

Is everything okay over there?

O.M.G. How did he know?

We're fine. Why?

My mom stepped back inside and closed the door. I slipped the phone behind me and out of sight.

"Oh, Mrs. Thompson," Kylee said weakly, wiping a hand across her sweating forehead. "I'm so sorry. I don't... I didn't mean to be so loud."

My mom smiled at her. "I know. Don't worry. I think

we got to Mrs. Alonso before she called the police. That's something we can't always manage, believe me!" she laughed under her breath.

"Thanks, Mom," I said. "I forgot about the neighbors." I didn't want to think about them now, either. Mrs. Alonso could be a real pain.

"Try to get some sleep at some point, okay?" my mom advised us unnecessarily, in true motherly fashion. Then she followed my father downstairs.

Tara came and sat down on the other side of Kylee, who was shaking like a leaf. Tara looked at me. "What was it?" she whispered.

"She must have seen a ghost," I explained. "I didn't see anything. But I could feel it. It was... not the happy kind of spirit."

Kylee's dark eyes shifted toward mine. "That," she said through chattering teeth, "was the understatement of the year, Kalia Thompson."

"Well, at least she's still got her sense of humor," Tara quipped, pulling a blanket up around all three of our shoulders as we huddled. "So what did this ghost look like? Was he tall, dark, and handsome?"

Kylee's moist brow furrowed with thought. "Yes, yes, and only to his mother. I swear, I thought he was real. I thought he'd snuck up the staircase and was going to kill us in our beds." She turned to look at Tara. "He was so close to you. When you stood up, your arm actually passed *through* part of him. Until then, I had no idea he was a ghost. I mean, I've only seen a couple, and... well, what do I know?"

"What did he look like, Kylee?" I asked, having a feeling I already knew.

"He was huge," she answered. "Tall and broad. With a big belly, but strong, too. And mean looking. He wasn't wearing much. Shorts, I guess. And he had all kinds of tattoos. He just looked so *angry*. And menacing. I swear he glared at me like I'd just run over his dog or something! He was scowling and flexing his muscles and *trying* to intimidate me!"

Kylee's breathing was still ragged. "I was *so* scared. I mean, he was right there! Out of nowhere, with no warning. I was sure he must be some deranged maniac but, still... I couldn't just do nothing while he started attacking us, you know? So I picked up—" she glanced around in confusion. "What was it?"

"My laptop," I answered.

"Oh," she said, embarrassed again. "Sorry. I didn't break it, did I?"

"Its fine! Go on."

"Well," she continued, "that's what was so strange. When I picked that up and acted like I was going to throw it at him, he... well, his expression changed. Like, he actually looked *surprised*. And then he started to fade out really quickly."

I heard the rooster ringtone again, faintly, from somewhere in the tangle of bedclothes.

"Do you think the Colonel scared off the ghost?" Tara asked.

Kylee shook her head. "He was gone already. I really only saw him a couple seconds. It was so weird!" She turned to me with a wounded look. "Why would a ghost be mad at *me*, Kali?"

I had no answer for her. Never mind that it was the second time today I'd been asked that question. I was fishing around behind me for my phone, but couldn't find it. The rooster crowed once more.

"Did you text Zane about this already?" Tara asked disbelievingly.

"No!" I defended, perhaps a little too quickly. If I was determined not to be a creepy-controlling girlfriend, I was doubly determined not to be a clingy-dependent one.

Of course, the truth of the situation was pretty disturbing itself. "I think he already knew," I admitted. I got up and turned around so I could see where my phone was hiding.

They stared at me as I finally found the phone and sat back down. "How could he?" Kylee squeaked.

I braved a glance at Zane's text. They both leaned in and read it with me.

Would you believe I saw a flash of your dad packing a pistol in his pajamas?

Holy crap.

"What does he mean he saw a flash?" Tara questioned. Then she groaned out loud and fell back on my mattress. "On second thought, don't tell me. I am *so* unqualified for this."

"What does he mean, Kali?" Kylee asked more quietly. "Tell us."

I took a deep breath and spilled it. I spilled it all. I described the ghost Zane had seen earlier by the car, and I explained about the new ability he seemed to have, but that we didn't completely understand yet. They listened to everything without interrupting, although once or twice I was afraid Tara might need to be sick.

Poor logical, scientifically minded Tara. She accepted me and all my weirdness. She pretty much had to, after seeing my gifts in action. She had even helped my equally stubborn and like-minded father to deal with me. But that didn't mean she enjoyed it. She was far happier sitting behind a nice, safe computer somewhere doling out advice to the rest of us than she was experiencing anything remotely... *unusual* herself.

Kylee's mood, on the other hand, improved steadily. The more I talked about Zane and his visions, the less she dwelt on her own fear of the menacing ghost.

"It sounds like it could be either astral projection or remote viewing," Kylee told me confidently, using terms she had learned from her *ba noi* (her Vietnamese grandmother, Joan) and her *ba noi's* social network of psychics and psychic wannabes in San Jose. "And it makes perfect sense, really. Zane's already shown the ability to travel outside his body when he was a wraith; it would be easier for him to do something similar now, even if he wasn't consciously trying. The flashes are pretty common, really. But this whole moving through a scene, thing... wow. That's pretty powerful."

"That's only happened twice," I explained. *I hoped.* I was trying not to think too much about Zane being able to spy on my dad in his pajamas. Zane had insisted he only saw flashes at my house, not whole scenes. Of course, he'd also told me that up until tonight, he'd only seen empty rooms.

I really didn't like where this was going.

"What's interesting is the perfect timing of his vision, coming in the middle of the night like that," Kylee mused. "It's almost like he has a sixth sense for danger where you're concerned."

"That would make sense," I debated, "if I was actually in danger. But I wasn't. None of us were. Remember?"

Kylee frowned. "Speak for yourself. *You* didn't see the guy."

"But he wasn't real!" Tara insisted, sitting up again.

Kylee glared at her. "He wasn't living. And he wasn't solid. But that doesn't mean he wasn't real."

Tara sighed and moved back to her own mattress. "Look, if he comes back again, just tell me where he is, okay? I'll kickbox his ass — no problem. For now, I need sleep. In Wyoming, it's like tomorrow already. Goodnight." She yawned, pulled up a sheet, and rolled over to face the wall.

Kylee's dark eyes caught mine and held them. "I know most ghosts are harmless, Kali," she whispered so low I could barely hear her. "The ones who come back from the other side are only here because they want to help someone. And the others, the ones who can't cross — they're just troubled souls who need some kind of help themselves. But my *ba noi* has told me that every once in a while, the kind of help they want..."

Her voice dropped lower.

"Well, it isn't always something you'd want to give."

chapter 7

"You guys can either make yourselves some nachos or some spaghetti," my mother suggested, rubbing her temple like she always did when she was fighting a migraine, "or you can order pizza. I'm going to take a shower and turn in early. Kali, your dad says he's staying over at your grandfather's place tonight. So lock the doors before you go upstairs. Okay?"

"Right, Mom." I looked up at her from the heap on the carpet into which Tara, Kylee, and I had collapsed after returning from our full day out on the town. We were hot, tired, hungry, thirsty, and painfully sore in the ribs from laughing so much.

It had been fabulous.

We'd gotten off to a late start, for obvious reasons, but we'd all perked up as soon as the sun hit our faces. I had driven them straight to Waikiki, making sure they got the token tourist experience out of the way early. They'd taken off their shoes and splashed in the Pacific a bit, but as expected, Kylee refused to "do" any beach for real until Tara had a swimsuit, so all too soon we were off the sand and hitting the shops. After multiple hours and several epic battles, Kylee at last emerged triumphant. Tara not only had another new one-piece, but Kylee insisted it was even sexier than the first one.

The rest of the day had been consumed with driving around aimlessly in a sea of Saturday afternoon traffic. I'd taken them past the Iolani Palace and the Punchbowl and Diamond Head, and we'd threaded our way up the hairpin turns of Tantalus Road and roamed around the lookout to admire its sweeping views of the city. Just like me — and despite the traffic — they were already hopelessly in love with Oahu, and I still hadn't shown them any of my most favorite places on the island.

The only disappointment of the day was that the hours had flown by so quickly. Not seeing Zane all day was another bummer, but at least I had expected that. My grandfather Emilio had called during dinner last night and invited both my dad and Zane to go surfing with him today, and I knew that nothing — and I do mean nothing, including *me* in a sexy new swimsuit — would keep Zane from jumping on that offer. Zane practically worshipped "Milo," as he preferred to be called, and although my grandfather was well beyond prime surfing age, he knew every break on the west side like the back of his hand. Not only that, but he was a fixture of the surfing community there, and he always made sure that Zane as well as my dad got treated like family.

So, my dad was fleeing the house tonight altogether, was he? What was up with these men and their fear of estrogen?

Kylee squealed and sat up. "Ew! Tara! I can smell that wretched suitcase from here!"

"Oh, you can not," Tara grumbled.

"I'm afraid she can," my mother deadpanned. "When the breeze blows just so, the smell comes right in that window. I've been noticing it on and off all day."

I sat up and sniffed. Then I grimaced. "Oh, yeah. Got it. Did anybody from the airlines call the house while we were out?"

"No," my mom answered. "Were they supposed to?"

"Not unless they found my suitcase stuffed in a closet somewhere after all," Tara sighed. "Or if Tim Jones only just now reported his missing."

"We were hoping he made the same mistake Tara did and took her bag," Kylee explained. "Her cell number was on her ID tag, though, so you'd think if he did, he would have called her by now."

Tara sat up and pulled her phone out of her back pocket. Her eyes went wide. "Crap! I did miss a call! It looks local, too." She jumped up and held out her phone while Kylee and I crowded around her.

The voice mail message began with a long, breathy pause. When we finally heard a voice, it was masculine, relatively young sounding, and completely distracted. "Yeah... Um... Hey. I think I got... something of yours. Um... call me back, okay? Um... Bye."

We all exhaled simultaneously. "Oh, yay!" Kylee exclaimed. "Now you'll have *two* sexy swimsuits!"

Tara called the number back, but her call went straight to his voice mail. "Yeah. Leave me a message," the same voice said lethargically.

"Loquacious fellow," Tara mumbled sarcastically.

"Nobody *normal* even knows what that means!" Kylee scolded.

Tara rolled her eyes again and gestured for Kylee to hush. She turned aside and left a detailed message for Mr. Jones, including my parents' landline number, just in case. Then she turned back to us with a smile. "Well, that's a relief!"

"Glad to hear it," my mom acknowledged. "Goodnight." Then she went into her bedroom and closed the door, shutting out both the noise we were likely to make and the smell wafting in the front window.

"Ugh," Kylee said again, waving her hand in front of her face. "Can't we close the glass louvers on that window or something?"

"We can," I answered, "if you want to sweat to death.

We really need it open for the breeze. But we can move the suitcase."

Kylee recoiled in horror. "*You* touch it. I'll start dinner. You guys want nachos or—"

"Move it, nothing!" Tara interrupted. "I've had enough of smelling Tim Jones' stink. Who knows how long it's going to take for him to pick that thing up?" She turned to me. "Where does your dad keep his tools, Kali? Like his pliers?"

I blinked at her. "All his tools are in that little shed out back." I gave her the code to the shed's combination lock, and she nodded and took off.

Kylee and I stared at each other. She shrugged. "I'm thinking nachos," she announced.

I headed after her into the kitchen and started pointing out where we kept everything, but when we heard strange sounds out front I left again to see what Tara was doing. I walked to the carport to find the lid of our washing machine standing open. Tim Jones' black suitcase was laid out on the floor next to it, still zipped. Tara stood poised over the case like a surgeon, her brow creased with concentration as she held a pair of pliers in each hand. I laughed out loud. "Are you serious? You can't wash that stuff!"

She seemed angry with me. But no... Tara wouldn't be angry! She was looking back at me with a good-natured smirk.

"Believe it or not, Kali, I've washed worse than this," she insisted, affixing one set of pliers to each zipper pull. "I've been a professional laundress since the age of thirteen, remember?"

"I know!" I argued. "But these aren't your clothes!"

"Well, they're at your house," she insisted, pulling back the zippers an inch at a time, rather like she was defusing a bomb. "You didn't ask to have custody, but now you do, so hey... somebody's got to change the baby's diaper, you know what I'm saying?"

She pulled the flap fully open. The smell that wafted out was beyond foul.

So angry...

"Tara," I said, thinking quickly. "Wait a minute."

"Not on your life," she argued, poking around in the suitcase's contents with the pliers. "I may not be conscious that long." She threw her head to the side a moment and took a breath, then dived back down. "Hmm... looks like the usual recipe for man stink. Nothing dead, here. Just some seriously gnarly foot odor on these water shoes... stowed dripping wet, no doubt, tossed with sweaty clothes and baked till done." She grimaced again. "No valuables, at least. Just laundry and the shoes. Okay, watch out. Heads up!"

I heard the front door open. "Kylee!" I called, scrambling in her direction. "Don't scr—"

Kylee stopped dead at the entrance to the carport, swayed dangerously for a second, then clapped her own hands over her mouth.

"Yes, I know!" I said, wrapping my arms around her shoulders. "The ghost is back. Maybe if you just don't look at him this time?"

Kylee squinched her eyes shut tight. "Tara!" she squeaked in terror. "He's right on top of you! He's... he's pounding you over the head!"

In one hand, Tara held the cuff of a gnarly, balled up, disgustingly dirty crew sock in the jaws of a pair of pliers. With the other hand, she used a second set of pliers to grip the toe. She pulled her hands apart, unrolling the ball, then dropped the sock in the washer before bothering to glance in our direction. "Yeah?" she said with disinterest.

"The suitcase," I murmured. "Kylee, weren't we talking about the suitcase when the ghost showed up last night?"

She opened her eyes and looked at me. "I think so. We were joking about—" She turned her gaze back toward Tara. "Oh!" She shook herself and plastered both hands over her eyes. "I can't look!"

Tara pulled out a grungy tee shirt and a pair of men's underwear, holding them at arm's length with the tools. The tee shirt was speckled with gray spots of mold. "*Nice,*" she commented.

"Tara!" Kylee squealed again. "Can't you tell he's hurting you?"

"Nope!" Tara answered jovially. "One of the benefits of being an ordinary human, I guess." She unrolled another sock.

"Kylee," I pressed. "I know this is going to sound stupid, but does it seem like he's attacking for no reason or is, well... does it seem like he's trying to protect what's in the suitcase?"

Tara snorted. "Tell him I'll use the delicate cycle."

"This is nothing to laugh about!" Kylee exclaimed, her voice close to breaking. She seemed like she was about to cry.

Tara's expression softened. "Look," she cajoled. "It's almost loaded, and nothing's going to get damaged." She looked up at the air around her. "You hear that, whoever you are? I know how to do a friggin' load of laundry, okay? I have five brothers whose odor-production capabilities can take on this Tim Jones dude any day, so *chill out.* I'm going to wash this stuff and dry it all nice and fluffy and then I'm going to give it all right back to his majesty. Okay? Sheesh!"

She poked the pliers back into the suitcase and pulled

out the remaining articles of clothing, which included some casual shorts and a bunch of synthetic-type sportswear. Most of it seemed damp, much of it was moldy, and it all smelled horrible. Tara dumped some laundry detergent into the washer, closed the lid, and started the cycle. "There," she said proudly, slapping her hands together and then gesturing with her palms in the air. "We all good, ghostie?"

Hot, red anger. And yet...

Kylee reluctantly cracked open her eyes. Her expression changed from horrified to confused.

"What's he doing?" I whispered.

She shook her head. "He's gone now. But he... well, he was just sitting on the washer. Staring at Tara, like right in her face. But he was... well, he wasn't hitting her anymore."

"How big of him," Tara cracked. "These shoes need to be hosed off. Then I'm thinking disinfectant spray and a sun dry for them and the suitcase both. They're still going to stink, but that's TJ's problem." She picked up her tools and the suitcase with the sneakers inside, and without another word to me or Kylee, she headed out of the carport and around to the back of the house again.

"I can't believe her," Kylee mumbled. "If she only knew what he—"

"It's better that she doesn't," I pointed out. "What were you going to say? Did something change before he faded?"

Kylee nodded slowly. "He was still furious at her. At all of us. But he seemed somehow... well, I don't know how to describe the way he looked at her. It was almost like maybe she *amused* him somehow."

I thought about the feelings I had sensed, even through my normal barrier. Hostility... and yet a begrudging sort of respect? Or was it more the sadistic thrill of a cat playing with a mouse? "Maybe," I mulled. "Anyway, we've narrowed it down a little. Whatever the ghost's problem is, his appearance must have something to do with the mysterious Mr. Tim Jones."

Kylee made a face. "There can't possibly be anything mysterious about anyone named *Tim Jones*." She stared at the running washing machine a moment, then whirled back toward the house. "Hungry. Need nachos."

We all needed nachos. By the time we had consumed the large, sticky pile of lime-toasted tortilla chips bathed in colby-jack, black olives, sweet cherry peppers, fresh tomatoes, and part of a mango, we were all feeling a whole lot better about life in general and scary ghost dudes in particular, and the excited text I received from Zane shortly after dark was like the icing on my cake.

> Great Day! Fun-size waves, super clean – your dad did awesome. Milo's so proud of him! Way cool to see them shredding together. Gotta work on Gen3!

"Gen3?" Kylee asked, shamelessly reading over my shoulder.

"He means me," I answered with a grin. "He has this thing about three generations of the family surfing together. If he doesn't drown me with his obsessive safety training first, that is."

"Like he would ever let that happen," Tara commented, scraping the last of the melted cheese off the aluminum foil. "We see the way he looks at you, you disgustingly lucky wench."

My grin broadened. I knew exactly how lucky I was. A flush of warmth reddened my cheeks, and I started to say something mushy that my unattached friends probably didn't need or want to hear, but they were spared by the sound of the washing machine alarm.

"I'll move the clothes along," I offered, rising from the table. "It should be safe to touch them without pliers now, right?"

Tara nodded. "Better put them on low, though. We don't want Tarzan having a cow if any of Tim Jones' undies shrink."

Kylee scowled. "He does *not* look like a 'Tarzan.'"

"So, what does he look like?" Tara teased. "A Vinny, maybe? How about a Clarence? A Herbert?"

I walked out the door quickly, hoping to escape before any violence started. But once outside, I realized that the dark carport was no improvement. Maybe Tara could laugh off Kylee's descriptions of the grisly assault, but I couldn't. Not being able to see the ghost was poor consolation when I was still able to feel him. If he *did* want to hurt me, the fact that he could get to my emotions made me vulnerable. Vulnerable to *what* exactly, I didn't want to find out.

Wimp.

Just do it, Kali!

I forced my feet forward and up to the washer. What I needed to do was fight fire with fire — and that meant shoring up my empathic defenses. I took a breath and concentrated deeply, imagining a solid wall that surrounded me like a sphere in every direction. My wall was thick and glowing and impenetrable, and there was nothing and no one in it besides one human, a bunch of wet clothes, and two inanimate appliances.

I breathed out, slowly, and checked for any stray emotions battering around in my brain. I felt nothing out of place and smiled with relief. I was still pretty good at this stuff, even without Zane around. His presence made everything easier for me, which was nice. But I also knew that because of his effect, when it came to my own shield I'd been getting kind of lazy.

I reached into the washer and began pulling out the clothes. They didn't smell great, and the socks would never be white again, but at least nothing reeked. I tossed the wet handfuls in the dryer, pausing when I came to a baby-blue garment with black print that looked familiar. I held it up and shook it out. It was a surfer's jersey, made of a lightweight synthetic fabric and emblazoned with the logo of the Billabong Pro Tahiti, which as the girlfriend of one Zane Svenson I happened to know was a stop on the World Championship Tour of professional surfing. And as someone who had watched a good part of that contest — as well as every other leg that was held around the world since Zane and I had been together — I knew darn well that no guy named Tim Jones had surfed in it. So was he a fan who'd picked up a castoff jersey somehow? Or did vendors sell imitations, just like football jerseys? I shook my head and tossed it in the dryer. Zane would be amused. Where had this suitcase come from, anyway? We had all assumed it came into the Honolulu airport on Tara's flight, but multiple flights did use the same carousels. The contest in Tahiti had ended only a few days ago. Was it possible?

I swept my hand around the bottom of the washer and pulled up the last of the clothes. This time I couldn't help but study them more carefully. The underwear I tossed in the dryer immediately. But the boardshorts... *whoa*. Tim Jones was one serious fan, if not a serious surfer himself. The boardshorts were top-of-the-line AirTides.

A sharp pain exploded across the left side of my head, and the carport swayed. I reached out to brace myself, but my hands didn't move. The air around me grew blurry and thickened, and my eyes could no longer focus. There was no sound. My feet were floating and my body was weightless. I tried to feel for what was causing the pain in my head but my arms were still immobile; my body was being carried along like a ragdoll. The carport with its bright light over the white appliances morphed and swirled into a shimmering haze of sunlight over water, and threads of aqua filtered in from below. All at once I was suspended in various shades of blue, but before my eyes ran a river of red... a wispy stream of solid I knew to be my own blood.

My eyes closed then and I couldn't reopen them. I couldn't move at all. But I could feel that I was sinking. I could feel the weight of the water around me, the pressure that grew stronger with every inch I dropped. I could see nothing, still, but I knew. I knew that I was going down. Going down where it was darker. Colder. Deeper. Lonelier.

Down where I would never breathe again.

"No!" I forced out hoarsely. My eyes flew open and I drew in great gulps of air. I was staring blankly at the dryer controls in the middle of my well-lit carport. I was still standing upright. Still holding the boardshorts in my hands, exactly as before. I tossed the shorts and put my hands to my head, feeling for a bump, a gash, the slickness that would mean I was bleeding. There was nothing. My skin was damp with perspiration but my curls were dry. I wasn't injured. Shaken, disoriented, and completely baffled, yes... but not injured. I had been so certain that I had passed out... yet my knees hadn't even buckled!

I slammed the dryer door and started the machine. I walked to the front of the house, stopped, and leaned against the back of the door, still gasping for air.

What the hell?

I put my hand to my head once more. I was fine, really. Whatever I thought I felt, it was clearly an illusion. The ghost couldn't hurt Tara, and he couldn't hurt me, either. Not physically.

I tried to slow my breathing. But it wasn't easy when my heart kept on pounding. I had spent most of life fighting against an irrational fear of water and drowning. Zane and I had worked so hard to get me over it. And I was over it. I *was*.

What had that horrible specter done to me?

How had he done it, when I'd been so sure my defenses were solid?

And why would he want to hurt *me* in the first place?

I felt an incredibly strong, incredibly embarrassing urge to cry, and I realized that if I'd done one thing correctly just now, it was not yelling loud enough to bring everyone in the house running. That humiliation would be more than I could bear.

Get a grip, Kali.

He's the one who's dead. Remember?

Good point!

I clenched my teeth. Then I clenched my fists, just for the heck of it.

I turned toward the perfectly innocent-looking empty carport and gave the space in front of the dryer my best girl-power glare. Try to mess with my head, would he? "Okay. So you surprised me that time," I said icily, drawing up my shoulders with my best imitation of dignity. "But if the only weapon you've got is fear, you can prepare to lose."

I opened my front door and walked through it. Then I closed it quietly, without a slam.

Stupid ghost didn't deserve the satisfaction.

chapter 8

I awoke the next morning to the pleasant sound of a gentle rain pattering on the roof above my head. The air was comfortably cool for the first time in days, and Kylee and Tara were both still sound asleep. A few moments later, Zane's rooster ringtone sounded.

Seeing that he was calling rather than texting, I hopped out of bed and slipped out the door to my lanai. I leaned against the near wall under the eaves where I wouldn't get wet, at least not *that* wet, and answered with a smile. "Good morning."

"Good morning," he returned gaily.

The sound of his voice, as always, did something electrical to my bone marrow. I hadn't talked to him for real since Friday night, and I was already going through withdrawal. We'd only texted a little bit yesterday, since he'd been out on the water most of the day. I had wanted to call him immediately after the ghost encounter — actually, I'd wanted to drive myself out to the North Shore and bury my head in his chest — but it had taken me nearly an hour to work up to telling Kylee and Tara what had happened. And after the three of us had talked it through and I'd dealt with their reactions and theories and suggestions and my own aggravation about leaving myself vulnerable, I was too exhausted to do anything but crawl into bed and get unconscious.

Now I didn't want to think about it — much less talk about it — at all.

"So what's next on the girlfriends' agenda?" Zane asked. "You guys going to spend another day in

Honolulu? You might as well, you know. Sunday traffic's as good as it gets."

My spirits dipped a little. "Oh. We hadn't really planned anything yet. You're, um... not coming out?"

He was quiet for a beat. "Well, no. I was going to hang out with some of the guys today."

"That's cool." I felt so sad I couldn't stand it. We hadn't talked about any plans together — I had just assumed. We'd seen each other almost every day over the summer. But I shouldn't assume. And I shouldn't be so sad either. I was being ridiculous. I was being... that dreaded word... "clingy."

"Kali?" he asked tentatively.

"Yeah?" I replied, faking a happy tone.

"What's wrong and do *not* tell me nothing."

I sighed and smiled at the same time. "I just miss you, that's all," I said with perfect honesty. "So sue me, okay? I know we just hung out on Thursday, but I'm spoiled, and it seems like longer. That's all."

He was quiet another moment. "I miss you, too," he replied, his voice so warm I got electricity arcing in my spine again. "But, Kali, aren't you, like... occupied? I mean... I thought you guys would want to spend some time alone, just the three of you. To do girl stuff. Or whatever."

Buzzing warmth zipped through my veins. He was only trying to be considerate. In addition to avoiding the squealing, of course. "We do," I explained tenderly. "And we're having a blast. I don't mean to sound ungrateful — having them here is beyond fabulous! It's just that I'm anxious for my three best friends in the world to get to know each other, that's all."

"I see. Well, all right, then," he proposed brightly, "why don't you bring them out here tomorrow? We can spend the day on the North Shore. I'll make you guys a picnic."

"That would be perfect!" I gushed. "I can't wait."

"Don't get too excited," he quipped. "I'm only going to Foodland."

I heard stirrings from inside my room. Somebody else was up. I knew I should fill Zane in on what had happened with the ghost, but I didn't want to bring either of us down right now. "Will you have your phone with you today?" I asked. "There's something I need to tell you, but... I'm not sure how much time I'll have, here."

"Oh," he answered, a new awkwardness creeping into his voice. "Yeah, I should have the phone. Surf's no good here. But I was hoping... I mean, that's why I called early. There's something I really need to talk to you about, too."

I tensed. The tone of his voice had changed. It had that guilty ring to it again.

The door of my lanai opened and Tara's head popped out. "Oh! There you are! In the rain, of course. Sorry to intrude." She threw me a knowing smirk and dodged back inside. I could hear from the voices that followed that Kylee, too, was awake.

"You're standing out in the rain?" Zane asked.

"Um... only partially," I defended.

"Never mind then. We'll talk another time, okay?" The relief in his voice was painfully obvious.

Now I was really tense. What exactly did he feel so guilty about?

"I'll let you go, Kali," he rung off. "No picking up guys in Waikiki, by the way. And don't tell me they won't be following the three of you around, either. You're lucky I don't insist on chaperoning you."

I grinned. "You trust me."

"I do, actually."

"Likewise."

There was a pause. "I'll talk to you later, Kali. Bye."

"Bye." My heart took another dip into my stomach as we hung up. A pause? Seriously?

Like, a *guilty* pause?

No. I had only been imagining it.

When I pulled myself out of the community pool a few hours later, the smile on my face was genuine. First because I had gotten myself back in the water again, despite what happened with the stupid ghost. And second, because Lacey and Kylee were sitting on beach towels on the grass, laughing and talking like old friends already. I knew the two of them would get along. I had no idea where Tara had gotten to at the moment, but so far she and Lacey had hit it off, too. I was also happy because I was giving myself permission to stop this particular workout before the usual point of exhaustion. I wouldn't have dragged Kylee and Tara out here at all if I didn't feel so funky after missing one day's workout already — which was entirely Zane's fault for having trained me so consistently all summer. I still wasn't sure what I would do when the pools closed. But coming here this morning had been a good idea all around. Not only did I feel better physically, but seeing Lacey laugh and smile lightheartedly again was priceless.

She and Kylee were in the middle of comparing scores on some app where you listen to sound clips to pick out "guy lies" when I walked up — not surprisingly, Kylee had done much better than Lacey — but we were interrupted almost immediately by Tara. She stomped up to her towel and plopped down in a fury, her rough manner a hundred percent at odds with the sleek turquoise one-piece she was wearing, which made her look like a ballerina Barbie doll.

"Since when," she barked with annoyance, "does '*no*' mean 'follow me around and put your hand on my butt?'"

Kylee's eyes widened. "Is this guy still breathing?"

"Yes," Tara replied darkly. "But only because I could tell where his hand was going and my reflexes are quick."

Lacey sucked in a breath. "Where did this happen? Here at the pool?"

"Out in the parking lot," Tara answered, making herself more comfortable on the towel. "I went back to the car to look for something that fell out of my bag, and I found it and turned around and there was this guy — a really good-looking guy, by the way — and he just smiles at me and says, 'I've never seen you before.'"

"And what did you say?" Kylee asked.

"What am I supposed to say?" Tara retorted. "I mean, how many answers to that question are there? He's cute, yeah. But I don't know who he is, and I'm only here for a week!"

Kylee sighed. "You know, your attitude is really—"

"Kylee!" I reminded. "He was a jerk!"

Her face reddened. "Oh, right."

"Anyway," Tara reported, "he asked me why I was at the pool and if I wanted to go out to lunch with him instead, and I said no. Then he said, 'Oh, come on. I think you're hot,' and *whammo*."

"Wow," Lacey said sympathetically. "That's gross. I'm sorry. We can report it to the manager if you want. Did it look like he was on his way into the pool, or was he just hanging around outside?"

Tara shrugged. "All I know is he didn't follow me in. Don't worry about it on my account. I'm fine."

"We'll all walk out together this time," I announced,

toweling off. "You guys ready to do Oahu, Part Two, Southeast?"

"Totally!" they chorused in unison, pulling their clothes back on over their swimsuits.

"I'll walk out with you, too," Lacey offered, glancing at the clock. She had finished her shift a while ago, but didn't seem in a hurry to leave. "And if we see this dude, I'm threatening to call the police. This is a family establishment, after all!" She threw her shoulders back with bravado, and I tried hard not to grin. It was tough to take Lacey seriously as an authority figure for the pool when she looked more like some cherub out of a medieval painting. But you had to admire her chutzpah.

"Any chance you're not working tomorrow?" I asked as we walked out the gates. It would be fun to take Lacey to the North Shore with us. Maybe we could even get Matt to show up.

"I wish," Lacey said solemnly. "But I'm working *every* day now. The best I get is a two-hour break at noon, like today. But that actually works out all right, because—"

"There he is," Tara said grimly, pointing. "The blond one."

I looked up to see three guys in their late teens hanging out around a parked car about thirty feet away from us. The blond one was Austin.

Lacey's face went deathly pale.

I didn't need to ask Tara if she was sure. I was sure. I was sure because I already knew that Austin was a jerk and because it was pretty obvious in retrospect that Lacey had been about to say "because Austin's coming to take me out to lunch." Unless, of course, he found something more enticing to do in the meantime.

"Don't go over there by yourself, Lace," I said quickly, stepping between her and the guys, who as yet hadn't noticed any of us. "Maybe you should just tell your manager. Anyway, we'll definitely have to hang out sometime this week. Even if it's for a late dinner or something. Just text me and let me know. Okay?"

Her thick lashes blinked back tears, even as her cheeks flamed with red. Her cornflower blue eyes burned with a fiery mixture of fury, hurt, and gratitude. "Sure, Kali. Thanks," she squeaked, turning away from us and back toward the pool gates. "Bye, guys."

Kylee and Tara called back their goodbyes, and we all moved towards my car. Fortunately for Lacey's pride, no one but me had witnessed her distress. Kylee and Tara had been keeping their eyes on the Neanderthal. Austin never did notice Lacey, but shortly before we reached our car, we heard him whistling at Tara again. We got in the car without responding and I revved up the engine, trying hard to suppress lurid fantasies of mowing the guy down on our way out.

I had driven several blocks before I realized that Kylee and Tara were arguing.

"That was *one* guy," Kylee insisted. "You cannot—"

"Oh, yes I can!" Tara fired back. "I barely had that stupid suit on an hour! Why don't I just hang a sign around my neck that says 'harass me?'"

"What happened with that one jerk was not the suit's fault!" Kylee raged. "Most guys aren't like that and you know it. What matters is that you look gorgeous in it! You *have* to wear it today!"

"I do not!"

My head swam. I was sick with sympathy for Lacey's crushed feelings, but I had to confess I was also a tiny bit relieved. It was well past time she put "rebound guy" aside and moved on with the business of realizing she should be with Matt. And although I probably should be bothered by the strife between Kylee and Tara, I had missed them so terribly all summer that their familiar bickering was like music to my ears.

"But if I don't want guys to paw me, and I *don't*, why should I even wear a suit like this?"

"Because it makes you feel good about yourself and because the nice guys will enjoy it, that's why!"

"Who says it makes me feel good about myself?"

I hummed merrily as they continued to argue all the way down the H1. The rainclouds had thinned to a partly sunny sky and the temperature was holding nicely in the upper seventies. I had a nagging feeling that I should be concentrating more on what had happened with the ghost last night — trying to figure it out, trying to keep it from happening again — but in the happy light of day it was all too easy to shove such dark thoughts aside. Kylee and I had agonized forever last night worrying over what to do with the clothes in the dryer and how to remove them before anyone else came under attack, only to find out that even as we debated, Tara had snuck out and quietly folded them all. She'd put them in a paper sack in the tool shed to store until Tim Jones' suitcase was completely dried and de-scented, and she had experienced no ghostly problems whatsoever. Her opinion was that the two of us should just stay away from the stuff and let her handle it.

So, hey. Why stress?

"By the way, Kali," Tara asked cheerfully, the swimsuit argument apparently forgotten. "Where are we going, exactly?"

I grinned. "The spitting cave of Portlock."

"Ooh," Kylee cooed. "Sounds awesome! What does it spit?"

"You'll find out!"

We parked in an upscale residential neighborhood and

walked beside a chain-link fence along a path between two houses. The brush was thick, and if it weren't for the fact that we kept passing people coming the other way, I'm pretty sure Kylee and Tara would accuse me of leading me them either into the middle of nowhere or straight off a cliff, as I did when Zane first led me down this path and which, ironically, was not far from the truth.

When the brush opened up I turned around to enjoy my friends' expressions as they took in the view. We were high above the ocean, standing on bare, sloping rock. It was impossible to tell how far up we were. The slope was so abrupt that from where we were standing it appeared as if you could walk straight out and drop straight down. Naturally, there was no guard rail. This was Hawaii. I chuckled as their eyes widened and they unconsciously braced their feet beneath them.

"This way," I instructed, picking my way along the side of the cliff. Above us, all along the ridge of the cliff, were magnificent houses with spectacular views that none of us could ever afford to live in. But the beaches of Hawaii were open to all, and this cliff, technically speaking, was a beach. Unlike the twisted, spiky lava rock common to the North Shore, the rock here was laid down in smooth circular bands, kind of like cake batter looked when you poured it into a pan. The whole cliffside was made of the smooth, rippling layers of rock, and it wasn't difficult to climb on... if you weren't afraid of heights. The path I followed was a well-traversed zig-zag that led down the gentlest possible slope, and Kylee and Tara followed me bravely until we had descended enough to see the main attraction. I picked out a relatively flat spot and sat down, then encouraged them to sit beside me. I had to double-check my empath blind, because the shadows here were numerous and my first visit had been made all the more harrowing by the feelings of those whose companions had not come back. But like most spots of raw natural beauty, the cumulative awe and wonder of those visiting before did help to balance out the element of danger.

"Oh, my God," Kylee breathed with reverence. "Kali, this is *so* amazingly gorgeous!"

Indeed it was. Our new vantage point was halfway down to the water, and from here we could look across to see the waves crashing into the foot of the towering cliffs all along their scallop-shaped banks. The striated layers of rock gleamed red and gray in the sun, and the dark blue water turned frothy white as it exploded upon their meeting.

"Wow," Tara exclaimed. "I love that sound. I could listen to crashing waves all day!"

"See that hole?" I said, pointing to an unremarkable looking divot in between two scalloped arms of the cliff. "The one that looks like the entrance to a sea cave? Keep watching it."

As the waves continued to crash into the rocks, the mysterious mechanism within soon met its requirements. We heard a bumping, rocking sound, then a gush, and with a spew and a hiss, the spitting cave of Portlock showed its opinion of the Pacific by shooting a giant stream of water straight back out of the cave mouth. As the frothy rejects sprayed back over the ocean, the assembled onlookers laughed and cheered.

"That is so cool!" Tara and Kylee proclaimed together. "How does it do that?"

They continued to watch in wonder as the cave did its thing, with Tara pondering the physics involved and Kylee pretending to care, while I pulled out my phone for a quick check-in with Zane.

Watching the cave spit. And you?

His answer was almost immediate.

Waiting for BBQ chicken at Ted's.

I smiled. A plate lunch at Ted's Bakery was always a treat, no matter how long it took.

Jealous! All we've had today is cereal and fruit.
Kylee starving us for sexy beachwear purposes.

His answer both warmed my heart and embarrassed me, as always.

Hey, while you were pigging out on nachos last night, I had PB&J! Your sexiness for beachwear purposes already maxed out.

Sometimes I didn't know how to take his compliments, since it was clear to anyone with a halfway objective eye that I was nowhere near the female equivalent of his own ridiculously good looks. But he seemed to think he knew what he liked, so who was I to argue with him?

Thanks for that. :)

I stuffed my phone back in my pocket, and after my friends had spent a suitable amount of time ogling the natural wonder before us, I rose. "Okay, guys," I announced. "That's enough spitting. We're off to the blowhole."

Kylee raised an eyebrow at me. "The blowhole? Is that what it sounds like?"

I chuckled. "Probably."

"Awesome!" Tara declared. "Let's do it."

We were all the way back in the car and pulling out of the neighborhood when the critical words from Zane's texts popped out front and center in my brain. There they floated, like a pregnant rain cloud — dark, ominous, and waiting for just the right moment to drop their heavy load.

I ran back over our limited conversations in my mind, replaying everything I had said, everything I had texted, and every other possibility by which anyone else might have transmitted the information in question.

Nope. I hadn't said a thing. Nor could anyone else have.

It seemed like such a small matter. But the implications scared the crap out of me.

I'd never once told Zane that we'd eaten nachos last night. And there was no way he could have known that.

Unless he had seen it himself.

chapter 9

I kept my mouth shut all the way down the Kalianaole Highway. With chiseled cliffs towering above us to the left and dark rock and blue ocean below us to the right, the scenery was way too beautiful to be spoiled by my brooding. I let Kylee and Tara ooh and aah and squeal in peace as we snaked along the southeast coast of Oahu.

The Halona Blowhole Lookout, which unlike the spitting cave was actually a sanctioned tourist attraction with signs and a parking lot, was one of my own favorite spots outside of the North Shore. The multi-level, paved overlook was built right into the side of the mountain that sloped down into the sea and was easily accessible with wide concrete steps, stone walls, and actual guard rails that conveniently showed where an intelligent person should and should not stand in order to avoid certain death. The lava rocks here were different again from those of the cliffs near the spitting cave, being rougher-edged and tossed in an unruly jumble. They were more difficult to walk or climb on, and definitely more painful to fall on — although pain was a relative thing, depending on whether you stopped at that rock or went tumbling helplessly on down to the ocean.

We filed out of the car and went to stand at the railing with a handful of other tourists whose attention was fixed on... a bunch of wet rocks. "Wait for it," I promised.

From the sharp tips of the green peaks behind and above us, the earth swept out and down in tumbled stages, forming a series of plateaus. The highway and the lookout we were on rested at one level, and the chaotic expanse of rocks we were currently staring at formed another beneath us. As the waves crashed relentlessly into the base of this rocky pedestal, billows of white frothed up and splashed onto its jagged edges.

"Oh, I see it!" Tara exclaimed, pointing. "Is that it?"

From the middle of the rocky area in question came a sudden burst of white, much like a puff of cigarette smoke. It erupted from a hole in the floor and released straight up into the air.

"Keep waiting," I instructed.

The blowhole puffed again. Then after a few seconds it made a sort of gurgling sound, followed by an uncoordinated, unbalanced plume of white that pitched to one side.

"Was that," Kylee began. "Wait, whoa!"

The blowhole made its grand entrance. A huge fountain of bright white shot straight out of the ground with a mighty roar, towering high up into the sky before plummeting back down to spatter the rocks around it with a mighty smack. Lesser plumes completed the show, huffing and puffing and chugging until the pressure was released. Then the swirls of white froth wriggled their way among the crags and channels back into the ocean, and the unassuming hole lay quiet again, looking innocent as a cat.

"Awesome!" Kylee praised. "Just like Old Faithful!"

"Except it's not faithful at all," Tara mused. "It's totally at the whim of the tide and the ocean swells. That was *so* cool!"

I could stand it no more. "You guys enjoy," I heard myself saying. "I'm going to step over here and call Zane real quick."

They paid no attention to me as I backed away and moved to sit on a low stone wall away from the main attraction. I was practically sitting on the laps of two different overlapping shadows, but I refused to let that bother me. The blowhole was always crawling with shadows, and right now I was so preoccupied that their faint and fleeting concerns barely registered. I made my call.

Zane didn't pick up till the third ring. "Hey, there," he answered, sounding ever so slightly nervous to my well-trained ear. "What's up?"

You know exactly what, I thought grimly. "How did you know we were eating nachos last night?" I asked.

His response came a beat quicker than expected. And his voice was way, *way* too chipper.

"They looked really good, actually. Was that mango mixed in with the peppers?"

"Zane!" I fumed.

"Okay, okay!" he said with a guilty chuckle. "I know, I shouldn't joke about it. I'm sorry, Kali. Really I am. I tried to tell you about it this morning."

My teeth gritted. That was true, he had. I closed my eyes. *This is not good.* "Please tell me that you're still just seeing flashes," I begged. "Of... almost empty rooms."

"Well, yes, but—"

His next silence was nearly unbearable.

"It's still nothing like the long scene at the beach or when I saw the car accident," he finished. "But the flashes have gotten a lot more frequent. Not so much when I was out surfing yesterday, but last night and then again today... it seems to happen whenever I'm thinking about you."

"What are you seeing?" I asked, bracing myself. "Tell me *exactly*."

He blew out a breath, and I could imagine a shock of his adorable curls ruffling up off his forehead. "Nachos," he reported. "Your room with air mattresses on the floor. This morning I could see the rain outside on your lanai."

"What about right now?" I asked hopefully. "Can you see my mother working at her computer?"

"Um... It doesn't work like that."

"What do you mean?"

He paused. "Look, Kali, there's something else going on here. I'm really sorry. I didn't ask for this, and I'm not trying to do it. But I can't control it, either. Whenever I think about you, it just—"

My pulse raced. "Tell me what you've seen!"

"You guys eating breakfast," he answered tightly. "The pool. Lacey meeting your friends. Driving down the H1. I knew you were at the spitting cave before you told me and I know you're at the blowhole now. I'm sorry, Kali."

HOLY CRAP!

"Listen," he pleaded into the silence that followed. "I promise I haven't seen anything embarrassing. I really haven't. I haven't actually even seen *you*. What I get is a flash of a room, or the car, or the area you're in, and sometimes I catch the people around and sometimes I don't."

"Why can't you see me?" I croaked. I really, really hoped he was telling the truth about the nothing embarrassing part.

I was pretty sure he was.

"I don't know," he answered. "All I know is, whatever's going on, it keeps changing. The first flashes were really quick and not too often. Now they're all the time, and it seems like there's more to them. I don't know for sure because with the whole stalker thing I've really been trying not to look. But the truth is, if I *tried* to see more? I'm almost positive I could."

"Don't you dare!" I snapped. Then I got a grip. "I'm sorry. Defensive reflex. Dialing back now. What I *meant* to say is that I appreciate your not taking advantage of the situation." *Which you still could*, I reminded myself. Geez, this was a nightmare! "Please, Zane, can you just keep trying to ignore it until we figure out what's happening, here? Because this is really creeping me out."

"I get that," he said quickly. "And I am trying." His voice deepened. "It'll be better when we're together tomorrow. Neither one of us will have to worry about it then."

I thought about how nice it would be to feel his arms around me again, and tomorrow looked like a better day for any number of reasons.

"There has to be a way for you to shut it off," I said hopefully. "I'll ask Kylee. If she doesn't know, surely her grandmother will have some idea."

"Okay," he replied, his voice tense again. "But... you do realize that this is going to make your friends think I'm totally twisted now, right? I mean, I may not see you, but I *have* seen them."

I froze. "You've seen—"

"No, no," he clarified quickly. "I told you I didn't see anything embarrassing. I just mean that I've literally *seen them* in the flashes."

I exhaled loudly. "Oh. That's a relief."

"Still. Those swimsuits they were wearing, I have to say, were totally—"

"Zane!" I warned, even as I smiled. He was clearly teasing me now.

"I was going to say totally decent!" he insisted, managing to sound unjustly accused. "As was everyone's sleepwear, by the way. But I've got to tell you, I am totally disillusioned now. I was led to believe that when girls had sleepovers they ran around half naked snapping towels at each other."

I snorted. "Where do guys get this garbage?

"Hard to say," he speculated. "Seems like a middle school impression. R-rated frat-boy movies, maybe?"

I cracked up laughing.

"So set me straight!" he cajoled. "What else do I have wrong?"

"Not my problem," I said with a smirk. Then I wondered, uneasily, if he could *see* me smirking.

Yikes.

This was difficult. Despite our being able to laugh about it at the moment, I was not at all looking forward to confessing this conversation to my friends. Zane was right. His uncontrollable spy-vision *was* going to creep them out. And who could blame them? But they had to know. Telling them was the right thing to do. Besides which, we needed their help.

"Listen, I've got to talk to them about this," I explained. "I'll call you back a little later, okay?"

"Okay," he returned. "Sorry. Again."

"I know you are," I assured. We said our goodbyes and hung up.

Kylee and Tara had given up their prime spots closest to the blowhole to more newly arriving tourists, but they were still enjoying a killer view of the coast from a spot a little further up on the lookout. They were laughing and pointing, no doubt watching the bodysurfers do their thing at Sandy Beach. The surf might be flat on the North Shore, but here on the other side of the island it was kicking up nicely for August, and Sandies was booming.

I suspected I should take them to a more private place somewhere, butter them up a bit, and then carefully plan a way to explain everything so it didn't make my favorite guy in the world — who I wanted desperately for them to adore — sound like some kind of pervert. But I was better at winging it. So I just opened my mouth and started talking.

"Whenever Zane thinks about me he gets flashes of wherever I am," I announced before they'd even realized I was standing behind them. "He knew we were eating nachos last night and he knew we were at the pool and the spitting cave and he knows we came here. He can't see me for some reason but he can see you, although he swears he hasn't seen anything embarrassing. And he says he feels bad about it and he's trying not to encourage it, but he feels like if he wanted to, he could see a lot more."

Kylee and Tara turned around. They stared at me with their jaws slack and their faces unpleasantly colored.

"Oh, that's not right," Tara said after a moment, her tone grim.

"I know," I agreed miserably.

They were both quiet for another long while. The blowhole spewed again, but nobody looked at it.

"But that doesn't make any sense," Kylee argued, staring at me. "He can't constantly be popping in and out of his body all day long, whenever he thinks about you. He wouldn't be able to function. Besides, if any part of his spirit was actually present *here*, you should be able to sense it, just like you did before."

Her words struck me. I hadn't thought about it quite like that. "I... I don't feel like he's been *with* me, no. I certainly haven't seen anything."

"This is too weird!" Tara said defensively, her eyes getting the glazed look they always got when she overloaded on woo-woo. "I'm going to go contemplate some nice, tame fluid dynamics for a minute, okay?" She took a step back towards the blowhole.

Kylee caught her by the arm. "Be a man!" she hissed. "This *is* physics! You've said so yourself. What we all need to figure out is—" She breathed in sharply. Her lids fluttered and her dark eyes swam with thought. "Wait! Kali, you said he can't see *you?* Like, ever?"

I shook my head. "That's what he says."

"Will you let go of me?" Tara demanded as Kylee's nails dug into her wrist.

"No," Kylee replied offhandedly as she flashed a smile at me. "I think I get it!" she gushed. "You're a beacon!"

"I'm a what?"

"A beacon for remote viewing! Zane isn't leaving his body at all. At least not with these flashes. I was thinking OBE or astral projection, and it still sounds like that with the beach scene and the car accident thing, but this sounds different. It's—"

"Will you talk English instead of psychobabble please?" Tara ordered.

Kylee frowned at the word choice, but she did let go of Tara's wrist. "Remote viewing isn't the same as actually traveling someplace else. It's getting impressions about a distant target in some other way. Like telepathy."

Tara rubbed her arm. "So what you're saying is that Zane is able to see whatever Kali is seeing? Like he's seeing through her eyes?"

I stiffened. Seeing through my eyes was *way* too close to being inside my brain.

"Not exactly," Kylee said, looking at me with concern. "It's not like he's inside your head looking out. But if he's focusing on you, and you're his beacon, then he's picking up on whatever you're focusing on, if that makes sense. He's getting visual images that are like snapshots of your day, in real time."

I processed that information slowly. I decided I didn't like it. "And what if there are things I see, like when I'm *alone,*" I stressed, "that I don't want Zane — or anybody else — to see?"

Kylee blinked back at me uncomfortably. "Oh. I guess that's... awkward."

"Awkward?" I practically choked. "Are you kidding me?"

Her brown eyes swam with sympathy, making me feel a whole lot worse. I whirled away from both of them and headed... somewhere.

This was too much. Really. All of the other psychic stuff was annoying. It made me feel like a freak, it intruded on my otherwise normal life. But giving my boyfriend unlimited access inside my eyeballs was taking the concept of personal intrusion to a whole new level — and I wanted off the whacko bus. *Now*.

"Kali! Where are you going?" Kylee called after me.

"I don't know!" I fled across the parking lot, then stood gazing out to the south. Beyond the overlook and far below me lay a protected cove with a small, sandy beach. The rock walls surrounding it were steep and forbidding, but nevertheless a narrow, unauthorized trail led down to it from the corner of the parking lot, and a dozen people were swimming in the aqua shallows and frolicking on the sand.

Kylee caught up with me. "Kali, I'm sure Zane can learn to control this thing. It's the same with all these abilities, isn't it? He just has to learn how, that's all."

I didn't look at her. It was a nice thought, and Zane was a nice guy. But he was a *guy*.

I really didn't want to think about this anymore.

Tara caught up with us and stared over my shoulder at the cove below. "How did those people get down there?"

"Tara!" Kylee protested, "Can't you see that Kali is upset?"

Tara drew back and looked at me. "I'm sure you can keep it under control, Kali. You're good at that. What are you so worried about? He said he hasn't seen anything embarrassing yet. And now you know. Right?"

"But it's not under my control!" I practically shouted. Dangerous heat rose up behind my eyes. I would *not* cry.

Tara looked from me to Kylee as if she were confused. "Sure it is," she said gently. "I mean, if some form of Zane's own energy were actually present in this place, like when he was a wraith, that would be one thing. He could see you like anyone else here could see you, and you couldn't do anything about that." She looked at Kylee as if for confirmation, and Kylee nodded slightly. Then Tara looked at me. "But if Zane and all of his energy is physically located on the North Shore right now, and he's getting whatever info he's getting by tapping into his emotional connection to you, then it seems to me like the ball's in *your* court. Somehow or other, *you* have to be letting him in. Ergo, you should also be able to—"

"*Block* him!" I shouted for real, throwing my arms around Tara's neck in a spasm of happiness. "Yes! Of course!"

"Damn, Tara," Kylee said approvingly. "I think you're right. And you say you don't have a sense for this stuff. Been reading up behind our backs have you?"

Tara had gone beet red. "No!" she protested, detaching me. "I just... Well... isn't that common sense? It does follow... well... scientifically."

Kylee smirked.

Tara rolled her eyes. "Oh, shut up."

I laughed out loud and group hugged them. "Thank you," I gushed. "Both of you. Surely I can figure out how to block him, at least when it matters the most. I *am* really good at that now!"

My high lasted only a few seconds. Then an unwelcome memory brought me right back down again.

Pain. A river of red. Sinking. Dropping. No way to breathe...

I had not been able to block the ghost last night. Perhaps I was not as good as I thought I was.

"Where to next, Kal?" Tara asked merrily.

"Yes, I can hardly wait!" Kylee chimed in. "Every view here is more gorgeous than the last one!"

But you ARE good at blocking! I told myself forcefully, refusing to lose my mojo. If I had slipped up with the ghost, it was only because I had gotten lazy having Zane's comforting presence around. What I needed to do was train myself in blocking, just like I had done with swimming. And what better place to start than with some good, old-fashioned exercise?

I drew in a breath, then blew it out with determination.

"To the Pali," I declared.

chapter 10

I had not been back to the Pali, a magnificent overlook of Oahu's windward coast set in the cleft of a mountain peak, since the day I had first met Matt. He had been taking me on a tour of the island and thought I would enjoy the view, which I probably would have if I had actually managed to reach the overlook. Sadly, however, the plateau was also the site of a horrific battle that resulted in hundreds of men being pushed to their deaths over the side of the cliff, and it was inhabited by the one of the densest, most miserable assemblies of shadows I'd ever encountered. Their emotions of fear, failure, and horror had completely overwhelmed me before I'd learned how to block such feelings.

Not too long ago I had considered going back, this time with a living, breathing Zane at my side, to test how far I had come and how much better I could tolerate the place's oppressive gloom. But I had never quite gotten up the nerve.

"Are you sure you want to do this, Kali?" Kylee asked me hesitantly as she popped open her bottle of KonaRed. We were standing by my car outside the 7-Eleven in Waimanalo where we'd stopped to buy snacks. At least, that's why they told me they had wanted to stop before driving on to the Pali. I suspected that what they really wanted was to get the car keys out of my hands before I drove them anywhere near the place. Since they had heard me describe in detail my near nervous collapse on my last visit, I couldn't blame them.

"Yes, I have to go," I said stubbornly. "Trial by fire

and all that. These abilities only seem to get stronger once they show up. At least that's the way it's happened so far."

Kylee looked back at me with sympathy, even as a flicker of amusement danced across her dark eyes. "Love'll do that to you," she teased. "You and Zane definitely seem to have some weird kind of synergy going on. My *ba noi* says that's really rare, but it can be super powerful when it happens."

"Power's fine, as long as it's divided up equally," Tara commented, studying me as she dug into her bag of Maui onion chips. "I think you're taking the right approach, Kali. As long as you're careful about it. In fact, I think we should set up a test."

"Like what?" I asked, intrigued. Sometimes, Tara's cool, detached way of looking at problems made Kylee and me both want to scream and shake her like a rattle. At other times she was our calm in a storm, and her level-headed observations and careful plotting were priceless.

Tara considered a moment, crunching her chips. "How about this? First, we'll get you settled where you can feel the shadows. Where exactly do you need to be?"

A shudder rocked my shoulders, and I looked away with embarrassment. Seriously? Was that all it took? Just thinking about how close to the edge of the Pali I would have to walk? How many of the yelling, bleeding, moaning—

No! Did I really need to do this? Today?

Wimp.

"I'm not sure I can go that close to the edge," I admitted. "It will be too humiliating if I fail and flip out. The shadows are freakin' *everywhere*... for a first test, I'll probably be fine staying in the car. They're bad enough in the parking lot."

"Perfect," Tara said encouragingly. "So here's what

we'll do. You make yourself comfortable and get your empathic blind in place, just like we all learned in the spring. It should be easy enough to test. You'll have a gauge for how strong your blind is, because the shadows will be pushing its limits every second, right?"

"Right," I agreed.

"Once you get to the point where you think it's pretty solid," Tara continued, "we'll run a test for Zane. We'll put up a flash card that *you* can see with a message for him."

"Oh, cool!" Kylee enthused. "And if he doesn't get it, her blind worked!"

"Well, not necessarily," Tara explained. "Not if he only sees occasional flashes. But we'll leave the sign up for a while to increase his chances."

My pulse sped up with anticipation. This *had* to work. "But he's trying not to look, remember? Should I text him and tell him to reverse that?"

Tara shook her head. "Not at first. First we see what happens when he's clueless. That'll be our control round."

"Let's do it!" Kylee urged.

I turned toward the car, only to find Tara's outstretched hand in front of me. "Um, Kali? Keys, please. You can give me directions."

"Right," I agreed again.

Tara drove us up into the high part of the mountain range in the center of the island, and as expected, the sky grew cloudier as we ascended. The misty shrouds that encircled the dramatic green peaks only added to the air of romance for Kylee and Tara, but I suffered the same feeling of foreboding this stretch of highway always dredged up in me. The feeling only got worse as I directed Tara to turn off onto the narrow lane that led back to the Pali.

"Ooh, it's so pretty here!" Kylee cooed, unaware of

how the dense, jungle-like surroundings seemed to be closing in on me with every inch we drove.

I didn't know if the effect of the soldier shadows could stretch this far, or if I was really just psyching myself out with memories of the last time, but the cold feeling settling into my limbs was already distinctly uncomfortable.

"I'm going to start working on my blind now," I told them, closing my eyes as I tried to relax in the passenger seat. "The lot is straight ahead. Just drive up to it and park."

I couldn't seem to get the memories of that day with Matt out of my head. Never before or since had I seen so many shadows, so many suffering bodies, all in one place. I didn't doubt there were worse places on earth, but with the exception of a Civil War battlefield that I had visited when I was little — and not yet as sensitive to emotion — I had not been subjected to them. Nor would I ever, if I had a choice about it. Battlefields of any kind were a nonstarter, including Pearl Harbor. No amount of money could get me to tour someplace like the Tower of London or a concentration camp. In fact, I never wanted to go to Europe, period. The more people that had lived in a place, the thicker the shadows were. And although generally that meant as many happy moments as sad, in some places, the imprint of human grief could be overwhelming.

The battle of the Pali might be relatively recent and unknown to the history books. But it was definitely one of those places.

"Are you okay so far, Kali?" Kylee asked. "We're not there yet."

No, I was not okay. But it was my own darn fault. I had to stop remembering the last time! "I just need to focus," I murmured.

I tried to clear my mind and start with the simple

empath tactics I'd learned. It didn't help my confidence that the wall I'd thought was so great back at my carport had failed so epically, so I decided to do something slightly different. First I visualized the blind coming down, the way I blocked out the everyday shadows. Then I brought in a layer of... platinum. Yes, why not? I wrapped sheets of platinum — whether platinum actually bent or not, I didn't care — around and around me like bandaging a mummy. It seemed secure, and oddly, I began to feel better. Then I decided to make my barrier glow.

Awesome.

"Kali," I heard Tara saying. I had almost forgotten what we were doing. "Are you okay? We're there."

"Seriously?" I questioned, not believing her. "Where exactly?"

"Parked in the lot. Right up front, against the sidewalk that leads to the overlook."

A smile spread across my face. My cheeks warmed. "That's amazing," I breathed. "I feel perfectly fine. Really. I don't feel bad at all."

I could hear stifled cheers from Kylee in the back seat, then various shuffling noises from Tara. "Hang on Kali," she said quietly. "Just keep your eyes closed for now."

I sat back and relaxed in my happy place. I could visualize where we were parked and I knew how I had felt the last time I was here. The shadows weren't terribly dense this far out, but the bad ones were near enough, and I was more sensitive now. There was no question that without any protection, I would be in misery.

Glowing platinum was the bomb.

"Okay," Tara said after a moment. "Do you think you can keep your concentration if you open your eyes?"

"I think so," I said with optimism. Nothing could prevent me from seeing the shadows, but if I had learned how to keep the regular blind down in the background of my mind, I could figure this out, too. If not, I could always shut my eyes again.

I opened my lids slowly. The transparent outline of a man's bare shoulder moved across my lap. His spear stuck up in my face.

Fear. Anger.

Glowing platinum!

It took only a second to make my emotions stable again. I focused on the solid part of the car in front of me and looked through the wispy image to see a little spiral-bound notebook propped up on the dashboard. Written on it in Tara's clear block letters was "Zane, text Tara now if you see this!"

I chuckled. "How is he going to text you?"

"He has both our numbers," Kylee added from the back seat. "We had to arrange your little surprise, didn't we? Good thing we were in communication, too, since our flight kept getting delayed. Are you still okay?"

"Perfect," I said proudly. "I'll just sit here and stare. Why don't you guys check out the view? I hear it's amazing."

They seemed to be exchanging a glance. "We'll go one at a time," Tara announced, and I heard Kylee open the back door.

"Pay the parking machine!" I called after her before it closed again. Then I relaxed and enjoyed my glowing platinum some more. It was warm and cozy inside.

"You seem awfully chipper," Tara said suspiciously a few minutes later.

"I can't help it," I said, still smiling. "This is going to work. I can block the emotions of these shadows a hundred percent, and I can block Zane's access too. I know I can. I've been staring at this sign for what, five minutes now? He'd text if he saw it. I can't tell you what a relief this is. I've been going crazy thinking about what it would be like to lose every shred of privacy for the rest of my natural life. Because that's exactly what would happen if anytime Zane wanted to he could just—"

Tara's phone buzzed on the dash.

No, no, no!

Terror shot through me. Tara grabbed her phone.

Rage. Fear. Horror. Pain...

I closed my eyes quickly and cursed myself for losing focus. *Walls up!* The emotions of the soldiers left me, but my own panic remained. I opened my eyes again to find Tara staring at her phone with a disgusted expression.

"What?" I practically screamed. My platinum couldn't have failed. It just couldn't! Everything had been going so wonderfully with Zane all summer. I knew that no relationship was perfect, but ours had seemed like it was starting out pretty darn close. As long as he felt the same way about me that I did about him, nothing could get in our way. But *this?* How could I ever deal with *this?*

I wasn't sure that I could. And even though I knew it wasn't Zane's fault, I was still irrationally angry with him for having such an unfair advantage over me.

I wasn't sure I could ever get over that, either.

"It's Kylee," Tara said with an eye roll. "She can't figure out how to pay the stupid machine. You mind if we switch off?"

I collapsed back into my seat. For a long moment, I couldn't seem to move. "No," I murmured.

Tara got out of the car.

I couldn't handle much more of this. The uncertainty was killing me. I pulled out my own phone, called Zane, and closed my eyes. Then I set my platinum walls on high glow.

"Hey," he answered, still sounding a little on the nervous side. "Everything okay?"

"Not sure on that," I answered honestly. "Could you do me a favor? Wait exactly three minutes from now, and then I want you to *try* to see what I'm seeing. For one minute, maybe. Then give up. Okay?"

I heard an uncomfortable exhale. "Are you sure about that?"

"Yes, I'm sure."

"All right. Then what do I do?"

"You'll know. Or if you don't know, I'll call you."

"Okay, then. T minus three minutes," he agreed, trying to sound cheerful. It was a half-hearted effort for him. He knew that I was uptight, and I was too uptight to convince him otherwise.

We hung up. I checked the time on my phone and settled in. When Kylee returned a few moments later and popped into the front seat beside me, I explained my plan. She quickly crossed out Tara's name on the sign and replaced it with her own, then put her phone on the dash and waited with anticipation. When the three-minute mark arrived, I stared at the sign. But inwardly, I was focusing on those glowing bands of platinum with all my might.

Safe and secure. Impenetrable. Just me and my own brain, thank you very much. Warm and cozy. A thousand light-years thick...

Either I almost hypnotized myself, or I almost fell asleep, because I heard nothing until Kylee shook me by the shoulder. "Kali! Can't you hear me? Snap out of it! It's been a minute and a half already!"

I snapped out of it. "Has he texted?"

She flashed a brilliant smile at me. "Not a peep!"

The back door of the car popped open and Tara jumped inside. "Well?" she asked eagerly. "What's happening?"

"Did you get a text?" I begged.

She shook her head.

My body went rubbery with relief. He was *trying* that time. He told me he would. And he hadn't texted. Which meant he hadn't seen it!

Was I safe? For real?

Kylee explained the experiment to Tara, then looked at me proudly. "See there, Kali! You can do it!"

"Very promising," Tara agreed. "But let's verify. Kali, what if I drive you down the road a ways where you're more comfortable, and then you can drop your defenses? Then we'll have him try again. Kylee, you should check out the Pali while we're doing it. Shame to miss that view, particularly since we just fed the meter."

"Check!" Kylee agreed. She hopped out of the driver's seat to let Tara in. "Good luck, Kali!" she chirped, moving off to take her turn at the view.

Tara wrote a third message for Zane, then started up the car. "Why don't you text him?" she instructed. "Tell him to try again in exactly five minutes. But keep your defenses up until then."

I nodded. She didn't have to tell me the last part. I was close enough to an emotional wreck without feeling the shadows. She drove down the narrow road away from the Pali until a dirt pullout appeared. She turned in, splashed through a leftover rain puddle, and stopped again.

"Okay here?" she asked.

I checked the time and looked around. I couldn't lower my walls for twenty more seconds, so couldn't say for sure, but since I could only see a few shadows scattered about, their emotions couldn't be too bad. Tara propped up the notebook in front of me again and as our time target struck I let my mummy-bandages fall away.

Ouch. So exposed!

"How do you feel?" Tara asked.

"Like one of those dreams where you walk into elementary school and realize you're in your underwear," I said honestly.

Tara chuckled. "That bad, huh?"

I stared at the sign. *Zane — If you see this, Text Tara now.* I felt open to sensations from around me, but the few shadows made little impression, I saw no living people other than Tara, and I could never "feel" my closest friends anyway. So I was not surprised to be unbothered by external emotions. Within myself, however, the fuses on all hell's firecrackers sizzled away.

Tara's phone buzzed.

Her eyes met mine. She scooped her phone off the dash and looked at the screen with a smile. "It's him," she announced. Then she held it out towards me.

As you wish.

I grabbed my phone and dialed his number. "Zane!" I gushed, as soon as he answered and before he could even speak. "Do you know where I am right now? Tell me exactly what you've been seeing ever since we left the blowhole."

"Oo-kay," he said, his voice tentative. "I told you I would try not to see anything. I started to get a few flashes, but I mainly just saw the inside of your car."

"Could you tell where we were?" I demanded. I knew I sounded harsh, but I couldn't help it. Once I got my questions answered, everything would be all right again.

I hoped.

"I wasn't trying to," he answered, sounding slightly hurt. "But if I had to guess, I'd say you were headed up the windward side, because I think I saw the ocean to your right once."

"I know you weren't trying to," I said, feeling guilty. "I'm sorry. What about in the twenty minutes or so right before I texted you? Anything then?" My heart was thudding. I had kept my defenses up ever since we'd turned off the Pali Highway onto the access road. If my block was effective, he shouldn't have seen any of the "jungle" part of the drive.

"I saw mountains once," he admitted, sounding miserable again.

I could barely ask the next question. "And what about after I called? When I told you to try hard in exactly three minutes? What did you see then?"

Please, please, please!

"Well, that was kind of weird," he explained. "It was the first time I'd *tried* to connect with you, so I'm not sure what should have happened. But I got nothing."

I closed my eyes and exhaled slowly. *Thank you, God!* All was now officially right with the world. "Nothing?" I repeated weakly.

"No. It was like I was trying to see in a tunnel or something. There was just nowhere to go. Totally weird. So I thought maybe it only worked when I wasn't thinking about it, like the other visions."

I had a tiny moment of panic again. "But that wasn't it?"

"No," he agreed. "Because when you texted and told me to try it again, I did the exact same thing, and right away, I saw the dashboard of your car, clear as day. That sign really freaked me out, by the way. Nice touch. Was that Tara's idea?"

"Yes," I replied, beginning to feel wonderfully warm again, even without my glowing platinum.

"But, Kali," he continued, sounding miserable again. "I have to tell you, when I *tried* to think about you, and connect with you like that — well, it was more than just a flash. It still wasn't anything like the other visions. But I don't think I should be practicing it like that anymore. Because, well—"

"It's okay, Zane," I interrupted swiftly, feeling bad about the self-reproach in his voice. "It's going to be okay. Tara figured it out." I smiled across the car at her. "I can block you. Just like I can block the shadows. That's what I was doing the first time I texted. That's why you got nothing. In fact, I've been at the Pali this whole time," I finished proudly. "Blocking the whole irritating lot of you."

He was quiet for a moment. "You can block me?" he repeated quietly. "Then, *you* can control it? Even if I can't?"

"Deal with it, Svenson," I said smugly.

The deep rumble of his laughter did that electrical thing to my spine again.

"Kali," he said warmly. "That is the best thing you could possibly say to me right now. Do you have any idea how impossible it is *not* to try to think about you, ever?"

I grinned. "Particularly when you know that the three of us are running around beach-hopping in sexy swimsuits?"

I could tell he was grinning back. "Yes. Particularly then. But *you're* in control. This is fabulous! I'm totally off the hook, now!"

That worried me a bit. "Off the hook?"

"Oh, yeah," he said mischievously. "From now on, whatever fun stuff I get to see, it'll totally be *your* fault!"

chapter 11

Tara pulled up her phone again, looked at it, and sighed.

"We're all annoyed that Tim Jones still hasn't called you back," Kylee lectured lazily as she adjusted the straps of her bikini. "But to *sigh* in a place like this is just wrong."

I had to agree. The sun had finally won an edge over the clouds and had been shining for a good twenty minutes straight now. The bright sky had turned the waters of Kailua Bay to a soothing shade of sapphire, contrasting with the green peaks encircling its sides and the dark chain of rock islands that rose out of the ocean in the distance, sheltering the beach from the strongest of the swells beyond. We had backtracked to the windward side because I knew this would be the ideal spot for some low-stress, late afternoon R&R. Close to the light tan, powdery sand of the beach, the calm, shallow waters of the bay were great for swimming and splashing. Farther out, the deeper waters were enjoyed by standup paddleboarders, kitesurfers, kayakers, and windsurfers. For the three of us on a lazy summer afternoon, the possibilities were endless.

"You're right," Tara agreed, dropping her phone back in her beach bag. "I should let it go. The man's obviously in no hurry. *He's* got other clothes."

"We all know you look better in Kali's things anyway," Kylee said unsympathetically, her eyes trained down the beach. We had parked the car and walked to a spot where we could see the water, at which point the two of them had stopped in awed wonder, basically unsure where to start.

"Should we go for a dip?" Tara suggested, ignoring the

dig at her wardrobe.

"I want to pick up guys," Kylee said matter of factly.

"You're wearing that bikini aren't you?" Tara snapped back. "Just let nature take its course. Come on, Kali. That water looks *so* gorgeous! Too bad I won't be able to see it from now on," she lamented as she took off her glasses and stashed them in her bag. Then she kicked off her flip-flops and headed for the aqua-white froth.

"I want to stay dry for now," Kylee said absently, her eyes surveying the various groups of locals and tourists milling about the beach. "You two go ahead."

We went ahead. Aside from Tara's introduction to Waikiki yesterday, she had never been in the ocean before, and I was glad I had started her out someplace tame, because the jagged, wild beaches of the North Shore could be pretty intimidating, even when the surf was flat. And as much as I hated to admit it, I still couldn't completely shake the images the vile ghost had foisted upon me in the carport. Whatever I had seen or imagined in those few seconds had definitely taken place in the ocean. But, I consoled myself as we frolicked, it hadn't happened in water this clear — or this shallow. And fortunately, Tara's joy at the novelty of the sea was contagious. We had a great time joking and splashing around — until she stopped suddenly and stared at me like I was some kind of alien.

"Crap, Kali!" she protested. "I totally forgot about Zane! Are you blocking him right now?"

I had to laugh at the look of horror on her face. "I think so," I assured. "I'm working on it, anyway. I've been doing this thing where I make my normal blind stronger. I'm hoping it will work like the regular one, where I don't have to concentrate on it every second. I won't know for sure until I quiz Zane about it later. But Tara," I chuckled again, "you do realize we're in a public place and *anyone* can see you, right?"

She made a face and pulled up the plunging neckline of her swimsuit. "Yeah, but they don't know me."

I stifled another laugh and shook my head. Tara was so amazingly *not* self-aware. She saw herself as an intellectual that no guy could possibly be interested in, unless, of course, he was smart enough to appreciate her mind. And although it was true that she hadn't attracted much lasting interest from the guys we knew in Cheyenne, it was also true that (1) half of them had known her since kindergarten when she had a reputation for biting people and (2) she actively discouraged them on a daily basis. What Tara couldn't seem to grasp was that if she was going to ditch those hideous frames of hers on a public beach and go splashing around in the ocean wearing a swimsuit that was perfectly suited to her coloring and figure, Zane's spy-vision was the least of her concerns.

A flying disc skipped over the water and nearly collided with Tara's thigh.

"Oh, no!" a male voice exclaimed. "Sorry about that!"

We looked up to see a guy in bright green boardshorts splashing through the water to retrieve the disc, which had landed a few feet away. He looked around our age, maybe a little older, and he spoke with a southern accent. Tara and I exchanged a quick glance. He walked over to us with a sheepish smile and gave his shaggy dark hair a shake.

He was pretty cute.

"Hi, I'm Curtis," he introduced, his manner friendly. "It didn't hit you, did it?"

"No," Tara said shortly.

Curtis blinked at her as if he was wounded. He looked at me. "I'd blame my brother for a bad throw, but really, I should have caught it. Sorry again."

"That's okay," I answered with a smile, taking pity on him. Tara really was awfully good at the discouragement thing.

He smiled back at me, gave a nod, and moved away again. He drew back the disc and flicked it to another guy standing knee-high in the ocean about forty yards away. That guy, who was taller, looked a little older, and was even cuter, made an impressive leap in the air to catch it.

Tara was unmoved. "I tried to look up Tim Jones on your laptop while you were in the shower this morning," she said as if the guys didn't exist. "I thought it would be hopeless, and it was. I did trace the flight number on the luggage tag, not that that was any help either. He wasn't on our flight from Denver. His bag came all the way from Tahiti. You believe that?"

"Tahiti?" I said with a gasp. "As in the Billabong Pro Tahiti?"

Her eyebrows knit together. "Say what?"

Tim Jones had been there himself? For real? "This is too cool, Tara!" I gushed as I tried to explain about the contest jersey, which I was sure now was genuine. "I know it doesn't mean much to you, but Zane will flip when I tell him. Tim Jones must be a major surf fan with major bucks to make a trip like that! He must know people!"

Tara was not impressed. "Whatever," she replied. "I just wish he was a little more considerate. He might be rich enough not to need his stuff, but is it so much to ask that he give me a chance to pick up mine? No offense, but a girl likes to wear her own underwear, you know?"

I did sympathize with her on that one. "Sorry."

Tara shook her head. "Well, hey, if we don't connect by the time I have to leave, it's his loss. Whatever's in his suitcase that isn't moldy, my brothers can fight over. Damon would like those boardshorts."

"Hey, Kali!" a happy voice chirped. "Catch!"

I turned to see Kylee, who had been sitting on the beach what seemed like five seconds ago, now up to her knees in water standing next to Curtis. She was preparing to fling the disc at me, and I put up my hands, but it was only for show. Kylee and I both knew the disc had zero chance of ending up anywhere near me. She flung it with all her might, and it spun out sideways high up in the air.

"I got it!" Curtis's brother yelled playfully. But no — Curtis's brother was standing on the far side of Tara. The one currently splashing after the disc was a new guy with sandy red hair and freckles. There were three of them.

"Fished in," Tara murmured.

"Hey!" Kylee called out to us enthusiastically, greeting us as if we hadn't seen each other in weeks. "Have you met Flynn and Wes?"

Tara shook her head. "How *does* she do that so fast?" she muttered to me as the other two guys took the cue and all of them approached us. Kylee was grinning from ear to ear as she splashed over, but as soon as she arrived the smile on her face evaporated.

I cast a quick glance over Tara's shoulder to see where Kylee was staring. I saw nothing but blue ocean and a handful of kayakers farther out in the bay. Kylee swallowed hard and turned to hold my gaze.

Ghost!

Gotcha.

Curtis made a bunch of introductions and I pretended to pay attention. Kylee didn't seem afraid of what she was seeing this time. She just seemed... intrigued. She even managed to get some small talk going within the group, even as her eyes kept darting to the space on the water behind Tara. Then she looked at me expectantly.

I made some small talk too, although I have no idea

what I said. Then, very carefully, I attempted to lift my new and improved blind. I didn't want to get socked with a sucker punch of hostility again — or worse. This time, I intended to stay in control.

I began at the bottom of the blind and visualized a tiny crack where the glow lessened and a draft blew through. Then I braced myself.

Lust.

Oh, come on! I looked up at the three smiling, perfectly friendly guys from Tennessee. Curse Kylee's bikini and Tara's sexy one-piece! Either the ghost had disappeared already or whatever feelings it had were getting drowned out by those of the living.

I pretended to cough, then took a step back behind Tara's shoulder, roughly in the area where I thought Kylee had been looking. Then I removed my blind completely.

Lust.

I groaned internally. I tried my best to screen out that particular emotion and search for something else. And there *was* something else, but it was hard to describe. Kind of like... steadfastness. Or loyalty. Along with a certain defensiveness. And pride.

Say what?

"So, you live here, Kali?" Curtis's older brother asked. I straightened up to find him smiling at me. "You go to the University of Hawaii?"

I had no idea if he was Flynn or Wes. "No, I'll be a senior at Frederick High," I answered. "But my boyfriend is starting at UH next week."

"Oh, that's cool," he replied, even as Kylee frowned at me.

He didn't *look* disappointed, but I could feel that he was. Not only that, but his friends were disappointed, too. Guess I'd just ruined the numbers game. Still, Curtis — at least I think that vibe was coming from Curtis — was optimistic. He really, really liked Kylee's bikini.

Did I want to know all this? I put my blind back in place.

Much better.

Curtis and Kylee kept up their flirting, but lacking suitable encouragement from Tara or me, Flynn and Wes moved off and went back to throwing their disc again. Kylee gave no further signs of seeing a ghost — or if she did, she no longer cared — and after Tara and I had enjoyed a leisurely swim, we returned to the beach.

"No!" Tara shouted the second she replaced her glasses and took a look at her phone. "I missed another call from TJ!" She punched through to her voice mail messages and held out the phone where I could hear.

"Hey. Yeah, sorry. Been on the Big Island. Family thing. Can we maybe, um, do tomorrow? Or... well... just call me back, okay? Bye."

Tara exhaled with relief. "Well, at least he's not blowing me off completely. Still, this may go on a while. How much you want to bet he doesn't answer?" She tapped *call.*

"I bet nothing," I answered.

"Me neither." She waited about twenty seconds, then tossed the phone back in her bag. "As expected. I'm not leaving another message yet. I'm going to keep calling him. I may start texting him, too. In fact, I am about to become Tim Jones' worst nightmare."

Kylee skipped up to us. "That was so much fun!" she chirped. "Bummer they have to leave tonight! Wes goes to the University of Tennessee, and Curtis is about to start at crap he's right behind you again!"

Tara and I both stared at her. "Curtis is what?" Tara exclaimed.

"Behind you!" Kylee insisted. "The new ghost!" Her eyes were fixed between our shoulders. We turned. Of course, we saw nothing.

"I thought he had to stay in the water, what with his board and all!" Kylee continued. "But he's just holding it now."

This was getting weirder by the minute. "Another surfer?" I asked.

Kylee nodded. "Well this one is, anyway. I'm not convinced Jabba the Hutt does anything but beat up on people, but this one's different. He's normal. He's not threatening or anything."

"Describe him to us," I begged.

She cocked her head as if to study him better. "He reminds me of those soldiers you see in London in those little box things. You now, the ones who are supposed to stand guard with no expression on their faces for hours and hours? He's short, and he's bald, and he's pretty thin, but still muscular. Looks about thirty, maybe. He's wearing those dorky mid-thigh swim trunks from the seventies, and he's got tattoos on his arms. He comes and goes, but every time he looks the same. He never moves. There — he's gone again."

I considered the idea a moment. "I did get the feeling he was guarding something," I admitted. "Like by being where he was, or doing what he was doing, he was being loyal. He was defending something he cared about. Something he thought was really important."

All three of us started looking around on the ground.

"Well, I give up," Tara announced. "I don't have TJ's suitcase here."

"But we were talking about it!" I recalled. "You had just said that if Tim Jones never called back, you were going to give his clothes to your brothers!"

We stared at each other.

"Please, Kali," Tara said heavily. "I have enough trouble believing in empathic perception, spectral visualization, and now remote viewing. Do not ask me to believe that all the powers of the afterlife have been unleashed in defense of Tim Jones' boardshorts."

Kylee and I dissolved into laughter. "Well," I said, "if you put it like that, it does sound pretty ridiculous."

"There must be *some* other explanation!" Kylee agreed. We began walking towards the car. We had taken about a dozen steps when she stopped in her tracks.

"What?" Tara and I cried together.

"He's following you," Kylee whispered, gesturing with her head to the air right behind us.

"So, tell him I got dibs on the front seat," Tara threw over her shoulder, walking on.

Kylee looked at me. "Can you feel him?"

I shook my head. "I'd rather not try. I need practice with my new blocking technique."

We started walking again. "He's gone already anyway. That reminds me," Kylee asked curiously, "what has Zane seen since we left the Pali? Did he see the guys?"

I shook my head. "He shouldn't have."

"But you dropped your blind long enough to feel the ghost, didn't you?"

Whoops. She was right. What if Zane had tuned in right then? It was pretty unlikely. But still...

I reached into my bag and felt around for my phone. I hadn't actually checked it since before we went swimming.

"Uh-oh," Kylee teased. "Hope Zane's not the jealous type! Didn't you drop your defenses right when all three guys were there and Wes was hitting on you?"

I frowned at her. Zane was never controlling, but that didn't mean it wouldn't bother him to watch some other guy flirting with his girlfriend. The reverse certainly bugged the heck out of me. I pulled up the phone. "I do have a text," I murmured. "But nobody was 'hitting on' me!"

"Unless Zane can read lips, he wouldn't know what Wes was saying," Kylee pointed out. "And if you put your block back in place in the middle of that conversation, and it's still working, it could look like you intentionally shut Zane out from that moment on."

Oh, no. She was right! I pulled up the text feeling terrible.

"Well? Did he tune in then?" Kylee prompted worriedly. "Did he see you with the guys?"

I read the text, then breathed out with relief. My face broke into a smile. "He did," I answered warmly. "But he's okay."

I turned the screen so she could see it.

Good thing I trust you.

chapter 12

Lacey jumped into my back seat the next morning with a smile wider and more genuine than any I'd seen on her face in ages. "I cannot believe I have an entire day of freedom!" she gushed, dropping her beach bag by her feet and buckling up. "Even if the mechanic fixes the pump today, it'll still take us all day tomorrow to get the pool ready again. And every day longer it takes to fix the pump is a day I'm not yelling at kids to stop drowning each other! Hoorah!"

Kylee, Tara, and I all laughed as I pulled my dad's car out onto the street and pointed us toward the North Shore.

"I'm so glad you could come," I exclaimed, meaning it more than she knew. "Matt told Zane yesterday he didn't think he had to work the lunch shift today, so we asked him to join us, too. I'm hoping he'll make it, but so far this morning he isn't answering."

"Good luck with that!" Lacey scoffed. "Matt was impossible enough to catch up with *before* football practice started. Now that he's working lunch and graveyard and driving back and forth in between, he doesn't even sleep at home. He and his friend have just been crashing in that room above the restaurant. He's been bugging me to come hang out on the North Shore all summer, but he knows I don't have a car, or any time off."

"Well, I hope he makes it," Tara offered from the passenger seat beside me. "The more, the merrier."

I grinned at Tara's unusually social attitude. She was in a good mood this morning. Not only had we all finally gotten a decent night's sleep last night, but she'd even managed to have a constructive text exchange with Tim Jones. We were meeting him later this afternoon in Mililani, partway between Honolulu and the North Shore, to pick up Tara's suitcase and to dispose of its troublemaking counterpart, which was currently stowed in my trunk.

"Matt had *better* make the effort to join us, at least long enough to say hi," Lacey proclaimed. "Or else we're breaking into that restaurant so I can go wake his lazy butt up!"

I chuckled to myself. So far, my plan was going splendidly. Matt and Lacey were finally both single, and slimeball Austin had at least helped Lacey get over her longtime boyfriend and Matt's erstwhile best friend Ty. Surely now the two of them could get over the crazy big brother/little sister thing they had going on and wake up to the obvious.

We cruised through the middle of the island, up the valley between Oahu's two mountain ranges, passing an army base and the Dole pineapple plantation before popping out on the coast again, this time on the glorious North Shore. I took the bypass around historic Haleiwa town, not wanting to entice Kylee and Tara with a view of the shops there. But once we passed Haleiwa there was only one road that ran up and down the shore, and between us and Zane lay almost everything else I'd been raving to Kylee and Tara about for months now.

Unfortunately.

"Wait," Kylee protested, her face glued to the window as the ocean flew by to her left. "Why are all these cars stopped here? What is everyone looking at?"

"Sea turtles," I said flatly.

"What?" she squealed, practically pulling on the door

handle. "Let's go see!"

"Later," I insisted, checking the door locks. "There are other turtles."

We climbed in altitude and came to a bend in the road. I bit my lip as everyone turned to look at the striking panorama — a square white tower on a rocky cliff, overlooking a calm blue bay and crescent beach below. "This is Waimea Bay!" Tara cooed. "Ooh, let's stop a minute!"

"No!" I barked defensively. "We're in a hurry!"

The three of them stared at me a moment, then cracked up laughing. "Geez, Kali," Lacey chided, "you've got it bad. You just saw this guy like, when? Thursday?"

"Friday," I mumbled, leaving the Waimea Bay parking lot behind. They all laughed at me again, but I didn't care. I didn't even care that there seemed to be a record number of shadows prowling around on the Kamehameha Highway this morning. If they were transparent, I drove through them. (Although, as always, I was really careful to make sure about that first.)

I didn't bother to point out Three Tables or Shark's Cove. I zipped right by the Foodland and didn't even mention when we passed Ehukai beach. (In my defense, it's not like you can see the Pipe from the road anyway.) When we finally reached Sunset Beach and turned off onto the narrow lane that led to Zane's place, I was practically bouncing in my seat. I snagged one of the few parking spots hidden away in the tiny public access area for Kaunala Beach, then handed Tara my car keys. "Lock it up, will you?" I hopped out and pointed down the street. "Zane's door is around the far side of that blue house, the one with the yellow kayak in the carport. Just give me two minutes first!"

I was off.

Their cackles affected me not at all as I set off down the pitted street at a jog. It was going to be a lovely day. The sky was blue, the sun was shining, and it would be warm but not too hot. The trees were raucous with the cries of myna birds, local kids were out biking and skateboarding, and tourists were wandering in the bizarrely charismatic neighborhood, which was packed tight with small dilapidated cottages and junky yards. Without knowing what world-renowned attraction loomed nearby, who would guess that even the least of these modest little houses would fetch a cool million?

I jogged up to Zane's door, which was slightly crooked on its hinges, had peeling paint, and was underwhelming in every possible objective sense. I was breathless with anticipation as I knocked.

Open up, you!

He did. The sight of him was like nectar. He smiled at me with those perfect teeth of his, his face tanned to just the right shade, his green eyes shining with welcome and his still-wet-from-the-shower curls dangling every which way. "Hi there," he said, drinking in the sight of me with equal enthusiasm before throwing a cautious glance over my shoulder.

"Hi, yourself," I replied, pushing him inside without apology and kicking the door closed with my foot. "We have two minutes."

I saw his smile widen briefly before I wrapped my arms around his waist and buried my face in his shoulder, hugging him tightly. "I feel like I haven't seen you in a week," I mumbled, letting his familiar warmth radiate through me in heavenly, healing waves.

Bliss.

He chuckled softly, his breath tickling my ear. "Tell me about it." He was holding me every bit as tightly as I held him, which made me near dizzy with glee. He had missed me, too. Even if it was only a couple of days. I wasn't *that* crazy.

I could have stood there, just like that, for a very long time. Maybe even the rest of my life. But after what was probably longer than two minutes, we heard a mixture of giggles and footsteps outside.

"Okay, I'm better now," I announced, pulling away reluctantly. "Fortified for another couple hours. If I'm lucky." I kissed him lightly on the lips, then stepped back.

He eyed me with a strange mix of contentment and frustration. Then he rolled his eyes good-naturedly and muttered something under his breath about gender inequality.

"What was that?"

"Nothing," he replied, puttering around the room a moment. "Are you going to let them in Chez Svenson? I cleaned up. Can you tell?"

I looked around the tiny cell that someone had the nerve to call an apartment. An amateurishly tacked-on addition to the main house, it consisted of a roughly eight-foot by nine-foot bedroom and a closet-sized bathroom with just a toilet and sink. The house kitchen was shared, and he used an outdoor shower behind the carport. But the room was private and it was practically on Sunset Beach, and Zane was content. Thinking again how he could have rented better, when instead he spent his money buying plane tickets for my friends, nearly brought tears to my eyes. "It—" I began with good intentions. "Well, no, actually," I finished with a laugh. "It looks the same. Sorry."

He made a face at me. "Come on. When have you not seen clothes on the floor before?"

I raised an eyebrow and pointed to a stack of folded

laundry by the door. There was no closet and no furniture except the bed — all of his belongings were in stacks and crates. "What is that?"

"Those are clean!" he protested with mock hurt.

I chuckled at him. "Oh. No *dirty* clothes, you mean. Then yes, I'm impressed."

"You should be," he insisted. "That hasn't happened since the first time you saw it!"

"It looks fabulous," I agreed. "As good as it can possibly look. I don't even see any ants!"

He made another face at me, and I couldn't help but laugh again. We both knew the place was a hovel, but it hardly mattered, since he literally did nothing but sleep here. Unless it was pouring rain, he spent his time outside. He even ate his meals in the carport, since any kind of crumbs brought on an invertebrate invasion.

Someone's knuckles rapped on the door. "Let us know if you need us, Zane," Tara called sternly. "Kali can get a little... carried away sometimes."

"It's okay to say no!" Kylee chimed in devilishly. "You must resist those mesmerizing gray eyes of hers. It's a trap, I tell you! A trap! Run while you can!"

Lacey snorted out a laugh in the background.

Zane threw me a wicked grin. Then he mussed his hair even more than it was already mussed, wrenched open the door, and leaned against it gasping for breath.

He rested there a moment, staring back at me with bewilderment and terror, his chest heaving. Then his gaze shifted slowly to Tara and Kylee, his composure nearly crumpling with relief. "I'm glad you're here," he croaked in a barely audible, raspy voice.

My friends' jaws dropped. As one, they turned to stare at *me*.

I rolled my eyes with a groan. "Oh, will you stop?" I

demanded, taking a step toward Zane and tickling his ribs, whereupon he immediately broke character and dissolved into laughter. I glared at my so-called best friends. "How long have you known me, anyway?"

They looked thoroughly unsettled. "But he—" Kylee pointed helplessly.

"Yeah, I know. Don't feed his ego, will you?"

Lacey, who had been doubled over in silent laughter, came to their defense. "Don't be too hard on them, Kal. If I don't know *him* better, I would have bought it." She shook her head at Zane with a scoff. "Trying to escape? From Kali? As if!"

Zane smiled knowingly back at her. "Good point."

I shot him a quick glance of smugness then, and he had the nerve to look away. Wimp! We both knew he pulled away from me — and the intensity of our unnatural attraction — all the time. But that whole phenomenon was a bit difficult to explain.

"Sorry to mess with you," he apologized half-heartedly to Kylee and Tara, "but I couldn't resist." He stood up tall and clapped his hands together, his green eyes twinkling. "Now... who's ready to do the North Shore?"

—⁓—

"I've died and gone to heaven," Tara remarked, stretching her lean body to its full length on her beach mat. The sand of Ehukai beach was thick and comfy, the sun was shining, and the wind was blowing just enough to keep the air temperature mild.

"Ditto that," Kylee sighed, her shoulders propped up on her elbows to keep an eye out for suitable males. "This is awesome."

"At least if anyone drowns here, it's on those hunky

lifeguards and not me," Lacey murmured sleepily, lying on her stomach with her eyes closed.

"Yes," Kylee agreed, stopping just short of licking her lips as she gazed up toward the guard tower. "Isn't it nice to have them watching out for everyone?"

I gave my own sigh of contentment. The Pipe was firing no barrels today, but the late summer waves were just high enough to make a pleasant shuffling sound upon the sand, and as soon as Zane returned from Foodland, we would have a feast. So far, the day had been idyllic. We'd packed into my dad's car and retraced our path along the coast, stopping first to let Kylee gaze her fill at a green sea turtle on Laniakea Beach, then splashing around at Waimea Bay and taking a long walk on the scenic bike path around Pupukea. We were now both hungry and exhausted, and I followed Lacey's lead by relaxing on my own mat and closing my eyes.

"Hottie alert, seven o'clock," Kylee reported. "Oh! He smiled at me. He's coming this way!"

Tara groaned. "Don't encourage him. If he sticks around he'll eat all our food."

"He can have my food," Kylee whispered, her voice dropping lower. "Check out those biceps. What a cutie! Wow, he really is coming over here! And just look at those baby blues, will you?"

I opened my eyes to find Lacey blinking back at me. Clearly having the same thought, we sat up.

"Let me guess," Matt said smoothly, flashing Kylee a killer smile. He was wearing an athletic-fitting tee and boardshorts, and he carried a faded towel slung over his shoulder. With his solid build and powerful limbs, tamed by that adorably vulnerable baby face of his, he cut quite a picture. "You look like you're from... hmm... don't tell me... Wyoming?"

Kylee's answering smile widened into a smirk. Thank God she wasn't *that* gullible. She was wearing no telling sports logos — not that Wyoming had a major league franchise anyway — and her half-Vietnamese ancestry certainly offered no clue. "And you must be Matt," she replied with amusement, extending a hand. "I'm Kylee. Nice to meet you."

"You too," he returned, holding onto her hand a little longer than necessary.

My eyes narrowed. *Excuse me?* I looked over to see Lacey's reaction, but she was half up already. As soon as she was on her feet, Matt turned and lifted her off of them, and I smiled as he twirled her about like a doll.

"Lace!" he exclaimed. "You're alive after all! Who knew?"

She chuckled, then beat playfully on his chest until he returned her to the ground. "Don't give me that crap! You're the one who's been AWOL all summer!"

"Hey, a guy's got to make some money."

"Well, so does a girl!"

"Yeah, okay. Fine. We're both guilty." He beamed down at her, one arm still wrapped around her waist, and my spirits soared. Matt was crazy about Lacey — I could tell from the twinkle in his eye. This was all going to be so easy—

He leaned down and planted a kiss square on the top of her head. Just like a doting uncle. Then he released his hold and she returned to her beach towel.

You've got to be kidding me.

"And you must be Tara," Matt said graciously, extending a hand to the second stranger to him, who returned it with her usual firm, businesslike grasp.

"I am," she confirmed. "Good to meet you finally. And I take back what I said earlier. Zane is bringing food for you, so it's okay if you stick around." She waved a dismissive hand at Kylee. "Go ahead. Flirt away."

Matt cracked up, and Kylee, who *should* have been embarrassed, had the gall to giggle. "Well, all right! Permission!"

"It's your lucky day," Lacey told Matt with a chortle. A totally unconcerned chortle.

No, no, no!

I stood and pulled my towel up with me. "Here, have a seat," I instructed, gesturing Matt toward a patch of sand in between me and Lacey as the group scooted into a circle. Matt launched into a series of friendly questions about life in Wyoming, which Kylee fielded with rampant enthusiasm while Tara corrected her exaggerations and Lacey looked on with a contented smile.

My feet twitched on my towel with annoyance. Kylee and I would be having words later. Had I, or had I not, been clear about *the plan?* The girl monopolized Matt's attention entirely until one of the lifeguards rolled by on his ATV, at which point her fickle gaze began to wander. Tara and Kylee started debating whether talking to a lifeguard on duty would compromise his ability to do his job, and Matt took advantage of the distraction to have a semi-private word with Lacey. "So," he began, dropping his voice, "how's it going with what's his name?"

"Oh," she said drearily. "That's over."

Matt's eyes studied hers, and his face darkened. "What happened?"

Lacey shrugged off his concern. "The usual. But never mind. It was just a rebound thing, after all."

"The *usual?*" he exclaimed. "Lace! I can't believe you just said that!"

Lacey sighed. "Yes, you can."

Matt's expression turned thunderous. "I'll kill him," he

said quietly.

Lacey's cornflower blue eyes moistened a little, and her lips drew into a smile. "You know, as terrible as it is of me, I really do like that image. Still, don't bother," she touched Matt's cheek lightly, then turned away again. "You're sweet to offer, but Austin really isn't worth the effort. I'm over him. *Movin' on!*"

Matt made a low, grumbling noise in his throat. "You deserve better. You know that. Don't you?"

Lacey flushed. "Yeah. You're right. I guess I have 'selection' issues."

"Yeah. So how about you let me pick him out next time?"

My heart skipped a beat. This was all too perfect. Except that everything had gone quiet, which meant that Tara and Kylee were also now eavesdropping.

Then suddenly, Lacey laughed out loud. "Matt, will you stop? You do not have to take care of me forever just because you almost killed me in the ninth grade, okay? I forgive you."

"You what?" Kylee cried.

"Excuse me?" Tara asked.

Through my friends' surprised exclamations and Lacey's chuckles, I could just make out Matt's grumbled, "It has nothing to do with that." He said it so sincerely and so sweetly... but of course, no one else noticed. And in the next second, he was smiling sheepishly and laughing with the rest of them. "Liar," he teased Lacey. "You will never forgive me. You'll hold that concussion over my head the rest of our lives."

Lacey grinned slyly. "Maybe."

"Concussion?" Kylee begged. "What?"

Lacey went on to tell how Matt had plowed over her backward while chasing a badminton birdie in gym class, and when she got to the point where she had blacked out, Matt picked up the story. I noticed that although Lacey treated the whole episode lightly, Matt's guilt and horror was still raw, even after nearly three years. I wondered if maybe Lacey wasn't right. Maybe he did feel some kind of responsibility toward her, even now. But that didn't mean he couldn't feel something else, too.

"That's awful," Tara sympathized, looking at Matt. "I bet you felt really weird about playing competitively with girls after that. Especially when there was a big size difference. I mean, it's not even a gender thing, really. Accidents are just going to happen."

Matt studied Tara with surprise. "I never wanted to play sports with girls again," he admitted.

"Zane's back!" Kylee crowed loudly. "Woohoo! Food!"

We looked up to see Zane standing by the picnic area, waving one arm at us while the other was weighed down with bags. My heart gave a little leap, as always, at the sight of him. I would have gone with him to the Foodland, but he insisted I stay at the beach with my friends. In retrospect, it was a good thing I had. *Somebody* had to keep Kylee in line!

We all rose and collected our towels. I was prepared to subtly steer Kylee away from Matt if necessary, but to my surprise, he moved away from her on his own. Straight over to Tara.

Crap.

I blew out a frustrated breath. Tara's no-nonsense demeanor didn't usually attract the attention of macho types, but Matt wasn't your typical jock. Tara's having grown up in a too-small house with too many brothers had given her rare insight into the male mind, and Matt had zoned right in on that, drat him.

"I've lost count of the number of injuries my brother Damon's caused," Tara told him easily as they walked along together. "They were all accidents. He's not mean or anything. He isn't even all that aggressive in sports. He's just a dumbass. He always felt bad, but the worst was a real little guy he fell on once. Damon's weight broke the kid's arm. He doesn't think anybody knows this, but..." Tara threw a wary glance at Kylee, then leaned over and whispered in Matt's ear. She was close enough that I could just hear her, although no one else could. "Damon cried himself to sleep that night."

Matt's feet stopped for a second. Then his eyes sparkled at Tara even as his expression sobered. "Oh, yeah," he said raggedly. "I hear that."

Tara shrugged. "Well, you're not the only one."

Matt smiled back at her, and a flush of red colored his cheeks.

"Come on, Matt," Kylee cooed, gesturing back at the stragglers. "Let's eat!"

"Do I smell garlic shrimp?" Lacey exclaimed as we approached the picnic tables. She was paying no attention whatsoever to the drama behind her.

This was *not* how things were supposed to go!

"You did get garlic shrimp!" Lacey cried, opening one of the bags. "Zane! I thought you were just going to Foodland! This is awesome!" She jumped up and gave him a friendly hug.

Zane smiled at her, then looked at me. He cast a glance at Matt, whose eyes were on Tara, and Kylee, who was now hanging shamelessly on Matt's arm. My lips twisted with annoyance, and Zane noticed that, too.

He arched an eyebrow, then shot me a knowing smirk. *Told you so.*

<h1 style="text-align:center">chapter 13</h1>

The picnic was awesome. Not only did Zane's spread offer all the usual deli fare from Foodland, including fresh cut pineapple, but he'd even sprung for some genuine North Shore grindz (good eats) from the food trucks. The grindz and the company were all so good I was tempted to start dancing and make it a luau, but I knew that if I did, Kylee would join me, which was the absolute last thing Matt needed to see.

"That chicken is stalking me," Tara observed, moving her feet away from the path of a bold red rooster that kept circling our table.

"Well, if it makes you feel any better," Kylee said, gesturing to a clump of bushes nearby, "that cat is stalking him."

We all watched as a scraggly gray tabby crouched in the sand. Its eyes roamed under our table as its tail flicked.

"You'd think," I agreed. "But as many cats as there are running wild on this island, I've never seen one attack a grown chicken. I think the cat and the rooster both are just waiting for our crumbs."

"Who's waiting? Stop that!" Tara pulled up her feet as a cream-colored hen made a dive for something inches from her toe. "Geez! Where'd she come from?"

"It's the females you've got to watch out for," Matt quipped.

"Tell me about it," Zane agreed.

I shot him a well-deserved glare, and he grinned back at me. As cool as it was to be enjoying a picnic in the shade of the ironwood trees beside a world famous beach break with my best buds in the world, I found myself seriously craving a few more minutes of alone time with my guy.

"Oh!" I remembered conveniently. "Zane, I forgot to tell you! Guess where Tim Jones' suitcase came from? Tahiti!"

I had his full attention. "You mean... you think he was at the Billabong Pro?"

"I know he was," I said smugly. "He has a contest jersey in his suitcase."

"Get out!" Zane cried aloud. "How would he get that? Who is this guy?"

The rest of us cracked up laughing. His outburst was so exuberant it scattered the chickens and scared the cat back under the bush.

"Are you sure it's a real contest jersey?" he challenged.

I smiled as he fell unwittingly into my trap. "Well, you can see for yourself if you want. His stuff is in my trunk. We're meeting the mysterious TJ this afternoon to drop it off."

Zane was off the bench and on his feet. "Show me."

Predictably, neither Matt nor Lacey cared about the jersey, and Kylee and Tara had already seen it. So Zane and I headed off alone across the carpet of scrubby grass that led to the parking lot, and I threaded my fingers through his with a smile, enjoying the feel of his arm against mine.

"You wouldn't lie to me about a thing like this would you?" Zane asked, looking at me suspiciously.

"Of course not," I said, trying to sound overly innocent.

"Because toying with me about something this serious would be cruel. You know that, right?" he warned.

I could not keep a straight face. "What could possibly

be more serious than professional surfing?"

He was very good at keeping a straight face. "Absolutely nothing."

I rolled my eyes. We reached the car and I popped the trunk open.

"Kali!" he cried, pulling me back.

"What?" I looked around, expecting to see some flying missile or charging dog. But I saw nothing, and as quickly as he'd tensed up, Zane relaxed again.

"Oh," I said dryly, understanding. "If the ghost is back, just ignore him. That's what Tara does, and he doesn't bother her at all." I hadn't had a chance to tell Zane what that same ghost had somehow managed to do to *me* in the carport the other night, but right now, I didn't want to. It wasn't going to happen again, because I wouldn't let it. I double-checked my blind to make sure it was reinforced with the new platinum, then turned back to Zane. "You okay?"

"I'm fine," he answered. "It's just that he was so close to you. But... it isn't the same ghost."

"Oh. Really?" I so did not want to talk about ghosts right now. I leaned in and unzipped the suitcase. The baby blue contest jersey was right on top, where I'd asked Tara to put it.

"This guy is short and bald, but he's ripped. Another surfer, for sure," Zane described. "He's kind of... well, he's gone now. But he was different. He wasn't aggressive or anything. Just watchful. Seemed like a pretty cool guy, actually."

"Yeah, that sounds like the one Kylee saw at Kailua Bay yesterday." Enough about dead people. I pulled out the jersey and shook it in the air in front of Zane. "Ta-da!"

He stared at it like I'd offered him the holy grail.

"This *is* a real world tour jersey," he murmured, taking

it from my hands and studying it with reverence. The shirt was lightweight and stretchy, meant to fit tight, and it had the Billabong logo on the chest and other sponsorship logos over the shoulders. Surfers in the same heat wore different colors, rather than numbers, to distinguish themselves for the judges.

"Would I lie?" I teased. "Tim Jones must know somebody. Or else he found it scrapped on the beach. What do you think?"

Zane shrugged. "He could work for the organizers. Maybe it's a spare?"

"If he works for Billabong, why's he packing AirTide boardshorts?" I questioned.

Zane folded the jersey carefully and returned it to the suitcase. "You mean these?" he asked, lifting out the red and black boardshorts. "*Nice.* When did you say you're going to meet this guy?"

"This afternoon. In Mililani."

"Any chance I could tag along and—" His head sprang back suddenly as if he'd been punched in the face.

"Zane!" I cried, stepping closer.

"Sheesh," he muttered, feeling tentatively along his jawbone. "That was pretty convincing."

"Try not to look at him," I begged. "That's the only way he can get to you. It's Jabba the Hutt again, isn't it?"

"Yep." He looked at me strangely. "Wait, how you'd come up with that name?"

"Kylee."

He studied the air, then nodded his approval. "I see the resemblance." He dodged another imaginary blow.

"Close your eyes!" I ordered. I could sense no hostility this time, which encouraged me. My platinum was working. The ghost's emotions weren't getting through. "Will you chill the hell out?" I hissed at the spot Zane had recoiled from. "You know we're giving all this stuff back to your precious Tim Jones in a matter of hours, and in better condition than we found it, even. So lay off!"

But of course Zane would *not* close his eyes, and I could tell from where he kept looking that the stupid ghost hadn't budged an inch. When Zane tensed up for an obvious third blow, I groaned aloud with frustration. "Oh, just put them back!" I urged, grabbing at the boardshorts in his hands.

Pain slammed into the left side of my head. Dizziness. Weightlessness. My feet... floating. The sun in the sky and the lid of the trunk swirled together in a molten mass like a witch's brew in a white-hot cauldron. Seconds passed and time blurred as the blood began to blend in. My blood, swirling through the other liquids, thick and red, even as everything else around me turned to blue. Streaks of aqua shimmered in from all sides while the sinking began. The slow but steady sinking of me as the pressure on my skull and around my chest tightened and the water on my skin grew colder and clammier and the light grew dimmer and then my eyes were so very heavy until at last I couldn't see at all... blackness... coldness and darkness and deepness and despair...

"Kali! Snap out of it!" Tara ordered, her hand none too lightly tapping my cheek. "Zane! Are you all right?"

I blinked at her. She was standing in front of me — in front of both of us — holding the boardshorts in her hands. I watched as she breathed out with relief, stuffed the boardshorts back in Tim Jones' suitcase, and closed the trunk. "Geez, these things are a pain in the butt!" she griped. Behind her clunky dark frames, her blue eyes held mine. "What was that all about? The two of you looked like you'd been turned to stone or something!"

The two of us?

I turned to Zane. He looked back at me with a gaze every bit as bewildered as my own. "What just happened?" he asked.

"You... you first," I stammered.

He looked warily around the car, but as far as I could tell from his reaction, he saw no more ghosts. "The... uh," he began uncertainly. "Well, Jabba the Hutt was laying into my face, and then—" he stopped and looked at me curiously. "And then you touched my hands, and it was like I was... transported. I was seeing something else, a whole different scene. And my head hurt. When the guy was hitting me before I didn't feel a thing, but all of sudden — *wham*. And then there were all these funky colors, and I was bleeding, and... I don't know. I think I drowned."

My heart nearly pounded out of my chest. "Where did your head hurt?"

He put up a hand and touched his left temple.

"And what colors were you seeing? Not the blood... the rest of it."

"Shades of blue."

I let out my breath in a rush. "We had the same... well, whatever it was, it was the same. And I've had it twice now." I felt a flush of heat as anger pulsed through my body. "It's that damn ghost again! He's trying to get to me. To scare me. I don't know if *he* knows I've always been scared of drowning... or if he just got lucky. But he's doing his best to scare the hell out of me!"

"You still think the ghost is doing it?" Tara said skeptically. "But how? How could he produce images inside your brain? He's just a marginally visible energy form!"

I frowned at her. "You have a better explanation?"

"I saw it, too," Zane reminded, perplexed. "And it

wasn't anything like the other stuff I've been seeing lately. The other times were just like being plucked out of one ordinary, everyday place and being dropped into another. This whole thing was just... weird. Like I was inside a brain that wasn't working right."

"Or like it was a fantasy created to scare us," I argued. "I'm telling you, Jabba has it in for me. You probably just tagged along for the ride. You know — saw it through my eyes?"

"Was your blind in place when it happened?" Tara asked. "The new and improved one?"

Her words made my blood run cold. "It was," I answered feebly. "And it was working great, too. Just seconds before, it was blocking the ghost's feelings completely!" I slumped against the car's bumper. "This makes no sense!"

Zane leaned beside me and hugged my shoulders. "Since when does it ever, at first?"

"Speaking of making no sense," Tara said begrudgingly. "You do see the obvious connection here, don't you?"

We looked at her. My brain was still spinning, although I was very much enjoying the feel of Zane's arm.

She gestured toward the trunk. "Oh, please. Don't make me say it. You *know*, don't you?" She winced. "The freakin' boardshorts!"

Zane and I shared a doubtful look. "Get out," he mumbled.

Tara groaned. "Look, you think I enjoy pointing this out? It's absurd! But Kali, you were *holding them* when it happened before and you were *holding them* just now. Both of you! And the vision stopped when I took them away. Have you actually held them in your hands any other time?"

I thought about it. I shook my head.

Zane cast a wary glance over my shoulder toward the trunk. "So... you seriously think that what Jabba and Baldy have a problem with is people dissing our boy's boardshorts?"

"Do *not* make me say it again," Tara replied dryly. "I have little enough respect for myself as it is."

"Hey!" Kylee called from a few yards away. "You guys okay? We're all done with lunch — Matt and Lacey are just throwing away the trash. I, uh... noticed you had company."

Zane stood up from where he was leaning against the bumper with me, and I felt his absence like a cold draft blowing.

"Kylee!" he cried. "I almost forgot... what did you see? How long have you been watching?"

She joined us, and her voice lowered. "Long enough to know I'm never touching those boardshorts again."

"She sent me over here," Tara explained.

"Did Matt and Lacey notice anything?" I asked nervously, casting a glance in their direction.

Kylee shook her head. "No, they were facing the other way." She looked at Zane. "I saw the big guy slug you," she explained. "But then you and Kali were both just standing still, like statues. What was that all about?"

"The same drowning thing as before," I answered shortly. "Why? What were the ghosts doing then?"

Kylee studied me a second, her dark eyes concerned. "Nothing. They weren't doing anything. One minute the ghost was pounding on Zane, the next minute you guys are frozen and the goon is just standing there. I swear he almost looked confused himself. Then both ghosts just faded out."

Zane and I looked at each other. Then we looked at

Tara. She held her palms up in the air. "Don't ask me," she said gruffly. "I don't get any of this. I thought I knew from weird already. But 'Attack of the Killer Boardshorts' is over the top. How about we all just go snorkeling already and forget any of this ever happened?"

We all stood silently and stared at each other again.

"You know, Tar," Kylee said finally, smirking. "For once, I actually agree with you. Screw the analysis. At least for now. Let's snorkel!"

Zane's green eyes twinkled into mine, and he put his arm around my shoulders again. "Sounds good to me."

I cuddled into his side. *So nice.*

"We ready?" Matt called cheerfully, reappearing with Lacey. He withdrew his keys from his pocket and gave them a jingle. "I can take somebody else in my car, if you want."

Kylee made a move, but I snatched at her elbow just in time. "No, we're good!" I called with equal cheer. "Meet you there!"

Matt and Lacey moved off toward his car and the rest of us piled into mine. Kylee glared at me as she slid into the back seat. "Did it ever occur to you," she said heavily as we all buckled up, "that I might not want to ride with two ticked off ghosts and a haunted pair of boardshorts?"

"Did it ever occur to you," I fired back as we pulled out of the lot, "that I am *trying* to facilitate true love, here?"

"I am *helping* with that!" she protested.

"How?"

"By showing Lacey what a hottie she's got, of course!"

"Oh, please," Tara rebuked from the other rear seat. "How convenient."

"Speaking of convenient," Kylee said, turning on Tara. "*You're* the one causing the distraction, in case you haven't noticed. Like, why do I even ask that? Of course you haven't noticed!"

"Noticed what?" Tara asked, baffled.

"See?"

"Noticed what?" Tara repeated, her voice rising.

"That Matt has a thing for you!" Kylee screeched.

"Oh, please! He does not!"

"How can you *not* know that? You are *so* like a guy!"

"Will you knock it off?" Tara ordered. "Acting like I'm one of the guys does not mean I'm flirting."

"That's not what I meant—"

"If anyone's a shameless flirt out here, it's you!" Tara griped. "Seriously, Kylee, we'll be gone in a matter of days. *What is the point?* Like you could ever tolerate a long distance relationship!"

"Who said I was looking for one? Or for a relationship at all? Why can't you just have fun for one afternoon? I still can't believe how cold you were to Flynn yesterday. He really liked you!"

Tara groaned. "This again? They were leaving for the airport in *hours!* We were never going to see them again!"

"You don't know that!" Kylee argued. "What if you end up at the University of Tennessee? How cool would it be to know somebody there?"

I squirmed with embarrassment. I loved my friends dearly. But... "Um, Zane—" I began.

"No worries," he said pleasantly. He was slouched in my passenger seat, dangling his arm out the open window while the breeze made his blond curls dance around his face. "I tune it out in real time."

I grinned at him, my heart swelling with emotion as the bickering in the back seat continued.

"Thanks for that."

chapter 14

Lacey and I sat on the sand beside the snorkeling cove at Turtle Bay, watching the tops of everyone else's heads skim along the surface of the water. The group had come up with five sets of snorkeling gear among us, but one of the masks had started to leak, so now we were down to four. I was more than content with the trade-off plan. The sky was still sunny and the water was warm, but the ocean's colorful underwater secrets were not holding their usual allure for me this afternoon. Besides, I'd been waiting all day for the chance to talk to Lacey alone.

Now... how to bring up the subject of Matt without being too obvious?

"I'm glad you and Matt are finally getting the chance to hang out again," I said casually, feeling her out. "Not that you wouldn't see him at school next week anyway, I guess!"

Lacey shrugged. She smiled slightly, but didn't say anything. A long pause followed. Just when I began to fear she really *didn't* care, she came out with a statement I was wholly unprepared for.

"He seems to really like your friend Tara."

Crap. "You think?" I said weakly.

Lacey smiled at me knowingly. "Knock it off, Kali. You know how he is. He flirts with everybody, but every once in a while he discovers a gem. He liked you right away, didn't he? He sees something in Tara, too. He does have taste — when he chooses to use it." She breathed out with a huff, then closed her eyes and tossed her head back in the sun.

I studied her peaceful expression. I honestly couldn't tell if she was jealous or happy for him.

"Tara's great, but she's going back to Wyoming," I said practically. "What do you think Matt *should* be looking for?"

She opened one eye and squinted at me curiously. I decided to go for it.

"I mean," I continued, "what kind of girl do you think would make him happy?"

Lacey opened both eyes and sat up. She dusted the sand off her hands and looked thoughtful. "I used to think you would," she said frankly. "But now I see how you and Zane roll, and I can tell I was wrong. I mean, let's be real. Zane is a little more evolved. Matt's no Neanderthal, but he needs somebody who needs somebody, you know what I mean? Or at least, he needs somebody who's willing to pretend she needs somebody."

My heart sped up. Yes! Lacey had Matt's number all right. And unlike either me or Tara, I had the feeling that Lacey herself would *enjoy* that kind of pretending.

"I think you're right," I agreed with enthusiasm.

"He doesn't know that, though," she continued, her tone turning melancholy. "The guy's social radar totally sucks. You and Tara are rare exceptions for him — usually he goes straight for the legitimately needy types, and then five minutes later he's bored out of his mind. He can't get it through his thick head that he doesn't actually *have* a thick head!"

I cracked up. Lacey seemed to have given Matt's love life a good deal of thought already. Come to think of it, she had a better handle on his needs than she did on her own.

"Have you ever told him this?" I asked.

She shrugged. "I try. He doesn't listen to me."

I inhaled sharply and decided to go for it. "He does realize you're not actually his sister, doesn't he?"

Lacey's head whipped around. She stared at me for at least five seconds. "No," she answered slowly, her voice serious. "I really don't think he does."

I made no response. I had expected her to laugh, to make a joke about it, to be lighthearted. But the blue eyes that normally danced with merriment were now all seriousness.

"I don't mind," she continued, speaking softly. "I like what we have. It's special. But it does seem a little weird sometimes, now that Ty's out of the picture. I mean, that's how it started, you know. I was always off limits because I was his best friend's girl."

I swallowed. Now was the time. "You could change that dynamic," I suggested mildly. "If you wanted to."

Lacey looked away. She seemed like she was about to say something, but before she could, a dripping giant blotted out the sun. "Hey!" Matt said, pulling off his mask and giving his muscular chest and shoulders a shake. Seawater flew from his hair, scattering droplets in all directions as we closed our eyes and cringed. "Who's next? Kali, you haven't been in much."

I opened my eyes. I knew I should take the mask he held out. He was right, I had only taken one turn, and then I'd only stood in water up to my knees hoping that no one would notice my lack of enthusiasm. But I didn't want to go any farther out; I didn't want to get in the water at all.

"No thanks," I said without thinking. "I'm good."

Lacey and Matt both looked at me strangely. *Whoops.* This was awkward. Maybe Matt wanted a chance to be alone with Lacey on the beach. Maybe Lacey wanted a chance to be alone with Matt.

Isn't that what I wanted, too?

I gazed out at the calm blue ocean, at the modest ripples of swell that broke in gentle white crests over the sand. A lamer, tamer, less intimidating body of water could not be found anywhere on the North Shore, unless you counted the stagnant, manmade shrimp lagoons up in Kahuku.

I didn't care. I still didn't want to go in.

"I'll go again, then," Lacey said finally, ending the awkward silence. Although she did throw me a quick, questioning glance, she smiled cheerfully at Matt as she reached out for the mask. "Who knows when I'll ever get back out here? Maybe I'll see a turtle this time!"

"I heard a guy saying there was a little one over that way a few minutes ago," Matt offered, pointing. "No more cooing about how cute they are, though. It's annoying."

She made a face at him. "Turtles are adorable. Deal with it." She adjusted the mask, they traded the flippers, and off she went.

Matt watched her walk away awkwardly, like a frogwoman, with a shake of his head and a smile that lit up his whole face. Then he dropped down on the sand beside me with a satisfied sigh. "Man, this has been awesome," he praised. "Thanks for inviting me. It's been great to meet your friends finally. Nice of Zane to get them up here, too."

I agreed.

"So, Zane said he's supposed to get you surfing by the end of the summer. How's that going?"

An icy rock dropped into the pit of my stomach. *Surfing?*

We had indeed been working up to it all summer, with the swimming lessons and the laps, and supposedly I was on target for the final exam next week. Zane wasn't the only one pushing the "three generations" thing — my father and grandfather had both been making a ridiculously big deal out of it. I had been looking forward to the big event myself, even.

Key word: *Been.*

"Um, I guess it's still on."

"You don't sound too excited about it," Matt observed.

"Oh, I am," I said unexcitedly. "I'm just a little nervous, that's all."

Colder. Deeper. Sinking. Darker...

"Aw, come on!" Matt teased, giving me a hearty back clap. "You're a great swimmer! And you're a dancer! If you can balance on your toes, you can balance on a board, right? Heck of a lot better than I can. I should offer to try it again, too. That'd make you look *really* good."

"Would you?"

"Hell, no," he laughed. "No way is anyone ever getting me on a surfboard again. Complete humiliation. I totally suck. But I'd go and cheer you on, anyway."

I smiled at him. A sweet, smart, good-looking, yet self-deprecating jock. What was not to love? Of course Lacey had feelings for him. She must just be afraid he wouldn't return them. Afraid of losing whatever special bond they already shared.

"Hey, do you have the time?" he asked, looking around him on the beach and grabbing his towel. "I left my phone in the car."

I hadn't brought mine either, but I sneaked a peek in Kylee's bag and made a report.

Matt swore. "I can't believe it's that late already. I've gotta go." He stood and dried off with the sandy towel.

I rose with him, disappointed. This would have been the perfect chance for a heart to heart. "Oh, no. Do you really have to head out to practice already? Surely traffic's not that bad."

He shot me a canny look. "It's not just that," he said in a low voice. "I have to go kill a guy first."

Uh-oh. It was convenient that he'd broached the subject of Lacey himself — not so convenient that beneath his good-natured exterior, I could now see so much bottled-up anger brewing that I could almost believe he was serious.

"You know that wouldn't help Lacey *at all*," I reminded, just in case he was more serious than I knew. "Right?"

He looked away from me, and his jaw muscles clenched. He didn't answer. He threw the towel over his head and rubbed at his hair. After a moment he stopped rubbing, but continued standing there with the towel over his head, motionless except for the slow, intentionally controlled movements of his ribcage. "Matt?" I urged again.

He made a growling sound and ripped off the towel. "I'm sick of it, Kali," he grumbled. "I'm sick of standing by and watching these jerks rip her heart out. She doesn't deserve that."

"I agree with you!" I said with enthusiasm, seeing my opening. "But she said herself, she has 'selection' issues. So if you really want to help, why don't you steer her toward somebody better next time?"

I watched with amusement as his forehead wrinkled into a frown. Never mind that he'd suggested the exact same thing a couple hours ago. "Like who?" he demanded.

"I don't know," I said innocently. "How about your friend who works at La Ola?"

"No way!" Matt barked. "The way he—" He cut himself off with a self-conscious look. "He's not going out with Lacey. Forget it."

I squelched a smile. Then I named two more friends of his.

"No," he said instantly, both times.

"Okay, fine. Forget your friends," I replied. "Then what about..." I struggled to remember the name of a guy Lacey had told me about from a rival high school. He was a star athlete, and supposedly really good looking, but he also had a reputation for being a player, and there were rumors that the ex he'd dumped last spring was about to be a single mother. "How about... Troy Ferg—"

"Over my dead body!" Matt exploded, his face turning six shades of purple. "Kali, how could you even *say* that?" He turned away from me and paced six steps, which was fortunate, because I really needed to let out a laugh. I barely had time to recover before he did an about-face and stomped back to me again. "I know you don't know who he is, but if that guy... *Ughh!*" He took both hands and mimed an action which the Troy in question would probably not survive.

"Sorry," I said sincerely. "Bad suggestion. But who do you think she *should* go out with, then?"

He looked at me, or rather past me, his chest still heaving a bit from the horror of imagining Lacey in the clutches of... well, anybody, apparently. He appeared to draw a blank. "I don't know," he said finally, his voice thoroughly agitated. "I have to go."

He hunted around through our piles of stuff until he found his sandals and keys, then he stepped over and gave me a hug. "Look, Kali, I'm sorry if I yelled at you. I'm just really ticked about... you know."

"I know," I said, hugging him back.

"I'm glad you guys asked me to come. Tell everybody I said bye, and to come to La Ola anytime I'm on duty — I'll make sure everybody gets free chips."

I chuckled at his worthless offer. All the customers got free chips. "Gee thanks."

"Later." He managed to grin at me as he walked away.

I watched him with just the teensiest bit of insecurity. I was almost a hundred percent sure he wouldn't kill anybody.

"Kali, where's he going? He leaving already?" a voice called from behind me. I turned to see Zane walking out of the ocean, his mask pulled back over his head, those gorgeous curls of his wet and dripping again. The boardshorts he was wearing were my personal favorites, with bold alternating zigzags of green and blue, and I noted that five months into his recovery from the coma, he was still adding muscle. It took me a second to remember who he was talking about.

I joined him at the water's edge and explained Matt's departure. But although I tried to do the noble thing and convince Zane that I was perfectly fine sitting alone on the beach and that he should go right back to snorkeling, I could tell from his expression that I wouldn't be getting away with that.

He pulled off the mask and snorkel, kicked off his swim fins, and sat down on a towel with me. "I know what you're doing," he announced, holding my eyes. "What that ghost made you see... made *us* see... it's made you afraid of the water again."

I looked away. In one way it felt really good to have him know me so well. In another way, it was scary. Not to mention humiliating. "I can't help it. I know it's stupid."

"It's not stupid," he said gently. "Look, the whole thing freaked me out, too. Of course it hit you harder. You've already been fighting that phobia your whole life."

I still couldn't look at him. But I did lean into his side a little.

He put his arm around me, and I cuddled up closer. I wondered, briefly, if enjoying his touch so much made me "needy," but I decided that was taking the independence thing too far. Could I survive without Zane's affection? Absolutely, and vice versa. But sharing it made us a whole lot happier.

"You don't have to hide this stuff from me, you know," he said, his voice bordering on reproachful, even as he held me. "We should be trying to figure it out together."

I humphed. "Like I *can* hide anything from you," I pointed out. "I'm sorry. I guess I just don't want to think about it. I had myself believing that this new and improved shield of mine was ghost-proof, and it really ticks me off that it failed. I don't like thinking that I let some dead guy get the better of me. *Twice.*"

"Hey, he got me, too," Zane reminded. "I just wish I knew how it worked. And *why*. Was it really about the boardshorts? I mean..."

I shook my head with a groan. "We're getting rid of those things *today*. Maybe this will all just stop then and we'll never have to figure it out. As long as it's not..."

My voice trailed off. My stupid mouth was about to blab stuff I didn't even want to think about.

"What?" Zane asked.

"Nothing."

"Kali," he pressed. "Spit it out. We're in this together, remember?"

I spat it out. "What if it's me? What if it's *my* blood in that water? Not because any ghost made up something to scare me, but because it was always meant to be?"

Zane's face darkened. "That's crazy."

"Is it?" I argued. "How can we possibly know? Doesn't it all make a weird kind of sense, if you think about it? I've always had these abilities. Maybe I've always been afraid of drowning, too. I've always thought that my fear of water started because I fell in that stupid fish pond when I was in preschool. But what if falling in water that shallow only freaked me out so much because I was *already* afraid?"

Zane drew in a ragged breath, and fear sliced through me as I watched the logic of my argument become clear to him.

"What if I've always been fated to drown?" I said roughly, my voice threatening to crack. "What if these windows the ghosts are opening up are actually... scenes from my own future?"

"There's no reason to think that!" Zane said sharply. "*None*. Since when does anyone know the future? It could be an attack aimed at where your confidence is weakest. Or it could be your own mind playing out your own worst fear. It could be a million other things!"

I released a pent-up breath. "It's my own mind I'm afraid of," I confessed. I caught his gaze and held it. "I wish it was as simple as a ghost 'attacking' us. But the more I think about it, the less sense it makes! We may not understand everything there is to know about our abilities, but one thing we do know for sure is that we're stronger when we're together. I've seen more shadows and been more sensitive to emotions since I've met you, but I also have a whole lot more power to block them when we're touching. You said yourself you've done more intense remote viewing when you're with me! So tell me this. Why is it that the worst ghost 'attack' *ever* happened to both of us when we were together at the car? My defenses should have been at their strongest then!"

A flicker of angst shot across his handsome face. "Were you trying to block... at that moment?"

"Yes," I answered heavily. "I made a point of it, because the same thing happened to me before when I handled the clothes in the suitcase. But it *didn't work!*"

I burrowed my head into his shoulder and wrapped my arms around him, as much for his consolation as my own. "Now you see what's bothering me. Either I'm being attacked by something way too powerful for my defenses — or it's not really an attack at all. It's just my own brain trying to tell me something."

I closed my eyes and held him tight. "And I don't even know which is worse."

chapter 15

We were back outside of Zane's apartment, dropping him off and getting ready to head back home, when Tara's phone rang.

I had done my best to hide my increasing angst, and so had Zane. But the truth was that sharing my fears aloud had only made them seem more real to me. And although his superior acting skills allowed him to hide it better, I knew that he was every bit as disturbed as I was over the drowning thing. I knew because even though the surf was pancake flat the whole rest of the afternoon, not once did he insist that I get back in the water.

For Zane, that was the equivalent of a major freakout.

"Who is this? Oh, hi!" Tara said happily into her phone. I noticed that her nose and forehead were shining bright pink, and I felt guilty for not pushing the sunscreen. My land-locked friend wasn't used to the glare effect of the sand and water; she was going to fly back looking like a lobster. "We're on our way to Mililani now." She paused a moment. "You what?"

Even as I watched, her face fell. Then her forehead knitted into a frown. "Are you kidding me?"

"Uh-oh," Kylee murmured. "Methinks TJ is blowing her off again. This will not end well."

"Look," Tara said sternly, using a voice I'd only heard her use on her little brothers. "I don't mean to be rude or anything, but I *need* my stuff, okay? If you'll just tell me where it is, I'll come there and *I will get it myself.*"

Zane stopped in the process of unlocking his door and looked at her warily. When Tara used "the tone," it didn't matter what actual words came out of her mouth. Everyone within hearing distance who was now or had ever been a mischievous little boy automatically felt their sphincters tighten.

There was a much longer pause, during which Tara's expression gradually softened. "Yeah, okay. I understand," she said finally. "No, that's cool. Sure, that'd be fine. I mean, hold on a minute." She put down the phone and looked at me. "He's offering to deliver it wherever we want first thing tomorrow morning. He has to leave Mililani right now — something came up. He says he feels really bad. Anyway, he doesn't want us to have to drive anywhere else out of our way again. Is that okay?"

I shrugged. "Sure. Just have him drop it off at the house. When exactly?"

We set up a time, I gave out the address, and Tara hung up. She dropped the phone into her bag and then stood still a moment, staring into space. "That was weird," she said finally.

"Weird how?" Kylee asked.

"I don't know. It's just that from his texts and his voice mails, I expected him to be some semi-literate clod, you know? But talking to him, he wasn't like that. He really did sound sorry about everything. He didn't say what was going on with him exactly, but he seemed really busy, like stressed out. Geez, I almost felt sorry for the guy."

Kylee snorted. "Well, that *is* weird. When he cancelled out again I thought you were going to give him TaraTime or something."

I laughed, then turned to Lacey and Zane with an explanation. "Um, it's kind of a twist on timeout as a babysitter's punishment. Except TaraTime involves being forced to clean things."

"I may still do that," Tara retorted, although she smiled

as she said it. "But I do really believe he's sorry. He was actually pretty nice about it."

Kylee and I exchanged a glance. Was it just the budding sunburn, or was our Tara actually glowing a bit?

"Hmmm," Kylee purred suggestively. "And about how old did this mysterious Tim Jones' voice sound?"

Tara shrugged. "I don't know, but his name's not Tim Jones. That's some other guy he was traveling with. He said his name is Makani."

Zane pulled his door shut again with a slam. He'd only just managed to open it. He stood there with his hand on the doorknob, his key still extended, his eyes wide and staring.

"What did you say?" I asked Tara, praying that Zane would remain standing. I sidestepped closer to him as I awaited Tara's answer. Maybe if he passed out, I could at least keep him from hitting his head on the ground.

"Makani?" she repeated. "I'm pretty sure that's what he said."

"Really?" Lacey asked with enthusiasm, her own eyes widening.

Zane made a gurgling noise.

"Steady," I teased, throwing an arm around his middle. "Try to breathe."

"What's wrong with the name Makani?" Tara asked.

"What's wrong with *him?*" Kylee asked, pointing to Zane with concern.

I laughed. "Um... I guess you could say he's having a fangirl moment."

Zane tried to turn and glare at me, but his effort was half-hearted. He took a deep breath and gave his head a shake. "Makani Marro," he announced to them both, "is not only a professional surfer, he is the next great hope for a Hawaiian World Champion! Doesn't the name even sound familiar to you? He's a superstar! Grew up right over in Waialua, blew away the pro juniors, made the CT as a rookie when he was only eighteen. He's nineteen now, and with the big win he just had at the Pro Tahiti, he's sitting in the number one spot — on track to win it all!"

Zane's delivery of this information, needless to say, was profoundly dramatic, and by the end of it he had Kylee and Tara blinking at each other, equally impressed and bewildered.

"Well if he's that big a deal," Kylee said finally, "why didn't he just say so?"

"Why would he?" Lacey pointed out. "If I were him, I wouldn't. Zane's right — around here, Makani's a rock star. For all he knows, Tara could be some stalker chick who stole his suitcase on purpose."

"We don't know for sure it's the same guy," Tara said skeptically. "All we have is a first name. Surely the name's not that unusual."

"But his bag came from Tahiti, and it had a contest jersey in it!" Zane reminded. Then he clapped a hand to his forehead and swung around to look at me. "Kali! The boardshorts! Just picture him up on that podium at the awards ceremony... I could swear he was wearing a pair just like that! Do you remember?"

I had watched the contest with Zane, partly on cable in my parents' living room and partly online. Since the various rounds took days to complete, I could hardly claim to have paid attention to every minute of it, and I had no memory of what any of the surfers' boardshorts looked like. But if Zane claimed to remember details of the final ceremony, I believed him. Surfers noticed surf gear. And Makani was sponsored by AirTide.

"It's almost certainly him, Tara," I agreed.

"This is so exciting!" Lacey cried with a bounce. "And

you'll all get to meet him tomorrow! That is so cool!"

Zane looked from Tara to me, and his green eyes danced. He flexed his biceps in cartoonish fashion. "Kali, I don't suppose you or your mom need any manly chores done around your house tomorrow? Say around ten *oh crap!*"

"Ten oh crap?" I laughed. "No, but maybe around nine oh crap?"

"No!" he exclaimed. "This is serious! I can't! I have orientation tomorrow!"

My smile faded. "Oh."

"I can't skip that!" he groaned. "It's registration."

"I'm sorry," I said, meaning it. "But you're right, you really can't skip. You won't get the classes you want."

He made a pained sound, and as I threw a sympathetic arm around him, I noticed that Kylee and Tara were communicating via some bizarre nonverbal gestures. "Well," Kylee announced, "we'll head on back to the car and leave you two alone for a few. But don't keep us waiting too long!"

The three of them thanked Zane again for lunch, then walked away down the road toward where my dad's car was parked.

"Something's up," I told Zane as they moved out of sight.

"Like what?"

"I don't know. But I wouldn't get too comfortable." I turned and nestled into his arms anyway. "I'm really sorry you can't meet Makani tomorrow. I know what it would have meant to you."

"It's okay," he answered. "I would have embarrassed you all anyway, what with the screaming and everything."

I chuckled. "Yeah, probably."

He gently brushed a strand of my hair across my

forehead and behind my ear. "You know what?"

"What?"

"This has been a really fun group to hang out with. But all day long, I've been dying to kiss you."

I smiled and lifted my head. He lowered his.

He stopped. "Incoming," he murmured.

"Sorry, sorry!" Kylee chirped, bounding up to us at a jog. "Yeah, I know, 'Go die, Kylee!' Whatever. Look, I couldn't say anything in front of Lacey, but... you guys are missing the obvious. Zane, dude, you may not be able to meet this guy, but that doesn't mean you can't be a part of the whole experience, you know?" Her dark eyes twinkled at us both. "Think about it!"

Zane and I looked at each other. Then slowly, a beaming smile spread across his face.

Oh, right. The creepy spy thing.

"Would you mind, Kali?" he begged. "Would you let me... um... watch the show? Or at least part of it? You can cut me out whenever you want to. But at least I'd get to see him!"

"Won't you need to be concentrating on something else?" I asked, envisioning him driving wildly across the grass of a quad or walking into a cafeteria wall.

"There won't be any danger," he said quickly. "Text me when he shows up and I can make sure I'm someplace safe if you like, but it really isn't necessary. The only time I've ever totally zoned out is when you're with me and I'm doing the remote drop-in thing. When I'm seeing through your eyes as a beacon, it's different. I'm channeling you, but I'm still mentally present in both places, if that makes sense."

"I really don't like the word 'channeling,'" I complained.

"But..." he begged, *"Makani."* Then he had the nerve

to throw me a starving puppy-dog look that was so over-the-top pathetic Kylee nearly rolled on the ground with laughter.

"My work here is done," she said finally, gasping for breath as she jogged away. "Don't keep us waiting too long!"

"Oh, knock that off," I told Zane playfully, smacking him lightly on the shoulder even as I cuddled up to him again. "Of course you can join us tomorrow. In your own creepy way. But only for a little while, while he's there. I'll have to lift my blind completely, and I've gotten spoiled now, enjoying the peace and quiet of not having other people's emotions poking at me. Let's just hope the stupid ghosts leave us alone once Makani has his suitcase back."

Zane pulled back a little. "Maybe that's it, Kali," he said thoughtfully. "Makani. Maybe it's him the ghosts have been protecting."

My lips twisted doubtfully.

"Well, why not?" he argued. "Both of the ghosts looked like surfers. And they were real, living people at one time."

"Oh, come on. So Jabba the Hutt came back from the dead, used all that energy following a suitcase around and throwing punches, and all that time he was just fangirling? Protecting the guy's dirty clothes?"

"You underestimate how important this is," Zane insisted. "No Hawaiian has won the world championship since Andy Irons in 2004! No *man*, anyway. The women are awesome — Carissa Moore's won three world titles back to back! But only three men have ever won it for Hawaii, and everybody loves Makani. He's your classic 'local boy makes good' story. Started out with no advantages at all and he's worked really hard to get where he is." He pulled me closer again and began rubbing my back. "Look, I don't know why ghosts do what they do. They're people after all... maybe these two are his relatives, and they're crazy overprotective? But I can't believe any of this is really about *you*. You're not in any danger. Do you hear me?"

"Mmm," I murmured.

"Kali?"

"Can't argue," I said, my voice muffled by his chest. "Getting backrub."

He chuckled. "Well, that's a trick I'll have to remember."

Unfortunately, it only lasted about five more seconds. Then he pulled back and lifted my chin with his hand. "You're not going to drown, Kali," he said intently. "Now, or ever. It's... it's just not going to happen. I won't let it."

There was worry in his eyes. A deep-seated, raw ache of fear that I longed to reach out and take away from him. But before I could think of anything to say, he leaned down his head and kissed me.

And then I forgot what we were talking about.

chapter 16

"This is so exciting I can't stand it!" Kylee said for the fortieth time. She was pacing between the front window of my house and the coffee table, where my laptop sat next to Makani's waiting suitcase. We had all been creeping on the guy pretty mercilessly since yesterday, and our favorite pic was currently on the monitor. It showed the shirtless surfer standing by his home break at Ali'i Beach in Haleiwa, smiling broadly as he toted his board under one arm. It was an advertisement for AirTide boardshorts, and we all acknowledged that his perfectly smooth, sculpted chest was probably airbrushed. But *still*. It wasn't hard to see how the guy had become a rock star — at least in those areas of the world where people watched surfing on cable.

His hair was an unruly mop of jet black, not curly, but a mass of glossy waves that blew around his face in the wind, revealing to the camera only one dark, twinkling eye. His skin tone was a rich brown, his cheek bones high, his jaw square. He had a swimmer's build, triangular and lean, with broad shoulders, slim hips, and long limbs. But what captured the imagination — at least of any female — was his smile. It was vintage Mona Lisa. Ever-so-slightly lopsided and puckering only one dimple, it was an irresistible mystery. At first glance it was casual, light-hearted, and friendly. But on further inspection, there seemed to be much more to it... much more that he was thinking, and that he wanted to say. But what?

"I wonder how the German got in there?" Tara asked with a yawn, referring to the bio she'd unearthed when she'd hit the search engines last night. She was sprawled on the couch next to me, sipping at her mango-flavored tea. We'd all overslept this morning, barely leaving enough time to eat some breakfast before he was expected.

"No telling," I replied with a grin. Tara was fascinated by Makani's self-reported ancestry, which he described as "African-American, Hawaiian, Chinese, German, Filipino... and probably a bunch of other stuff."

"However it happened," Kylee declared wistfully, staring out the window, "it worked out great."

I took a sip of my own tea and clicked back to a video clip of the final heat of the Billabong Pro Tahiti. Zane had been right. Makani had been wearing the exact same boardshorts that were currently in the suitcase in front of me.

"See how tall he stands as he moves through the barrel?" I pointed out to Tara, who still couldn't completely grasp the concept of competitive surfing. "He's always got that look. That casual grace, like what he's doing takes no effort. Like he's just chilling out there, having fun. The judges love that."

Tara's forehead wrinkled. "Is he supposed to fall off backward and send his board flying into the air?"

"He didn't fall off!" I said with a laugh. "He did a back flip just for fun, to get back in the water. The ride was over and his board's on a leash. See? He's back on it and paddling already."

"Car!" Kylee squealed from the window. "And it's... driving by," she finished with disappointment. "What time is it, anyway?"

"Five after," Tara replied. "He's late. What a shocker."

"Don't be so pessimistic," I chided. "Last night you said that you were sure he'd come through this time."

Tara was quiet a moment. "I know. I do think he

meant what he said. It's just that I got the feeling there was something else going on with him, you know?"

"Are you kidding?" Kylee chirped, bounding over. "Makani Marro is the ultimate man of mystery! A name that means 'the wind.' Those dark, steamy eyes. And that smile! How many nineteen-year-old hotties have *ghosts* to defend their swimwear? I mean, seriously! I am *so* in love right now." She bounced on her toes and returned to the window. "Love at first sight," she crooned. "Or at least it will be, whenever I actually get to see him."

Tara and I chose to ignore her. I certainly had no desire to be reminded of Makani's connection with the dead. All of the theories I had come up with so far to explain the ghosts and their bizarre manifestations either sounded stupid or they scared me, and with Kylee and Tara's visit nearly half over already, I really just wanted to be done with the whole macabre thing — no offense to Makani intended.

Tara's phone buzzed, and she pulled it up and looked at her screen. "It's him," she reported. "He says he's stuck in traffic and he'll be another ten minutes or so."

Kylee groaned and sank down onto the floor.

"See there!" I told Tara cheerfully. "You were right. He wasn't blowing you off. He'll be here."

She smiled to herself. A genuine, heartfelt smile. "Yeah. You're right. It was nice of him to let us know."

"I'll never make it," Kylee moaned, lying flat on the carpet. "I'll die of anticipation."

"Bummer," Tara remarked offhandedly. She sat up on the couch. "Hey, Kali, can you click back to that interview where he was talking about having to leave high school? I want to read that one again."

When a car did finally pull up outside, Tara was deeply engrossed in researching the legal history of the school·for children of Hawaiian ancestry that Makani had attended, and I was trying to amuse Zane via text as he sat in a campus auditorium watching a mandatory presentation on drug and alcohol abuse. The video annoyed Zane because it had "the production values of a middle schooler posting a health assignment on YouTube" and because we both knew that he could have done a better job himself if they had handed him the mic and let him tell everybody how he'd wound up in foster care. But they didn't make that offer, and he was lamenting how much he would rather be with me when I glanced out the window and saw a nondescript little Nissan slowing to a stop.

Kylee, ironically, was in the bathroom.

"He's here!" I shouted to my friends as I texted the words to Zane. I dropped my phone on the coffee table, took a breath, and closed my eyes. *Blinds... dissolve.*

I heard a door burst open and looked up to see Kylee racing out of the bathroom. "Let me!" She hustled around Tara to the front door, threw it open, and ran outside.

Tara rolled her eyes, then looked at me. "Well, I guess we're meeting him outside, then." She stepped toward the bag. "Don't touch it, Kali," she reminded.

"Don't worry," I assured. I had no intention of laying a finger on anything belonging to Makani ever again. Only Tara had touched the suitcase since yesterday, and she had handled it minimally and kept it zipped. Since Kylee had seen no more of the ghosts, we assumed this made everyone happy.

Tara picked up the bag and carried it outside, and I followed her. As I shut the door behind me I could just see the disappointed face of my mother as she slinked around the corner into the living room. She was supposed to be working on the kitchen deck this morning, but clearly she'd been eavesdropping, hoping the famous surfer would come inside. No doubt I would see her peeking out of the window soon. A middle-aged married woman! How embarrassing.

Kylee was standing in the middle of our small front yard, halfway between the door and the car, seemingly unsure what to do. The car windows were too tinted to see through, but the front ones were rolled down just enough that you could tell there was one person inside. He hadn't gotten out yet, though, and Kylee could hardly rush him in the street. But now that she'd left the house, she couldn't go back in and wait for a knock, either. The predicament was typical Kylee. Act now, think later.

After what seemed like an eternity, during which the driver appeared to have his head down talking on a phone, the car door finally opened.

"Hey," a surprisingly deep voice rang out pleasantly, even as wary eyes shot a quick look up and down the street. "I'm really sorry I'm late. There was a fender bender — took forever to get around."

"It's... no problem," Kylee answered haltingly, staring. "Are you—"

She didn't finish the question because Tara stepped up and poked her in the side. But it wouldn't have mattered anyway, because the guy couldn't hear her. He had opened the back seat of his car and was leaning inside.

We all knew what she'd been about to ask. Because the guy who'd just popped out of the car was not what we were expecting. I suppose if we'd given it any thought, we would have known that he wouldn't be toting a surfboard and flashing naked abs. But in none of our imagined scenarios did we expect to see an ordinary-looking guy in jeans, flip flops, a dull gray hoodie, and a grungy backwards baseball cap blinking at us through a pair of frames that were every bit as dweebie-looking as Tara's.

He pulled a suitcase out of the back seat, shut the door, then came around the back of the car and walked over. Only then did he take his first good look at the three of us. He was shorter than I would have guessed, slightly shorter than Zane. But despite giving an underwhelming first impression, he was definitely *the* Makani. A closer view revealed the same handsome face we'd been admiring all morning, just hidden behind the hideous glasses. But what I saw was one thing, and what I felt was another.

As soon as the guy stepped within six feet of me, the emotions started coming. They radiated out like he was a one-man nuclear power plant. But they weren't all coming from him. They couldn't possibly be.

Optimism. Dread. Anxiety...

His appearance might be ordinary and his demeanor cheerful, but the very air around him was tainted. It was choked so thick with a fog of gloom that I wondered how he could breathe. Whatever I was perceiving, I knew it wasn't really visible, it was only in my mind. But where was it coming from?

"Special delivery," he said with a note of self-deprecating apology. "Finally!"

Stress. His tone was breezy, but some of the anxiety I felt was definitely coming from him. *Lust.* Well, that one always seemed to show up, didn't it? I guess we were all wearing shorts and sleeveless tops. *Motherly love.*

Wait. What the hell?

"Are you Tara?" he asked, holding the bag out towards Kylee. She was the only one of us who had actually spoken yet. We were all kind of in a daze.

Kylee shook herself and snapped back into default flirt mode. "No, I'm Kylee," she said with a smile. "It's so exciting to meet you!"

"Kali," I greeted. "And ditto."

"I'm Tara," Tara announced, her face lighting up as she took possession of her long-lost suitcase again. "Thanks for bringing this out. Yay! *Now* I remember that zebra stripe!" She laughed as she put the suitcase down by its twin and looked at the two side by side. They were indeed identical, except for the ribbons. She picked up Makani's bag and held it out to him. "Here's yours. And I'm sorry, too. It really was my fault they got mixed up in the first place. I just grabbed yours and left. I didn't even look at it closely."

"That's okay," he replied, taking his bag eagerly. Then he cast another wary glance up and down the street.

"Oh, I get it!" Kylee cried suddenly. "Those glasses! You're like... wearing a disguise!"

Tara's face turned thunderous.

I didn't know if Makani was wearing ugly glasses on purpose or not. But as of now, I sure hoped he was.

"Kylee!" Tara fumed. "You are so amazingly rude! I don't suppose you happened to notice that he's wearing the *exact same frames* that I am?"

Kylee's brown eyes widened as she looked from one of them to the other. "Holy crap, Tara," she said with amusement. "You're right!"

I hoped that Zane was enjoying this. Personally, I wanted to crawl under a rock.

But Makani was as amused as Kylee.

"We do have the same frames!" he said to Tara, favoring her with a killer smile.

Tara offered one of her prettier ones back.

"I always said those were men's frames!" Kylee exclaimed.

"Actually, they're unisex," Makani corrected. "But I thought I was the only person in the world who liked them. Everyone hates the way they look on me, but I don't care. I wear them when I'm just hanging out because they're light, but they—"

"They don't slide around on your face," Tara finished for him.

They looked at each other. "Yeah," he confirmed.

Fondness. Lust. Mother love. Sadness.

The warring emotions were freaking me out. No way were they all coming from Makani. I cast a glance at Kylee. Mainly she was watching the couple, but her eyes were darting around a bit. I surveyed the front yard myself and saw only one shadow near the carport, and it was really faint. Clearly, we had ghost company. But on top of the scattershot emotions that kept hitting me, the doom and gloom that surrounded Makani like a cloud was like nothing I'd ever felt before, and it was beyond strange that he himself seemed totally unaware of it.

Despair. Tension. Excitement. Grief...

"I guess you know who I am, huh?" he asked matter of factly.

We all nodded. But although I knew what he meant literally, the larger answer to that question was blowing my mind.

He shrugged. "I wouldn't call this a 'disguise,' exactly, but sometimes life's easier when I don't call attention to myself, you know? Like when you thought my name was Tim, I just went with it."

"Totally understandable," Tara offered. "Who is Tim?"

"He works for AirTide, one of my sponsors," Makani explained. "He does the travel arrangements and stuff. I wound up with so much swag coming home from Tahiti that he and his girlfriend went out and got me an extra suitcase. She's the one who put the ribbon on it, but I didn't pay much attention to the colors, either." He grinned at Tara again. "Rainbow, zebra, whatever, right? I just hope..." He dropped down, unzipped the suitcase, and began to rummage. "Yes!" he cried triumphantly, pulling out the boardshorts. "I figured they must be in this one. Everything was so crazy when we packed up, I was just throwing stuff everywhere. And then when we got home it was even more nuts. I didn't finish unpacking for days. But they would have killed me if I'd lost them, I swear." He stuffed the shorts back in the suitcase, stood up again, and beamed at Tara. "Wow. Thanks so much. You have no idea."

He was spewing warm and fuzzy emotions like a volcano, but those balls of light barely made headway in the sea of gray surrounding him. My muddled mind tracked back to swimwear. "What's so special about the boardshorts?" I forced out.

To my surprise, Makani laughed out loud. *Relief.* It was bubbling off him. "Probably nothing. But when I told the uncles I wasn't sure where those particular boardshorts had gotten to, they were like..." He recoiled as if reenacting the moment. "Whoa. Coming of the apocalypse, man!"

"But why?" Kylee pressed.

Makani chuckled again. "It's just superstition. I was wearing them when I won at Gold Coast, and then again at J-Bay. I didn't even notice until people started telling me I had to wear them in the finals at Teahupoo, too. I guess I wore that pair other times and lost, but somebody noticed that whenever I wore them the day of a finals match, I won, so now I'm stuck. At least until I wear them in a finals match and lose, anyway!"

My mouth hung open. Superstition? This was all about a silly superstition? No way!

Amazement. The strong, focused emotion struck me soundly, and I watched as Makani's dark eyes widened.

"Wait," he murmured. He leaned down to peek inside the suitcase again, then he straightened and stared at Tara. His mouth opened wordlessly as his finger pointed downward. It took him a moment to speak. "Those weren't clean," he said roughly.

Tara snorted. "Clean? They weren't *clean*? Are you kidding me? They reeked! That bag stank so bad we couldn't keep it within ten feet of the house. We're talking air quality alert level, here. You're lucky I didn't drop it in the nearest landfill as a public service."

Surprise. Offense. Warmth. Desperation...

Argh! If it weren't for Zane, I would *so* pull my blind back down!

Makani's eyes twinkled at Tara, and slowly his lopsided smile appeared, looking exactly as it had in the AirTide advertisement. I had no way of knowing for sure which of the accursed free-flying emotions were coming from the ghosts and which were coming from Makani, but I would stake my life he was feeling no offense.

"I can't believe you did that," he said softly.

Kylee let out a muffled sigh that only I could hear. She had always been a sucker for sexy whispers.

Tara, on the other hand, merely shrugged. "No biggie. I've got five brothers. I've washed worse. Gotta warn you though — some of the cotton stuff's a lost cause. Mildew. Damage halted, but not reversed."

Makani was still smiling. "Gotcha. I've got three brothers myself. All younger. And yours?"

"One older, four younger," Tara returned. "You ever get stuck in the middle seat?"

He laughed out loud. "Never."

"Makani," Kylee broke in, "congratulations on the Billabong thing. We were watching clips of it earlier. I love the way you surf."

"Thanks," he said politely. He looked up and down the street again. There was only one little boy on a bike up the road. Makani adjusted his cap a little and turned his back to the child. "Well, I guess I'd better get going," he said. He faced Tara again, and they presented an amusing picture with his ugly frames mirroring hers, obscuring two uncommonly beautiful faces. "I still can't believe you washed my clothes," he said with embarrassment. "I should, like, pay you or something."

Tara waved a hand. "Please, no. Too weird. I'm just glad to have my own clothes back. Even if everybody does tell me that Kali's stuff looks better on me!"

Makani had picked up his suitcase. But now he dropped it again, stunned. "You..." he stammered weakly, "You don't live here?"

Tara's blue eyes shifted over to mine in puzzlement. I shrugged. "Um, no," she answered. "Kali lives here. Kylee and I are just visiting."

Makani swore, and the guilt that rolled off him combined with the sadness, dread, and worry already hanging in the air to whip up such a pall of dreariness I was seriously tempted to mumble a goodbye and run inside.

"I'm such an idiot," he berated himself. "Somehow I thought you were in the same situation as me — flying home. I never thought you might be a tourist, and that I had your *only* clothes! Oh, man, you should have said something!"

"I'm pretty sure I did," Tara admitted, although she was smiling as she said so. "It's fine now. No harm done."

But Makani looked stricken. "Yeah, there was," he insisted. "I should have called you sooner. I really am sorry about that. I got home from the contest and my mom wanted to see me but my aunt was in the hospital in

Hilo and so my mom had to be over there, and then we got back and there were all these interviews and stuff and they kept changing the—" he stopped himself. "It doesn't matter. The point is, I should have got it back to you sooner. I've been a total jerk, and now you go and *wash* my nasty clothes and make me feel even worse."

Tara chortled. "Yeah. *That's* why I did it."

Lust.

Oh, my.

"Let me make it up to you," he offered, his dark eyes twinkling again. "How long are you staying on the island? What have you seen so far?"

Tara started to answer his questions, but she didn't get very far. Somehow Kylee appeared front and center and began to recount our past and future itinerary. Or rather, her idealized version of it, which seemed cleverly designed to earn us all an invitation to go windsurfing at Kailua Bay. Kylee had admired both the colorful sailboards and the kites from a distance, and she no doubt envisioned herself sailing away with Makani on a sapphire sea. She would be less excited when she realized that both kitesurfing and sailboarding were solo activities.

Makani encouraged her interest, and even gave her some pointers about lessons and rentals. But then he turned back to Tara. "And what are you looking forward to doing?"

"Oh, I don't know," she answered with a shrug. "I've enjoyed everything. It's fun just being here with Kali. But I suppose if I were by myself..."

I turned to look at her. We'd discussed what we all wanted to do on their first night here, but Tara had said very little. I could only remember her mentioning one thing that didn't make our list. Kylee hadn't been interested in it at all, and when I said I didn't care one way or the other, Tara had acted like it didn't matter and never mentioned it again.

"What's that?" Makani asked.

"The Bishop Museum," Tara answered in a voice that, if I didn't know her better, I could swear sounded almost shy.

Excitement. Approval. Despair. Frustration. Adoration. Worry. More Lust...

Whoa! I really couldn't take much more of this.

Makani threw back his head with a laugh. "I love the museum! It used to be one of my favorite places when I was a kid. I haven't been there in ages, though. How about if I give all three of you a guided tour? It's the least I can do, really. For screwing up your vacation. What do you say?"

"The museum?" Kylee repeated, her disappointment obvious.

"We say yes," Tara answered over her. "We'd love to. Or at least I would. These two can do whatever the hell they want."

"Well, I want to go!" I said enthusiastically, smiling at him. "I haven't been yet, either, but I'd love to see the coat of feathers. My boyfriend and I have been meaning to, but we haven't got around to do it. Would you mind terribly if he came too?"

You so owe me for this, Zane! I thought, even though every word I said was true. I really did want to go to the museum, and we really had talked about going. I just felt a little weird about inviting him along. But if I didn't at least give it a try...

"Sure," Makani answered easily. Then he caught my eyes. "But... if you don't mind, could you not tell anybody else about it? We'll have a lot more fun if we can walk around without anybody knowing who I am. The cap and glasses are usually enough, but if there's a crowd, then people start wondering why..."

"Totally get that," I said quickly. "Just the four of us. Nobody else will know."

He smiled at me, too. "Thanks."

Gratitude. Death.

All the happy feelings within me sank like a stone. What the heck was going on with him?

Makani pulled out his phone, glanced at it, and winced. "Crap, I'm going to be late," he muttered. He looked at Tara again. "I've gotta go. When can we do this?"

She shrugged. "My schedule's open."

"Mine—" he looked crestfallen. "Is not." He looked at his phone again and began scrolling with a frown. "This is ridiculous... I don't know when... Wait. Are you doing anything later today? Like midafternoon? The museum closes at five, but we can get in a few good hours, maybe."

"Perfect," Tara answered. "Text us a time and we'll meet you there?"

"You got it."

There were smiles and goodbyes all around as Makani grabbed his suitcase and headed for his car. But just when I thought we'd seen the last of the trouble-making luggage, he stopped as he was putting it in the front seat and dug out the jersey. He found a pen in the car's glove compartment and scribbled something. "Hey Tara," he called, tossing the blue fabric through the air.

She reached up and caught it in one hand.

He grinned at her. "Little souvenir," he explained. "From Tahiti. If you don't want it, maybe you can score some cash on EBay."

Tara grinned back. "We'll see."

He got in the car, waved back at us once, then drove away.

"O.M.G.," Kylee said in an exaggerated whisper. "He was *so* totally adorable, wasn't he? A geek at heart, maybe, but still... totally adorable."

Tara said nothing. She just stood still holding the jersey and smiled to herself.

I breathed out with a sigh of relief and pulled my blind back down into place with a slam. *Glowing platinum... yes!* I could not go through that every day. It was exhausting. "Kylee, how many ghosts did he bring with him? I swear, it felt like there was a whole friggin' army!"

Kylee looked at me strangely and shook her head. "There was only one that I saw. An older woman. Maybe like his grandmother? She was kind of hovering and fussing and all that. I didn't see either of the surfer ghosts."

I blinked back at her with a frown. I started to puzzle out that information, and then I just gave up. Was there really any point in trying? Makani had his freakin' boardshorts back, and he seemed happy, so the ghosts should be happy, which meant everybody should be happy. My blind was back down and I didn't have to feel this crazy crap anymore.

Done.

"Ooh, let me see!" Kylee cried, taking the jersey from Tara's hands. "He has such cool handwriting! Bold, yet sensitive."

"All I see is a squiggle," Tara said. "But it was nice of him, wasn't it?"

I held out my hand and Kylee gave me the jersey. I grabbed it by the shoulders and spread it out to see the portion of the neckline that Makani had signed.

The shirt went blurry.

I drowned all over again.

chapter 17

I lay flat on my bed upstairs, staring at the ceiling. "Don't worry, Kali," Kylee soothed. "We *will* figure all this out. I promise. Eventually."

She did not sound particularly confident. The drowning sequence had been even more vivid the third time, and it had only ended when Tara took the jersey out of my hands. I felt so numb afterward that they had to guide me back inside the house, at which point my mom pounced on us begging to hear every word that had been said. My friends indulged her while I recovered, although retelling the actual words of our meeting with Makani only told a tiny fraction of the story. I was pretty sure, judging by the way my mom looked at me, that she picked up on that, but she didn't probe any further, which was a relief.

My parents knew about my abilities, and Zane's and Kylee's too, but I hadn't mentioned the surfer ghosts yet. My dad had more or less come to grips with the whole supernatural thing over the summer, but since hearing about it still weirded him out a little I usually kept the gory details to myself, and this latest drama had seemed harmless enough in the beginning. Now it had all gotten so complicated I had no idea where to begin. So I didn't even try. We just moved upstairs where we could talk without being overheard.

"But it doesn't make any sense!" I moaned, noticing how much I sounded like Tara. Things didn't always have to make sense to me. Many times I could be more like Kylee. I could shrug and say "whatever!" and decide not to think about it. This was not one of those times.

"Are you one hundred percent sure there were no ghosts around me?" I asked weakly, looking at Kylee.

Her dark eyes swam with sympathy. "No, Kali. I told you before. There was just the old woman ghost, and she left with Makani. And she wasn't hostile *at all*. She just seemed afraid."

Tara paced the floor beside my bed. "You touched the jersey before, though. Didn't you?"

I nodded. My head hurt. A rooster ringtone sounded, and I felt guilty as I ignored my phone. Zane must have sent a million texts in the last half an hour. He was even more frustrated than my mother at having to watch the exchange with Makani with no audio, and he couldn't call me to talk about it because he was in the middle of a registration session. But I couldn't answer his questions yet. Too much had happened to explain by text. He couldn't feel the emotions I'd felt, and since I'd put my blind back in place before handling the jersey, he had no idea that I'd drowned again, either.

"I touched it before I touched the boardshorts when I loaded them both in the dryer," I answered Tara. "The jersey didn't do anything then. At least not right away."

"It's strange," Tara said thoughtfully. "Makani did give the jersey to me, so it really wasn't his anymore. Even if some ghost was able to punish you from a distance, or without Kylee being able to see him, it seems... well... a tad *overzealous*."

"There would be no point," Kylee argued. "Ghosts aren't *insane*."

Tara scoffed. "Do you have any idea how ridiculous that just sounded?"

Kylee ignored her. "It's more like the clothing itself is cursed in some way. But only Kali is sensitive to it."

"Oh, no," Tara said quickly, hands raised. "I do not *do*

'curses.'"

"Neither do I," I agreed, sitting up. I really didn't like the sound of that. I grabbed my phone and scrolled through my messages. Zane was so excited. So stoked about starting college, about our meeting Makani, even about Tara's "souvenir." He would be horrified when I told him I'd drowned again, and I was sorely tempted not to. But I knew that he would want to know. And if our roles were reversed, I'd be plenty annoyed if he didn't tell me.

"All I mean," Kylee tried to explain, "is that maybe it isn't the ghosts that are doing it. I told you when it happened at the beach that the big guy was just staring at the two of you. Almost like he didn't know what was going on, either. Which makes me wonder if the drowning thing isn't separate. If it isn't some perception you're picking up from the clothes themselves."

"Like maybe a memory of Makani's?" Tara suggested. "Another imprint Kali is sensing?"

Optimism flickered. "Yes!" I cried. "Maybe that's something we have in common! Maybe he almost drowned when he was younger, too!" I liked that thought. Not that he had nearly drowned once, but that there was no current threat associated with the horrible images. "Why not? He's been surfing the North Shore since he was little, it would almost be more surprising if he *hadn't* ever been held under for a wave or two!"

Tara's sharp blue eyes did not seem convinced. "Didn't you say there was blood?" she asked.

I hopped off the edge of my bed. "Yes, but he could have cut himself on the reef or something," I said dismissively. "It doesn't matter. I still think it's the best theory we've got. For whatever reason, Makani has tight ties to the spiritual world. Maybe his clothes are radioactive with his energy. We already know I'm sensitive to imprints of past events, so it makes sense that I could tap into some visuals. Maybe touching his things brings out the drowning scene in particular because it triggers my own phobia."

"Now there's a thought," Kylee said. "I wonder if some of his belongings could be more 'radiant' than others? He did only wear the jersey one time. But I guess you could argue that it became more significant to him emotionally after he signed it and gave it to Tara."

"I still don't see—" Tara began.

"Well I'm glad that's settled," I announced cheerfully. I had an explanation that both made *some* sense and didn't scare me. Now I could move on.

I picked up my phone and began to text Zane. Not being able to hear what any of us had said earlier, he had no idea that he was about to meet Makani himself, in person, this very afternoon.

I couldn't wait to make his day.

—✺—

Zane's green eyes blazed with light as he caught sight of us at the appointed meeting place just outside the entrance to the Bishop Museum. He stepped up at once and enfolded me in a fierce hug, which he couldn't possibly know how much I needed.

Do you have any idea how much I adore you right now? His embrace said loud and clear.

Right back at you, mine returned.

"Any sign of Makani?" Kylee chirped, scoping out the area.

Zane shook his head as he released me. "Not yet." He grinned down at me, but after studying my traitorous face for a second, his enthusiasm dimmed a little. "You okay?"

I smiled back. He still had one arm around my shoulders. "Better now."

Tara looked up from her phone and back toward the parking lot. "He says he just got here."

"Listen, Zane," I said dutifully, trying to sound upbeat. "When we met him at my house, everything was a little more complicated than it looked. I was getting some really weird vibes that I couldn't explain by text, and I can't explain it all in sixty seconds, either. But we'll talk about it later, okay?"

"I see him," Tara announced.

Zane's gaze snapped from me to the figure striding toward us, then back to me again. The conflict was clearly painful. He was worried about whatever it was I had to tell him and he saw right through my fake happy face. Then again... *the next world champion of professional surfing! O.M.G!*

I laughed out loud. "I'm fine!" I insisted, meaning it.

He looked back at me skeptically, then turned his full attention to Makani. The disappointment on his face at his first sight of the Hawaiian icon made me laugh all over again.

The surfer looked even geekier than the last time we'd seen him. He was wearing neon orange sneakers, some seriously ugly dress pants, a baggy rain jacket, and a long-brimmed hunter's cap that was covered with guns and moose antlers.

Moose antlers?

Tara and Kylee chuckled along with me as he approached. "Very nice," Tara teased. "You go moose hunting often after a hard day's work at the office? And a run?"

He grinned and shrugged one shoulder. "I improvise. It helps to have a cousin who works at the airport and gets kicks out of raiding the lost and found." He looked at Zane, and I stepped forward to make introductions. But when I got closer to the famous surfer the same dismal pall of depression I'd felt before began to assault my senses all over again, even with my blind in full force. "Makani," I said quietly, careful not to be overheard. "This is Zane Svenson. Zane, Makani Marro."

The guys shook hands. I watched Zane closely to savor his reaction. To his credit as an actor, if I hadn't been watching him closely I probably wouldn't have noticed the shudder that passed through his legs and his back, or the way he braced himself as he fought the urge to recoil. I would only have seen what everyone else saw: a goofy, starstruck guy who was really, really happy to see his idol face to face.

"Awesome to meet you," Zane said with what was almost his normal voice. But the Zane I knew wasn't present — either in the voice or in his eyes. The response was given on autopilot... Zane was somewhere else.

My heart began to pound. I put an arm tentatively behind his back.

Makani nodded, and the guys dropped hands. Zane stiffened briefly, then relaxed again.

"I swear I don't normally dress like this," Makani said.

Zane's face showed disappointment. "No? I've got a hat just like that, man."

Makani snickered, and Zane smirked back.

Before anyone else could say anything, Makani had moved to the ticket window and paid for five admissions. He waved off our surprised thanks, gestured for us to follow, then led us through the building and out the other side to a large circular lawn area.

"I wasn't lying to you," Makani told Tara. "I love this museum. I've been looking forward to showing it off all day. First stop, Hawaiian Hall! Or as my brothers used to call it, 'the whale room.' Follow me."

I pulled on Zane's arm to get him to hang back as the others started walking toward the main building. "What happened to you back there?" I whispered.

He had the nerve to look at me like he didn't know what I was talking about.

I gave him a disgusted expression. "Don't even start! Yes, your acting was superb, but I *know* you. Now, what happened when you shook his hand? Are you all right?"

He threaded his fingers through mine and started walking after the others. "I'm fine. Can we talk about it later?"

I blew out a breath. Of course he was fine. Zane might be highly "evolved," as Lacey put it, but he was still a *guy*. He was also sharp enough to know when to quote my own words back at me.

I couldn't shake a continued feeling of angst as we followed the threesome into the castle-like building ahead of us. The museum, which bore the date 1889 above its entrance, was made of rough-hewn grayish lava rock and was Romanesque in style, with lots of arches and tall, narrow windows. On another day, it might have been beautiful. Today, as the sun that had shone all morning picked this moment to slip behind the gathering clouds, the only adjective that came to mind was "gloomy."

Or perhaps my blind was slipping somehow? The people shadows were certainly thick here, as thick as anywhere in Honolulu. Yet they were not unhappy as a group. For over a hundred years the museum grounds had been a site for school trips and family outings, weddings and galas. And I saw nothing among the scattered, fleeting shadows in the gardens to explain the strange, unsettled feeling that had come over me upon Makani's arrival.

We walked through the stone archway and into the Hawaiian Hall.

"This has all been renovated in the last few years," Makani explained, stopping to let us catch up with him in the entryway. "It was a huge effort. I haven't seen it since it's all gotten finished."

I had to smile at the enthusiasm in his voice, even as the chill in the air around him continued to oppress me. He began walking backward, moving as comfortably as if he gave tours for a living. "The wooden beam and the railings you'll see in here are all made of native koa wood. Later you'll want to walk around and read all the exhibits, but when you first walk in, it's cool just to stand back and enjoy the big picture for a second." His dark eyes twinkled at Kylee. "And I don't mean just stare up at the whale. It's fake, by the way."

Kylee giggled and widened her eyes. "Really?"

"Paper mache," he confirmed with a smile. "But it's still cool."

We walked on into the hall together, and I understood immediately what Makani meant. The room was a huge oval, three stories tall with skylights at the top and two levels of balconies that circled the whole way around. The bannisters, ceiling beams, and wooden trim on the elaborate third floor arches were all made of the gleaming, red-brown koa wood, and the space in between was filled with delights for the eye. Aside from the giant sperm whale that hung from the ceiling, I could see a shark, a ray, a turtle, and some fish sharing the vertical space. What looked like an actual ancient fishing canoe was also suspended along one wall, and in the center of the floor stood several giant tiki-type carvings and a full-sized grass shack. Various themed exhibits and artifacts in koa-wood cases ringed the periphery of the first floor, then spiraled up and around each balcony.

"Wow," I whispered to Zane. "This is neat."

It was also crowded. More crowded than any of the living humans currently buzzing about it were aware of, that was for sure. The place was absolutely seething with shadows. I suppose I shouldn't be surprised, since any spot of ground that was highly trafficked by people tended to host more than its fair share of emotionally charged life moments. But this building being as old as it was, funneling so many people along the narrow balconies... *Geez!* How many parents had nearly had strokes trying to rescue their idiot children as they dangled off one balcony or another? I saw three such shadow scenes in a matter of seconds. I lowered my eyes, afraid of seeing one that did not end happily.

"Oh, wow. Where do we even start?" Tara asked with glee.

"The realm of the sea," Makani answered dramatically, pitching his voice in a low, mysterious tone. "Pre-contact Hawaii. This way."

He led Tara off and Kylee followed, although I noticed that Kylee seemed to stumble a bit. She hadn't said a word since we walked in the hall, which was odd. She should have screeched or squealed. Or at the very least, oohed or aahed. "Did you notice—" I began to ask Zane. But I never finished the question. I took one look at his face and had a pretty good idea what was wrong with Kylee. "Zane?"

"Yeah?" he replied dryly. His eyes stared out at the room before us, not at one spot, but at the length and breadth of it. His gaze swept forward and back, stopping here and there at seemingly random places. His pupils were wide. His chest heaved up and down. He looked over at Makani and Tara, studying the area around them for several seconds as both worry lines and a fine sheen of sweat broke out on his suntanned forehead.

"Let me guess," I said, taking his hand into both of mine. "All these shadows I'm seeing are not alone, are they?"

Zane closed his eyes a second. Then he shook his head and shoulders and looked at me.

"Sorry," he muttered. "What did you say?"

"You were somewhere else?" I asked, confused.

"No," he replied absently, "I was here." He looked back up into the room again and blinked. "Just having childhood flashbacks of Disneyland."

Now he was really confusing me. *Disneyland?*

He nodded slowly. "The Haunted Mansion."

chapter 18

We moved around the first floor exhibits in a loose clump, with Zane and me staying a pace or two behind my friends and Makani. For someone who claimed he hadn't been to the museum in a couple years, Makani knew a surprising amount about the renovations and the older exhibits, and he easily answered every question Tara came up with about Hawaiian cultural history. He obviously enjoyed the topic as much as she enjoyed asking about it, and he was interesting to listen to. Unfortunately for me, he seemed not to want to speak too loudly, which meant I couldn't understand everything he said unless I also stood close enough to him to feel wretchedly depressed. Which was disturbing for several reasons, not the least of which was that unlike this morning in my front yard, my blind was now in place and fully functional.

It just wasn't working. At least not where Makani was concerned.

Zane was quiet. He spoke to me in monosyllables and watched the open air around us like a tail gunner spotting enemy planes. When he grabbed my hand suddenly by the miniature replica of the *heiau,* or sacred temple, my first thought was to duck. But he only wanted to pull me to the side so we could talk without being overheard.

"Kali," he whispered earnestly. "When you met Makani at your house earlier, did you shake his hand?"

I thought about it. Sometimes I shook people's hands and sometimes I didn't. It depended on the circumstances. I remembered the scene as Makani walked toward us... "No," I answered. "He was holding the suitcase when we introduced ourselves."

"Have you ever touched him?" Zane pressed. "Think hard. It's important."

I replayed both of our brief meetings in my head. "No. I don't think so." Standing close enough to him that I felt like I wanted to cry was plenty. "Why?"

Zane blew out a long, slow breath. "I need to think about it." His eyes darted across the room to rest on an older Asian man who walked with a cane. I had noticed before that the man seemed to be staring at us, or at least at Makani. Evidently, Zane had noticed too.

"Zane, something has obviously got you worried, and I'm warning you, you have exactly five minutes to tell me what it is and then 'later' officially expires," I demanded, refusing to be put off again. "I don't need to be protected. What is it that you're thinking?"

The old man took a step toward us, then wavered as if reconsidering. He was definitely focused on Makani. Did he recognize the surfer through his disguise?

"I'm thinking I have four and a half minutes left to stall," Zane quipped. Then he stepped away from me and up to Makani. "Sorry to interrupt, but I'm afraid your cover may be blown. The man at three o'clock has been staring at you and it looks like he's making his move."

Makani lifted his head with a sigh. But the instant his gaze connected with that of the elderly man, his face broke into a beaming smile. "Um... sorry," he said to Tara. "I'll be back."

He crossed the center of the room in a few hurried strides, then stretched out his arms and greeted the elderly man with a hearty embrace. When he drew back, the two began talking in hushed tones, all smiles. They didn't speak in English, but in Hawaiian Pidgin, a dialect that's a mixture of broken English and words from other local languages, like Chinese, Japanese, and Filipino. I'd lived in Honolulu for months now, and I still couldn't understand a word of it. But the two men were obviously quite close.

My heart warmed. "Do you think they're related?"

"Maybe. That's so nice," Kylee said approvingly, although her voice sounded a little off. "A lot of guys wouldn't hug their grandfather like that in public, you know?"

I took my first good look at her since we entered the hall, and realized that her voice wasn't the only part of her that was off. Her eyes were just as dazed and glassy as Zane's.

"He's a nice guy, period," Tara declared, leaving us to go back to the display she'd been reading. The normally observant Tara was so far off in museum geek la-la land she didn't even notice that half our party was losing it.

Kylee moved to Zane's side and threw him a beseeching look. "Please tell me this is freaking you out as much as it's freaking me out," she whispered.

"That would be a yes," Zane answered mechanically, his eyes glued on Makani and the elderly man. "What the—"

"Oooh, this is *so* weird," Kylee lamented, her eyes fixed on the same spot as Zane's. Her chin quivered a little and she leaned into his side. Then she sucked in a sudden breath. "Oh!"

Both she and Zane cringed.

"What *is* it?" I demanded, only just managing not to stamp my feet and scream. "Close your eyes for a second and tell me!"

"There are ghosts everywhere," Kylee moaned, keeping one eye half open as she hid the rest of her face behind Zane's shoulder. She was cuddling a little too close to my boyfriend, but I could see that she was genuinely afraid. "I wouldn't think they would bother me, but these... I mean..."

"They want something," Zane offered. "The one just now knew we could see her and she practically made a run at us. But..." He lifted his hands in helplessness. "I don't know what they want. How could we? Maybe they just want us out of here."

"But there are other people here!" Kylee complained. "This is a museum! People are *supposed* to be here!"

"What are the ghosts doing exactly?" I asked.

"Right now, they're hovering around Makani and that man," Zane answered. "But their expressions... I can't even tell if they're happy or sad!"

"I know," Kylee agreed. "It's so bizarre!"

Makani talked to the man for a few minutes, then rejoined us. "Sorry about that," he apologized. "Old friend of the family. Haven't seen him in a while. Where did Tara get to?"

Anguish. Torment.

Wordlessly, all three of us pointed to where Tara stood staring at the explanatory sign for the grass *hale,* or hut. She was completely absorbed, ignoring all of us. Makani rushed back to her side.

I breathed out with relief as the stifling aura surrounding him released its hold on me. "Describe what you're seeing to me. All the ghosts. Please!"

Zane and Kylee took turns filling me in as we made our way up and around the second floor. They spoke of ghosts from the semi-solid to the wispy, walking and floating, congregating on the hull of the airborne canoe and flitting about the banisters. Men and women, young and old. Some made sounds, but none of them could speak. And although several of the ghosts seemed to recognize the awareness in Zane's and Kylee's eyes, neither of my friends felt like their own presence mattered. The ghosts' focus was on one living person, and that person only.

Makani.

"Kali," Kylee admitted, her chin still trembling slightly, "I really don't like to admit this, because you know I've always thought of ghosts as normal people. Whether they come back to help a loved one or whether they're stuck here because of issues that need to be resolved, they're still just ordinary souls. But *these* people... there's something just not right with them!"

"I know what you mean," Zane agreed. "There's a vibe here that isn't healthy. I don't want to say it's evil, but I don't know what else to call it. Looking at their faces, they're just so..." He blew out a frustrated breath. "I don't know."

"Hostile?" I supplied, feeling slightly sick again as I thought of Jabba the Hutt laying into my boyfriend's face.

But Zane shook his head. "No, not exactly."

"We can't tell," Kylee said firmly, catching my gaze. "But *you* could."

I tensed. *Please, no.* "It's too crowded in here. It wouldn't work," I defended. "There's no telling what kind of a jumble I'd get! I'd have no way of knowing what was coming from the ghosts."

"You'll know," Kylee said confidently. We had all been talking low, both to avoid being overheard in general, and to avoid Makani's hearing us in particular. But gradually he and Tara had not only pulled farther ahead, they'd retreated into their own little world, too.

"There's a vibe in this place," Kylee continued. "And there's a vibe around Makani himself. You told us you'd felt it."

"Felt what?" Zane asked quickly.

I tried to explain to him about the sadness. The pall of depression that came over me whenever I stepped within a foot or two of the would-be world champion. "My blind doesn't seem to work on it, either," I finished.

"Nor did your blind stop the drowning attacks from the boardshorts or the jersey," Kylee reminded. "Those visions rolled right on in, like what was happening was a totally different mechanism from your picking up on other people's emotions."

My jaws clenched. I didn't want to think about that. I wanted the drowning scene to be a memory. *Makani's* memory.

"Wait a minute," Zane broke in. "The jersey?"

"Oh, right," I said sheepishly. I filled him in on how touching it had given me the drowning sensation all over again.

"And there were no ghosts around her then?" Zane asked Kylee.

She shook her head.

"And what about when I met Makani just now?" Zane asked. "When he and I shook hands?"

Kylee shook her head again. "Not that I saw. I didn't see any ghosts around him until we got inside the courtyard. Then there was that half-naked woman with all the tattoos—"

"Yeah," Zane said absently. "I saw her, too."

"Half-naked woman?" I asked, irked.

"But if the clothes can cause the visions to happen without any ghosts around, what does that even mean?" Zane continued.

Kylee cast a glance ahead of us at Tara and Makani, who were deeply immersed in discussion over some old farming tools. She nibbled on her lower lip. "I think it means whatever the 'energy' is with this guy, it's very strong. It radiates out from him. It sticks to his belongings. Things that are special to him seem to get a stronger dose of it."

"But what is *it?*" I begged, hating the quaver in my own voice. "I refuse to believe there's anything bad or angry or dark about Makani! He's a nice guy! A perfectly *ordinary* nice guy!"

Zane threw me a look of disbelief.

"Aside from the incredible surfing talent thing, of course!" I corrected impatiently. "Kylee, there just has to be something else going on here. What about the nasty ghosts? What is their problem?"

"Minions?" she suggested weakly.

"No! I'm not buying it," I said stubbornly. "Makani wouldn't do that."

Kylee pursed her lips at me. "You've known the guy for all of what? Six hours? And for what it's worth, *you* cannot see the expression on the face of that goon behind you!"

Like a fool, I turned around. All I saw were two middle-aged tourist women and the shadow of a preschooler heading for the railing. "Did you ever think that maybe they're all just frustrated?" I asked, facing Kylee again. "Makani doesn't seem to be aware of them himself! Maybe he's not."

"But how could that be?" Zane argued. "All I did was touch his hand, and I—" He cut himself off. "Wait. Maybe that's a good thing."

"What is? Spill it, Svenson!" I ordered.

"The drowning scene," he answered. "It happened to me when Makani shook my hand. At least it started to. It was playing out exactly like it did when you and I were touching the boardshorts, but when he dropped my hand, it stopped again. And this time, it was all me. No ghosts.

And you were standing beside me, but you weren't touching me. Not at first."

"I wasn't? Are you sure?"

He smirked. "Kali, I *always* notice when you're touching me."

I smiled.

"But that means..." Kylee murmured, thinking to herself out loud. "That means it *can't* be an imprint!"

Zane and I both reluctantly turned to look at her. It had been nice to get distracted for three seconds. "Why not?" I asked.

"Because Zane doesn't have that ability!" she insisted.

Tara and Makani moved up to the third floor balcony. We followed at a safe distance, making a pretense of staring at the exhibits and reading the signs. "He can't pick up imprints of the past any more than you can see ghosts or do remote viewing," Kylee continued. "This drowning business *must* be something else altogether!"

In a display case ahead, I spied an amazing cape covered with colorful bird feathers. If only we weren't so hopelessly distracted, both Zane and I would enjoy these exhibits, and I made a mental note for us to come back another day and do the museum justice. That outing was sure to be a whole lot more fun than this one.

"Kali, you *have* to lift your blind and get a feel for what's going on here," Kylee insisted. "You'll be perfectly all right. If you ask him nicely, Zane might even hold your hand."

I frowned at her. She was acting like there was no real risk in 'feelings,' but she didn't understand. I looked out over the balcony railing at the living people below, and at the faint and the not-so-faint looping shadows from the past. I tried to imagine the ghosts that Zane and Kylee saw superimposed on top of them all, and a shudder passed up my spine.

"Kali," Kylee said softly. "There's something about Makani that's drawing these spirits to him. And they're not happy spirits. I don't know what their problem is, but I know they're *with* him. They haven't been the least bit friendly to us, and both Makani and his stuff have pretty much caused psychological attacks directly *on* us. I don't want to say he's a bad guy, because he certainly doesn't act like it... but we've got to get real here!"

"Kylee's right," Zane chimed in miserably. "I can't believe it either, but if you sense anything really scary around this guy, we should get Tara away from him."

"I don't believe—" I started to argue. But I gave up. There was nothing even remotely sinister about Makani himself. I knew that in my bones, but I couldn't explain how I knew. And I had no excuse for not being willing to prove it to them. Especially not with Tara's wellbeing on the line. Forget the whole surfing prodigy thing — any guy who loved museums was a hero in her eyes. I hadn't seen the girl's face glow so much since the time we made the olive oil facials.

"Fine," I agreed, folding my arms across my chest and leaning against a koa-wood column. Zane immediately snaked an arm around my waist and pulled me into his side instead, which made me so warmly, wonderfully comfortable I almost forgot what I was supposed to be doing.

Almost. I breathed out slowly and focused on Makani and Tara. They both had their heads down, reading the text under a picture of a Hawaiian queen. "Where are the ghosts?" I whispered to Zane.

He looked around and shook his head. "All over. They move. Just tell us what you feel."

I decided to close my eyes. I leaned into Zane just a

tiny bit more, then began to roll up my blind. Slowly, inch by inch. Platinum... *disperse.*

First, I got what you would expect. Curiosity, awe. Perhaps even a wee bit of boredom. The feelings of living strangers were the strongest, while those of the shadows were often tough to distinguish in a crowd. Fear would be coming from the shadow parents of the climbing children, no doubt. Perhaps even from a few of the smarter shadow tots. The other shadows could be feeling anything.

Excitement. Enjoyment. Sadness. Fascination. Regret. Appreciation.

How could I ever tease out the feelings of ghosts I couldn't see from all the background noise?

"It's gibberish," I muttered to Zane and Kylee. "There's too much going on."

"Let's go closer," Kylee suggested. "There are three ghosts around them right now."

"Good idea," Zane agreed.

I opened my eyes, and we closed the distance between our group and the couple. Zane and I were about six feet away from Makani when I stopped short and clutched his hand.

Grief. Anguish. Sadness. Love. Confusion. Helplessness. Despair. Fear.

None of the emotions were new ones. I had felt them all around Makani at some point or other already. But now, suddenly, they were intense, heavy, *soggy.* They weighed me down as if I were underwater. But I was not, my eyes were seeing the room ahead quite clearly, it was only the emotion that dragged me down. Down to the depths of hopelessness. "Oh," I said without meaning to, my breath leaving my lungs with a whoosh. I staggered backward several paces.

Zane moved with me. "What?" he begged.

Kylee appeared at my other side. "Kali? What is it?"

I shook my head. Makani and Tara hadn't noticed us. They were reading something together now. They were smiling at each other.

Love. How had that gotten in there? The emotion hadn't come from either of them. No matter how cute they looked together, they had only known each other a matter of hours. There were no living people in the immediate area. Not even any shadows close by.

"The gh..." I stammered. "Ghosts. Where were they just then?"

Kylee huffed. "They practically sailed through us, my dear. Some of them have *no* respect for personal space."

Very slowly, my brain began to process it all.

"The ghosts," I whispered, as if I could keep the specters from hearing me. "They're not hostile. There's nothing evil about them. They're just... upset."

"Upset about what?" Zane asked.

My eyes focused on Makani. "About *him.*"

Love.

Motherly love.

"Don't you see?" I whispered more emphatically. "They're not minions! We were closer to the truth when we were joking about the stupid boardshorts! They're just people, or they *were* people, and in their own ways they're trying to protect him."

"Protect him from what?" Zane asked.

I shook my head. "I don't know. I can't read their thoughts. They're confused. I don't think they even know themselves. What they're feeling is a horrible sense of gloom and doom, and they're sad because they care about him. Makani, he..." I wasn't even sure how to phrase it. "He seems to be really special to a whole awful lot of dead people."

Zane cracked a sad smile. "Everybody loves Makani."

"Oh, no," Kylee said breathlessly, her dark eyes boring into mine. "The drowning vision."

I felt a knot twist up in my gut.

"It's not an imprint of the past, is it?" she whispered. "And it's nobody's memory, either. Your blind didn't work on it because it's not associated with anyone's feelings! In fact, the first time you felt it at the dryer, your blind probably *helped* you feel it because it shielded everything else and helped you focus on what was right in front of you."

"The boardshorts?" Zane said skeptically.

"A personal item important to Makani," Kylee corrected. "It carried enough of his energy that someone as sensitive as Kali could pick it up from a touch. You're not quite as sensitive, Zane, but you could do the same thing when you were touching both the boardshorts *and* Kali. And when you were touching Makani himself, you didn't need her at all."

Zane's eyes widened. "Are you saying something different is happening here?"

Kylee nodded. "It's a different ability. And this time I believe both of you have it."

"What?" I demanded.

"Precognition," she answered. "Seeing an event in the future."

"Hey, guys!" Makani said happily, walking over to us. "You have to see the *'ahu'ula* with us: the feather cape of Kamehameha. There's a great story I want to tell you about it." Kylee immediately plastered on a smile and stepped towards Tara, but for whatever reason, I couldn't seem to move. I looked into Makani's kind, dark eyes and could see that he was genuinely, incredibly excited to tell us all about the cape. I felt an unbelievable urge to cry.

"Come on," he said, touching me lightly on the arm. "It won't bite you."

Swirls of blue. Sparks of pain. My head, throbbing. Blood in the water, seeping. The light above, only darkness below. Going down, now. Far, far down...

"Kali, you're all right!" Zane whispered urgently, shaking me gently out of my stupor as Makani whirled away again. "Walk with me!"

I put one foot in front of the other and, assisted greatly by Zane, managed to cross the minimal distance to where the others stood, admiring the amazing cape of yellow feathers.

The famous surfer began to tell his story.

My eyes teared up.

"Zane," I whispered into his ear, my voice a barely audible, strangled whimper. "Makani's going to die!"

chapter 19

$\mathbf{Z}$ane and I sat on a bench outside on the garden lawn. I'd tried to fake it, but I wasn't that good an actress. Makani hadn't gotten three lines into his story before he noticed how upset I was, and I'd been forced to plead momentary sickness and make a run for it. Zane had an excuse to follow me, but since I hadn't needed two nursemaids, we'd had to leave Kylee to her own acting skills.

I really did feel sick. "Precognition," I muttered miserably as my head lay on Zane's shoulder. "What does that even mean? No one can know the future for sure. It's always changeable, to an extent. Isn't that what you always hear, anyway?"

"I have no idea how any of this works," Zane replied, stroking my hair gently. "I only know what I saw. And what I felt. If I was seeing the future through his eyes, then he's going to get a pain in his head, and he's going to feel like he can't move, and he's going to sink."

I shuddered. "Don't forget the blood. Did you see it?"

"Yes." He stopped stroking my hair and hugged my shoulders. "It's hard to tell what happened, exactly. Maybe something hit him. Maybe he had a stroke or a seizure of some kind and cut himself. A head wound could bleed a lot." He straightened up and turned to look at me. "How did it end for you?"

I swallowed uncomfortably. "It got interrupted at different times. But the first time was the longest. Everything went black, but I was still conscious, because I could feel myself sinking deeper. That's the last thing I can remember."

Zane's green eyes swam with angst. "How deep were you then? Do you have any idea? It did look like ocean to you, didn't it? Not a pool?"

"It was definitely ocean." I could see the movement of the layers, the frothiness of the surface water, the deeper murk. How deep was I? "I'm not good at judging distance," I admitted, trying to remember the sight of the slowly shrinking circle of light above me. "But I'd say at least ten feet, when I closed my eyes."

Zane closed his eyes a moment, then settled back on the bench again. "That's not good," he murmured. "I don't suppose you... saw anyone else? Any sign of anyone coming for you?"

I didn't care for the question. I liked my answer even less.

"No."

"There you are!" Kylee rushed up and sat down on the pavement in front of our bench. She lowered her head onto her arms a moment as if she, too, was feeling sick. "I got ahead and then told them I was going to run and check out the melting lava in the science center while they caught up," she explained. Her dark eyes bore into mine with an anguished look. "Oh, Kali, what are we going to do?"

Before I could respond, my phone sounded with a text from Tara. She was checking to see if I was all right. "I'm going to tell her that I'm better and we'll be back in in a minute," I said as I texted back. "We can't hide out here much longer, not when it was so nice of Makani to buy tickets for all—" My voice choked up.

"We can't know for sure what's actually going to happen," Zane said stubbornly. "We have no way of knowing if the scene in the ocean is something that *will* happen or something that *might* happen. Why should we assume the worst?"

I nodded my head in agreement, but I didn't feel nearly as optimistic as Zane was trying to sound. The sadness and grief I had felt around Makani was there for a reason.

Kylee shrieked and rose with a whirl.

She startled me so much I almost jumped into Zane's lap, and probably would have if she hadn't beat me to it. For the second time in an hour I felt an urge to strangle one of my best friends, only to snuff the feeling just as quickly when I saw the look on her face.

"What does she want?" Kylee squealed, backing up into Zane's chest as if she were being cornered. Both she and Zane stared straight ahead at a point in space not two feet from us.

I watched in both horror and fascination as the expressions on their faces changed from surprise to distress, to confusion, and then finally to sympathy. Kylee slid away from Zane and back onto the ground, her dark eyes practically teary. "But we don't know what to do," she said softly, still staring ahead at nothing — although it was a lower point of nothing. "What can we do?"

Then finally, their gazes looked different directions. They each let out a breath.

"That was intense," Zane said roughly, running a hand through his curls.

I looked from one to the other. "Talk. Now."

"It was the old woman ghost," Kylee said quietly. "The one who came with Makani to your house."

"Mother love," I mumbled.

"What?" Kylee asked.

"She's very fond of him," I explained. "I could feel her before."

Kylee nodded. "I thought she was being... aggressive towards us. At first. But she wasn't. She's just desperate."

She and Zane exchanged a pained glance. Then Kylee looked back at me. "She went down on her knees, Kali. She was asking for our help. She was begging us."

I began to feel sick all over again. "But what can we do?" I cried, repeating the same question Kylee had asked the ghost. "What does she expect from us?"

Zane shot a look at Kylee. "Doesn't the fact that she's even asking us for help mean that there's a chance for him? That this precognition stuff isn't a sure thing?"

I felt a spark of hope. "That's right! However ghosts know things, however they know that he's in danger, they must also know that there's a chance the future isn't written in stone!"

Kylee's face brightened a little. "That does make sense. Maybe we *can* do something. I need to call my *ba noi*." She got up from the pavement and smacked the dirt from her shorts. "One thing's for sure. Our top priority will be keeping our boy *out* of the ocean."

Zane's jaw dropped. He looked up at her as if she'd lost her mind. "Kylee," he said heavily. "The guy is a professional surfer. He's in the ocean every day. It's his job!"

Kylee blinked back at him a second, but the determination in her eyes didn't waver. "Yeah. That will make it harder."

It will be impossible, I thought dismally.

Kylee pulled out her phone. "I actually do want to see that lava melt," she admitted. "I'll call while I'm walking over there."

"We should go back in now," I suggested to Zane. "I want to catch them before they're finished with the third floor."

"They're only about halfway around it now," Zane reported, looking idly across the lawn. "They seem to be talking a lot and taking their time."

Kylee and I looked at each other, then stared at him. When he didn't respond, I bumped my shoulder against his.

"What?" he asked.

"How do you know that?"

He had to think about it a moment. "Oh," he said finally, seeming surprised at himself.

Kylee and I shook our heads in amazement. "Is it really that easy?" I asked. "Do you just think about a place and see what's happening there, just like that?"

"Well, not usually, no," he defended. Then he hugged me to his side again. "It's your own fault! You energize me. You're like a portable charger."

"That is so romantic I can't stand it," I said dryly.

"Romantic or not," Kylee said thoughtfully, "it could be very, *very* useful. I'm going to make that call. You two figure out the 'dry land' part."

She walked off across the lawn. I looked anxiously at Zane. "No challenge there."

"We barely know the guy," he agreed, his forehead creased. "It's not like we can tell him what to do."

"And if we told him the truth?" I threw out, knowing the answer.

Zane shook his head. "He'd think we were nutcases. And why shouldn't he? The only way he'd believe us is if he had some abilities himself, but we've got no reason to think he does. He didn't see those ghosts today, that's for sure. He might believe it if someone else he trusted had abilities, but how could we know that?"

"And if we take a chance on his believing us and tell him the truth, and we're wrong..."

"We'll lose any chance we have to get close to him," Zane finished.

I groaned. "I don't suppose the old woman ghost had any ideas?"

Zane frowned. "I wonder if that's part of the... well, part of all the despair you've been picking up on. These souls obviously have some connection to him, and they know he might die. The other ghosts we've known, like your grandmother and Kylee's great aunt, when they came back to help a loved one, they had a plan. But what are these guys doing? They're flying around like chickens with their heads cut off — excuse the metaphor. I don't think they have a clue what to do for Makani, and I think that's part of why they're so miserable."

"So Jabba the Hutt goes around randomly attacking people who mess with the guy's lucky boardshorts?"

Zane shrugged. "Hey, maybe Jabba's not such a bad guy. Maybe he was superstitious in his life and just wants to give Makani every advantage in the water. What else is he supposed to do with his energy, anyway? He probably feels as helpless and frustrated as we do."

I leaned my head against Zane's shoulder. "That's big of you."

He smiled a little. "You do realize the guy didn't actually hit me, right?"

"Doesn't matter," I replied, giving him a quick peck on the cheek before prying myself reluctantly away from him and up off the bench. "Nobody messes with my boyfriend. Now, let's go back in there and do some acting. We can't let Makani see any of this weirdness."

"Or Tara," Zane added, getting up with me. "Not when they're getting along so well. If she..."

"I know," I agreed. I didn't like keeping things from my friends, but he was right. If Tara was going to flip, it would be a hundred times better for everyone if she did it after she and Makani had said goodbye.

We made our way back to the third floor balcony and started at the beginning of the timeline again, waving an "all better now" to Tara and Makani across the open hall. We didn't get too close to them yet, since my eyes were puffy and I was still hiccupping a little. The pictures and artifacts describing the history of the Hawaiian monarchy actually did look interesting, but we couldn't begin to concentrate on them. We just milled about, lost in our own racing thoughts, grateful that Tara and Makani seemed too absorbed in each other and the exhibits to pay us much attention.

By the time the two of them had finished circling the balcony, Zane and I had caught up and Kylee had rejoined the group as well. None of the three of us had a clue what was written on any of the placards, but it seemed to have depressed the heck out of Tara and made Makani more thoughtful as well. "It's really sad, isn't it?" Tara said, stepping up beside me.

My eyes itched horribly. Hearing her say such a thing when I was still so miserable threatened to make me bawl all over again. But she couldn't know about Makani. She was talking about something else. What exactly, I didn't know, but I nodded anyway.

"I've read about all this before," Tara said soberly. "But I didn't really *get* it, you know? Why so few of the people living here now are descendants of the original Hawaiians. It's unbelievable how many of the native islanders died from disease after making contact with Westerners. And in such a short period of time, after they'd been living here so long!"

"Oh," I said sympathetically, understanding her melancholy now. "I know. It is horrible."

"And the way the queen got swindled out of power is just unconscionable!" Tara fumed. "No different than what happened in Wyoming with my own ancestors!" Her cheeks flared with red, and she muttered something else to herself and moved away.

The fire in her tone, I knew, was personal. Tara had found out through a DNA test in the spring that she was four percent Native American, a fact she was proud to boast about, more so because she knew how bizarre it sounded coming from a fair-skinned, blue-eyed blonde.

"I think we have time to see the Pacific Hall too, if we hurry," Makani announced, moving toward the stairs. Zane asked him some question about the history of the museum, Tara scooted closer to listen in, and Kylee seized the moment to whisper in my ear.

"My *ba noi* says that if you're sure the ghosts seem loving and that their intentions are good, we should let them lead us."

I sucked in a ragged breath. "Why does that thought make me really, really nervous?"

Kylee's dark eyes studied mine. "Because you're not sure their intentions are good?"

I shook my head. "No. I'm sure they care for Makani. But I don't think they give a rat's you-know-what about us. And I don't think they have a clue how to save him, either."

"But we could work together," Kylee insisted. "You may think that because they sense danger for Makani that they understand all about our abilities and what we're thinking, but *ba noi* doesn't think that's true, and neither do I. Maybe if we tell them what we can do and offer to help?"

"Be my guest," I said quickly. "You and Zane are the ghost whisperers, not me."

We descended the steps and made a series of turns through the lobby and into the Pacific Hall, a smaller but equally beautiful koa-wood room that featured a double-hulled sailing canoe and celebrated the various cultures of the Pacific Islands. Zane the actor was making a stellar effort to discuss the exhibits intelligently with Makani, and since Tara was an eager participant in those conversations, Kylee and I were free to chat while we wandered.

"It blows my mind that I've only seen a couple ghosts in my whole life before, and now they're all over the place," Kylee marveled, looking up in the air and over at Makani as much as she looked at the display cases. "*Ba noi* thinks that some places make it easier for them to appear because they're so rich in energy. Either because of the people gathered, or because of what's happened there in the past, or maybe even because of the energy in the objects stored there. Remember the old man Makani hugged?"

I nodded.

"Around him, the ghosts got, like..." Kylee struggled for words. "So much stronger. Like the ones that were only wispy got more solid. They seemed to draw strength from that man's energy. Or from his feelings for Makani. Or something. I don't know. It was just so weird."

"These ghosts don't look like real people?" I asked, thinking of how when Kylee had seen a ghost as a child, she had believed the ghost was a real person. The first ghost Zane had seen had appeared to be a real person to him, too.

Kylee shook her head. "No. None of them are that good. I mean, I think that takes more energy than they have. They can't talk and they can't stay visible long. Most of them are just wisps. I think Jabba and Baldy, maybe the old woman — they're the type that haven't crossed over yet. You know... the type with issues. They died near here, they haven't gone into the light for whatever reason, and they're more visible to us because of that."

"So the only ghosts strong enough to help us are the ones with... *issues?*" I said with discouragement, not even wanting to think about what actions might have landed Jabba in that nether zone.

"O.M.G!"

I jumped with alarm as Kylee whisper-hissed directly in my ear. I thought she was being attacked, but she was only looking at a display of ancient tattoo tools, which looked like combs and were made out of bone. "It's a good look on him," she said, staring with awe at a grainy, black and white picture of a nineteenth century Samoan man with an elaborate, repeating geometric pattern of tattoos covering the majority of his body. "But I would make a terrible warrior. I almost passed out when I got my cartilage pierced."

I looked away from the still-sharp implements. I'd never been the type to suffer for beauty, and the last thing I wanted to think about now was elective pain. I had just opened my mouth to ask Kylee if we shouldn't go somewhere away from the others to try to "talk" to some of the friendlier ghosts when I was interrupted by an announcement over the loudspeaker.

The museum was closing.

Zane, Makani, and Tara rejoined Kylee and me, and we all began walking back outside and toward the parking lot. "Sorry you didn't have time to see more," Makani said genuinely. "I hope you'll come back another day, if you can."

"Oh, we will," I said as cheerfully as I could manage, stepping back a bit every time Makani turned toward me or slowed down. I wondered if he noticed the odd distance I kept putting between us, but there wasn't anything I could do to stop myself. Now that I knew the truth, the soul-crushing sadness surrounding him was unbearable, even with Zane holding my hand.

"Tara says you live out by Backyards?" Makani asked Zane as we walked.

"For another week anyway," Zane answered ruefully. "Then I'll be moving into the dorms in town. Just in time to miss the fun stuff."

Makani chuckled. "Yeah, that's a bummer. But hey, I heard there might be a little something heading in up there."

Zane's eyebrows perked. "Yeah. I heard that, too."

When we reached the edge of the parking lot, Makani stopped walking. "Well, my car's this way," he said, gesturing. Then he offered Zane a friendly fist bump. "Thanks, man."

"Thanks for what?" Zane replied, managing not to flinch at the contact this time.

"For not bugging me with a bunch of questions. You know. About the tour and everything."

Zane's eyes twinkled a bit. "No problem."

Makani turned back to Tara. "You know, I would say I'm sorry about the suitcase switch again, but I'm really not," he admitted with a grin. "This has been too much fun. Just what I needed, with all this craziness lately."

"It's been amazing," Tara assured. "You've got a gift, Makani, you really do. You make history so interesting. If the surfing thing gets boring, you should seriously look into being a docent."

He laughed out loud. "I'll keep that in mind." He started walking backwards. "Hey, Zane, if the country does start pumping, maybe I'll see you out there."

Oh, wow. Zane's heart would be beating out of his chest at the thought!

"I'll be there," he called back, sounding suitably

restrained. I shot him a smirk, and he smirked right back at me while I knew his inner child was doing handsprings. *Yes, yes, YES!!!*

Only then did we remember. We were supposed to be keeping Makani *out* of the water.

Our smirks faded.

"Oh! If you do go out on the North Shore between now and Saturday, please text me!" Tara called after him. "I'd love to watch! But don't worry. We'll pretend we don't know you, I promise!"

"Tara," Zane said with a laugh, "If he shows up anywhere on the North Shore, believe me — it won't matter if *we* recognize him or not."

Makani chuckled. He reached his car and popped it open with a beep from his remote. We all called out another round of thanks as he opened the door and got inside.

"Don't forget The Plan!" Tara shouted just as he was closing the door. And after returning a smile to her that I could only call "secretive," he gave the rest of us a final wave, shut the door, and drove away.

We all stood silently, watching, for a long time after he'd gone.

"He has the most amazing intellectual mind," Tara said finally, turning around toward the rest of us. Her face was beaming. "It's a crime that a brain like his isn't in college right now. They wouldn't even let him finish high school! Did you know that? He was in the Kamehameha School, and probably at the top of his class, and he had to quit and do some stupid cyber school thing so he could traipse all over the world going to surfing contests! I mean, I know it's not every day that somebody has his athletic talent, but still, if you—" she cut herself off and stared at us. "What? Why are you all looking at me like that?"

Even with Makani's aura long gone, the urge to spout salt all over again almost overwhelmed me. Tara was not going to take this well.

"Tar," Kylee said gently. "Some things have happened. We figured some stuff out. About the drowning vision."

Tara's clear blue eyes transformed from bubbling over with joy to piercing the back of my skull with their sharp perceptiveness. She looked at me, inside me, over, and through me and then did the same thing to Zane and Kylee in turn. Her chest began to heave with rapid breaths. Her face paled. She blinked once, and then her eyes turned glassy.

She turned her back on all three of us and walked to the car.

chapter 20

I have experienced some uncomfortable family dinners in my life. There was one fast food meal, soon after I first told my parents about my abilities, when we were all so out of sorts we dumped three uneaten burgers straight into the trash. Then there was the dinner at which Zane and I told my dad that we'd found my grandfather, a biological father the Colonel didn't know he had. That one gave new meaning to the word 'awkward,' but at least it had included some happy news, too.

This dinner was just totally, unequivocally wretched.

My dad had started the evening in the best of moods. He was — of course — as excited as a little kid to hear all about our afternoon with one of the world's most famous surfers, and he had gone out and bought a huge plate of barbecued ribs and roasted pineapple to celebrate. Bringing him down with ordinary bad news would have been bad enough — kind of like poking him with a stick. But bringing the man down with a spooky tale of woo-woo had been like shoving him head first into a vat of ice water. He was now sitting in his chair on the kitchen lanai with his head hanging, his hands resting limply at his sides, and his eyes as glassy and unseeing as Tara's.

My mother wasn't much better. She had started out trying to cope with her emotions by fussing with the food, but now that it was clear no one wanted any more, she couldn't figure out what to do with her hands.

Almost all the talking had been left to me. Zane had tried to be useful when he could, describing the appearance of the ghosts, but Kylee — the traitor —

hadn't said a word. She had agreed with Zane and me on the ride home that we owed it to Makani to do everything we could to help him, and that meant making full use of the available brain trust — calling on every person who knew about my abilities for their ideas and input. Yet here Kylee sat, easily breaking her own record for longest stretch without a word, previously set the day after she got her wisdom teeth out.

Tara was even worse. All we'd gotten out of her since the museum were grunts and groans.

"So," I finished at last, letting loose with a long, slow exhale. "That's the situation."

Everyone was quiet for at least thirty seconds. My mom sprinkled salt into her napkin.

"Well," Tara said finally. "At least if he goes surfing, we'll know. I asked him to text me."

Zane and I exchanged a look of concern.

"You asked him to text you if he went surfing on the North Shore," Zane explained to her patiently. "But the surf in the country's usually flat in August. He only said maybe he'd see me out there this week because they're forecasting a swell that's kind of a fluke. But even if we do get something, I seriously doubt it'll get big enough to tempt him away from town. The South Shores are where the action is in summer. The surf's much better here."

"Guy like him could hop a plane to Maui or Kauai, too," my dad threw in.

Tara looked from one of us to the other. Her hopes seemed dashed, but only for a second. "Well, I'll just have to text him back, then," she declared. "I wouldn't normally bug him like that, but we have no choice. I'll say that I'd really like to watch him surf before we have to leave, that we're running out of time, and to please let me know the next time he heads out, wherever that might be. I'll promise him we'll stay out of his way and that we won't let on to anyone else that he's there."

The energy at the table ticked up a notch. "Perfect," Zane agreed.

Tara whipped out her phone and started typing.

"What will you do then?" my mom asked in a calm, reasonable voice, even as she lifted her folded napkin and methodically tapped out the salt into a line down the center of her plate.

"They don't know that the boy's going to drown, Diane," my dad answered irritably. My mom raised her eyebrows at him, but she knew he wasn't irritated at her. He was irritated at the whole annoying business of the supernatural that in one fell swoop had soured his family's brush with greatness *and* threatened harm to Hawaii's next best hope at a men's world championship. "They know he started to sink. Right? That's where it ended. So who's to say somebody doesn't rescue him? The point is to make sure that somebody gets to him in time."

The phrase "easier said than done" hung over the table like a flashing neon sign, but nobody said it out loud. Zane and I exchanged another uncomfortable look. *So far down...*

"Besides that, the whole scene itself could be a 'might happen,' rather than a 'will happen,'" Kylee said finally, her first words of the meal. "If we knew more specifically what happened *before* the vision starts, maybe there's a chance we could change the course of it."

"It starts with pain on the left side of the head," I reminded.

"And we shouldn't forget the blood," Zane added, causing winces all around.

My dad sat up straighter in his chair. "Have you thought about a shark?"

My muscles tensed. I didn't like to think about sharks.

Ever. I knew all the statistics about how rare fatal encounters were, how important sharks were to a healthy ocean ecosystem, blah, blah, blah. But I also knew that it wasn't at all uncommon for surfers to meet up with tiger sharks in Hawaiian waters, and whether the thought bothered Zane or not — and of course it did not — it terrified me.

"A bite on the head would be pretty strange," Zane said thoughtfully. "But not impossible. It would explain the blood, anyway."

Both Kylee's and Tara's faces seemed to have lost all their blood. My mother grabbed a fresh napkin and wiped all the rib sauce off the serving platter.

"We'll keep an eye out for sharks, then," I said crisply, moving on. "I guess the main thing will be to make sure there's a lifeguard nearby. To keep an eye on Makani at all times. To call 911 at the first possible hint of a problem. If that means driving all over the island trying to keep up with him without him seeing us, then that's what we'll have to do."

"And if he hops on a plane?" Kylee squeaked.

My dad's forehead wrinkled. He looked at Zane. "We'll fly if we have to. But if memory serves, the forecast's pretty decent in town this week, is it not?"

Zane nodded. "We know he just got back from the Big Island, and he was in Tahiti before that. Maybe if we're lucky he'll want to stay close to home for a while. After all, Trestles is coming up in a few weeks and then he'll be off to California."

My dad exhaled loudly. "Let's hope."

Kylee raised her hand. Then, with sudden realization, she blushed and jerked it down again.

The Colonel had a strange effect on people.

Kylee cleared her throat. "My *ba noi* said that whatever

Kali and Zane are seeing, it's very likely to happen soon. Precognition is a short-term thing, for a lot of reasons, and it tends to amp up the closer you get. She definitely thinks 'days,' not 'weeks.'"

"But..." I cried, "It's been three days already!"

"We have to think *logically!*" Tara practically shouted. Her face was still deathly pale, but her expression was resolute. Clearly, she was struggling to get a grip over her own emotions more than she was chastising anybody else. "What tools are at our disposal, here? We know there's danger in the ocean, and we know we can't keep Makani *out* of the ocean. All we can do is be on hand to intervene. We ordinary humans can find out where's he going, watch him like a hawk, alert the lifeguards, and call 911. Kali and Zane can touch the jersey again and see if they can pick up any more clues about how the whole thing starts. Kali can also see shadows."

She looked at me. "Any chance of that ability helping us?"

I sat back in surprise. I was still trying to process the concept of intentionally drowning myself again. "I don't see how," I admitted. "They can't *do* anything like ghosts can. And there isn't any knowledge from the past we're looking for."

"I guess not," Tara agreed. "What about feeling emotions?"

I considered, then shook my head. "All I've ever gotten from the ghosts is 'we're worried.' Even if they did know specifics, I can't read their minds."

"It's Zane that has the most useful tool," my dad said, sounding as uncomfortable as if someone were actively sticking pins in him. "You do realize the army spent years trying to figure out if remote viewing was a real thing or not? The CIA finally decided it wasn't, and they shut the program down. But hell, if Zane can do it, you've got a built-in spy machine right here."

All eyes turned to Zane. "I can see certain places I've been to already," he admitted. "But that doesn't mean I could track a person. I mean, I could only see Makani if he happened to be someplace I knew, and I happened to be looking at it then."

"Well," my dad continued, his voice smug. "In the months since you've lived on this rock, have you, or have you not, personally sized up every possible break that a guy like Makani would be likely to paddle into?"

Zane smiled with understanding. "Well, yeah. I guess I have."

"So there," my dad said triumphantly, crossing his arms over his chest. "We have a spy. As of now, you're on duty, son. Twenty-four, seven. Consider it a service to the state of Hawaii."

"But Dad," I countered. "Zane can only do that when he's with me. Survey a whole scene, I mean. He has to be touching me, or at least close by me. Otherwise he just gets flashes."

My dad's hawk eyes darted from me to Zane. "That true?"

Zane nodded.

My dad frowned. "Well. That's damned awkward."

"I think our most useful tool is the ghosts," Kylee piped up again. "They know who we are and where we are, and I'm sure that the old woman, at least, understands that we'd like to help. I don't think they're using up all this energy just to cry and moan. I think they're going to pop up again. And we should be ready to follow their lead when they do."

My dad threw a look at my mother. She threw a look back at him. I didn't need captions.

I'll take orders from a bunch of damn floating banshees when hell freezes—

Mitch! For God's sake, just roll with it!

My dad didn't follow anyone who didn't rank above him in the military. Unless, of course, he was married to her.

Tara jumped in her seat. She whipped a hand around to her back pocket and pulled out her phone. But then she tossed it down again, muttering one of her little brothers' names along with some unkind adjectives. "Like I care if he can't find his friggin' football pants!"

My mother stood and began to collect the dishes, signaling that the meal was officially at a close. "Well, it will only be daylight for a little while longer," she said in her best cheerful-mom voice. "Unless Makani was headed straight out to the beach when you left him, he's bound to be safe until tomorrow, right?"

She meant the statement to be comforting, I'm sure. But it had the opposite effect.

"How early do surfers go out in the morning?" Tara asked.

"Ever heard of the dawn patrol?" my dad answered her. "Makani would be just the type to get out there at first light, too. He's got every reason to want to avoid the crowds, never mind the wind."

Kylee was staring at Zane. "He's doing it again right now," she commented. "Look."

We all turned to Zane. He was leaning back in his chair, which he had scooted next to mine so that our shoulders were touching. His gaze seemed to be fixed on the cup of ice water in front of him, but his eyes weren't focused. If he knew that Kylee was talking about him, he gave no indication of it.

"Leave him alone," I suggested, trying not to move.

"He's probably scanning the south shores right now, checking to make sure Makani's not there."

We heard some dishes clink. I couldn't see my mom because she was behind me, but I'm pretty sure she almost dropped something. Her footsteps scurried into the kitchen and my dad made a funny sound that he tried to turn into a fake throat clearing.

Tara tapped something into her phone. "It'll be light before six tomorrow," she announced.

Kylee's lips pursed thoughtfully. "No offense, Tara, but we can't count on the guy answering your text to tell us when and where he's going surfing. I mean, he's not exactly been great at getting back to you."

"That was before!" Tara said defensively. But then her confidence deflated. "No, he's not the greatest about answering. Did you notice he didn't pull out his phone once the whole time we were in the museum? You know he had to be getting stuff, too. He was just ignoring it. I don't think he's much of a phone person."

"Even if he does answer," I pointed out, "I doubt he'd mention a dawn patrol. He wouldn't think you'd want to get up that early just to watch."

Tara groaned. "Well, how direct can I be? Should I call him up right now and say, 'Please, please, Makani, for the sake of our mutual love of museums, can you give me your minute-by-minute itinerary for the next three days?'"

"No," Kylee answered quickly. "We have to be careful. You can't all of a sudden go stalker-chick on him."

"I know!" Tara lamented. "I was only with him for a couple hours, but I'm pretty sure he'd know it was out of character, and then he would think I was just *weird*."

"Is that healthy?" my dad asked. He was paying no attention to any of us. He was still staring at Zane, who remained sitting motionless with his eyes unfocused.

I looked to make sure Zane was still breathing. "He's fine, Dad," I assured.

My mom finished clearing off the dishes, then began to wipe down the tabletop. I shifted a little so she could reach between me and Zane, totally forgetting the shoulder-to-shoulder contact thing. As soon as I moved, Zane snapped out of his trance and gave a little jump in his seat, which startled my mother so much she cried out and dropped the wet dishrag on my head.

"I'm so sorry," she apologized, extracting it from the curls beside my face. *Gross.* I could swear I tasted salt.

"What?" Zane asked, looking around in confusion.

"Did you see Makani?" I pressed, reminding him of his mission.

He gave himself a shake. "No. Actually, the surf sucks pretty much everywhere right now. I looked around at all the obvious breaks, but I didn't see him and I really don't think he'd be out. Not in this. It's not worth it. I'm pretty sure he's safe for the night."

We all let out a sigh of relief.

"Well," my mom said with authority as she collected herself. "Then I think the best thing we can all do is get a good night's sleep. Zane, you might as well head out to your place right now and get your things. The sooner you leave, the sooner you'll be back. All our air mattresses are taken, but the couch should be comfortable enough."

Three seconds of dead silence followed.

"What in hell's fire are you talking about, Diane?" my father bellowed. "Since when are we running a teenage dormitory?"

My mother made a huffing sound and came just short of rolling her eyes. "This is a group project, Mitch. You can't expect the boy to go home now just to get up and drive back over here in the middle of the night. If you think Makani is going surfing at dawn and you expect to have a prayer of getting out there in time to keep him safe, then of course Zane needs to be here with Kali to start watching the beaches as early as possible!"

My dad made a growling noise low in his throat. We could hear a gnashing sound as his teeth ground over each other.

"She's right, Dad," I said seriously, careful not to grin. "It's his service to the state of Hawaii."

chapter 21

Kylee, Tara, and I sat on the couch in my living room, staring at nothing. Zane sat beside me not even staring, but just sitting with his eyes unfocused, apparently running through a continuous loop of every happening surf spot on the island of Oahu. He'd been doing the same thing for hours now. He had to be getting exhausted.

Under any other circumstances, last night might have been fun. It wasn't every day a girl got to have her two best buds sleep over — and her boyfriend, too. We'd made a quick trip to the North Shore after dinner, packed up Zane's board and his backpack, and returned to a short but cozy evening of popcorn and surf videos. Once we'd all gotten familiar with how Makani looked out on the water, we turned in for the night, but I'm not sure how well anyone slept. I couldn't stop thinking about how Zane was tucked in on the couch one floor below, and I have a pretty good feeling he was thinking similar, distracting thoughts about me. The Colonel, I'm sure, considered it his fatherly duty to toss and turn all night listening for the creak of an unauthorized footstep going up or down the stairs, which would have kept my mother awake out of sheer aggravation. And I'm pretty sure that seeing my dad brandishing a gun in his pajamas earlier in the week might have been behind Tara's and Kylee's reluctance to make their usual trips down to the bathroom.

When our alarms had gone off in the wee hours, I'd slithered downstairs, my mom had heated up some island tea, and Zane had put his remote viewing ability to work. Kylee and Tara had devotedly gotten up with us, Kylee insisting that someone needed to watch for further communication from the ghosts and Tara checking her phone every three and half seconds. My dad made coffee and then went out to fetch us all some donuts.

Now it was late morning. Zane had seen no sign of Makani. And Tara had received no text.

I moved away from Zane, and his eyes fluttered. "Time for another break," I suggested. "We really don't know how long you can keep this up. You should pace yourself."

"I'm all right," he protested, stretching his arms. But he sounded groggy to me, and his eyes were still a little unfocused.

"Maybe you should get up and move around a little?" I pleaded.

"Maybe we should all go out for an early lunch," my mother proposed from her desk. "I'm used to sitting around this house, and even I'm getting stir crazy."

"Hear, hear," my dad agreed, practically jumping up from his recliner. "Can't stand another minute of this, myself. Why don't we move our base of operations a bit? Get a change of scenery?"

Everyone rose in unanimous approval as my phone buzzed with a text. My hopes skyrocketed for a second, and I could tell from the look on Tara's face that hers did too, before we realized that we were idiots. Makani didn't even have my number.

"It's Lacey," I announced. We hadn't seen Lacey yesterday, but she had texted to announce that the community pool's pump needed a part that had to be ordered, so the lifeguards were closing down for the season. Needless to say, she had been ecstatic.

Hanging in Haleiwa today!!! Hitching with Matt —

you guys gonna be around?

My smile was bittersweet. I would *so* much rather be playing on the North Shore this afternoon than face the specter we were facing! Then again, if Lacey knew what was good for her, she wouldn't be inviting us along in the first place. She would be spending quality time alone with Matt, waiting for his hormones to kick in.

Awesome! But sorry – doing town today. Have fun!

I sent off the reply and slid my phone back in my pocket. "Where should we go?" I asked Zane.

"We'll have to stay pretty much central, like we are here," he answered. "From what I'm seeing, the best action right now for a guy like Makani would be around Diamond Head, and I still think that's where he's most likely to show up. But your dad's right." He gave my dad a nod, and the Colonel nodded back. "Makani mentioned in an interview that he surfs around Ewa Beach a lot because he has friends over there. If there's even a small chance that he decides to go over and goof off with them while we're waiting for him all the way over near Waikiki, we'll have a terrible time fighting our way back through the traffic."

"Moanalua Gardens, then," my mother suggested. "It's right off the H1. We could take a picnic."

"Diane," my dad said fondly, crossing over to her and wrapping an arm affectionately around her waist. "You are a genius."

My mom was also really good at packing picnics. Between the week's leftovers and what she gathered from a quick run into the grocery store on the way, we had quite a spread laid out before us under the shade of a banyan tree at the picturesque city park. The food was tasty and the weather was gorgeous, sunny and warm with a light breeze that carried the scent of the park's abundant flowers. On another day, under other circumstances, we could all have had a fabulous time.

"I should try again," Zane said determinedly.

"It's only been ten minutes," I replied. He really wasn't himself. His appetite seemed fine, but the remote viewing was obviously draining him — mentally if not physically. He seemed fuzzy-headed and checked out, and it worried me. "Give it another five."

"I still haven't seen a ghost," Kylee said distantly, sounding more than a little checked out herself. "I haven't seen a whiff of *anything* supernatural since Makani drove away from us yesterday afternoon. And yet, I know it's not over. The silence is almost, like... eerie."

"I know what you mean," Zane said quietly. "There was so much activity. And now... nothing."

I looked from one to the other, and my heartbeat quickened. "You don't think—"

"No!" Tara cried with alarm.

"No, not *that!*" Zane and Kylee said together, a reaction that seemed to surprise them both. They exchanged a glance, and then Kylee explained.

"We would know if... well, if we'd failed. I'm sure of that. I'm not sure how I'm sure, but I am. I get the feeling that the ghosts are in some kind of holding pattern. Just like us. Like they're gathering their strength or something."

"Calm before the storm," Zane murmured.

I studied his too-serious face again. I really didn't like what all this weirdness was doing to him, and if it wasn't a matter of life or death I would make him cut it out right now. "Let's take a walk," I urged. "We can show Tara and Kylee King Kamehameha's summer cottage."

Zane didn't argue with me, but the zombie-like way he walked beside me across the grassy lawn was less than reassuring. I purposely moved away from him a little, just so he couldn't cheat and start viewing again while I wasn't paying attention. We both loved Moanalua Gardens, which was blessed with an abundance of happy shadows including some from my own family, but I couldn't focus on them now.

We left my parents to finish up their dessert in private while the four of us headed off at a brisk pace, trying to wake up our foggy brains. "I think you should text him again," Kylee suggested to Tara. "It's been long enough and he obviously liked you. He didn't mention having a girlfriend, did he?"

Tara frowned. "It wasn't like that! We didn't talk about—" She looked uncomfortable. "Look, I don't know whether he has a girlfriend. For all I know he has twenty. I really don't care. We got along really well yesterday, but it wasn't about *that*. It was like, I don't know... we were kindred spirits, or something."

Kylee arched an eyebrow. "Kindred spirits?"

"Oh, shut up," Tara snapped irritably. "We just think alike, that's all. We understand each other. Have similar interests."

"Whatever floats your boats," Kylee fired back. "Just text him again, will you?"

Tara glared, but pulled out her phone. "How about, 'We're heading out to the South Shore — you out here anywhere?'"

"Perfect," I agreed. "Friendly without being stalkerish."

Tara started texting.

"It's so frustrating we can't get more out of the stupid jersey!" Kylee moaned. "I was sure it would help us."

I looked at Zane, but he didn't look back at me. His eyes were on the ground. "Zane!"

"What?" he asked innocently.

"Just checking," I said with relief. He had been as annoyed as I was about the jersey. We had experimented with it at length, but all it had earned us was a pain in the head. He got nothing unless he was also touching me, and then the vision always began the same way — with a pang in his left temple. Every time I made contact with the baby-blue fabric I felt like my skull was splitting open. From there, the same drowning sequence began, and although Zane was willing to go through the whole thing and see where it led, he had blacked out at the same end point I had reached and then found himself back in the present. We had learned absolutely nothing.

"I have to check again," Zane said firmly, sitting down as we reached a bench near a meandering stream. "It's been almost twenty minutes now."

I sat down and settled against his side while Kylee and Tara walked off to explore the rest of the gardens. I looked out over the pleasant greenspace around the famous Hitachi monkeypod tree, where happy shadows cavorted in equal measure with shouting, running, living children enjoying their last full week of summer. To see what I was seeing when I could think of nothing but the pall of death hanging over Makani's head seemed so surreal... and so unfair.

We were all so incredibly anxious to *act*, to do something, that we were sure the endless hours of waiting would drive us mad. But though he searched and searched, Zane did not see Makani. And when Kylee returned, she reported seeing no ghosts. Makani had not answered Tara's texts, nor had he picked up his phone when she broke down and called him. My mom and even my dad, who had taken a rare personal day for the occasion, spent their time scouring the internet and making calls trying to find out if Makani had any media events or public appearances scheduled that could — at the very least — give Zane a couple hours off. But none of us knew where the surfer was. All we could find out was that although he shared an apartment somewhere in Honolulu with a cousin, he claimed he was "almost never there," since he had friends and relatives all over the islands and surfed couches as much as water.

By mid-afternoon, we were all in a such a stupor that even taking turns jogging around the lawn couldn't shake the cobwebs from our brains. It was just too quiet. Too peaceful. Too sunny.

The calm before the storm.

When the text finally came, I thought that Tara was going to pass out. The four of us were walking aimlessly across the lawn for the twentieth time when she stopped cold, pulled the phone out of her back pocket, stared at it, and swayed on her feet. "It's him," she said breathlessly.

"What does he say? Where is he?" Kylee demanded.

Tara shook her head. Her hands were trembling. "He says, 'Guess what? My dad thinks you're right.'" Her hands fell back to her sides. Her eyes closed.

No one said anything for a second.

"Well, what the crap does that mean?" Kylee shrieked. "Tell us!"

Tara drew in a long, shuddering breath. I was about to reach out a hand and steady her when she opened her eyes and smiled a little. "It means he told his dad about The Plan. Makani loves what he's doing and all, but he really does wish he could go to college, and I told him he doesn't have to completely put his brain on ice. I was encouraging him to enroll at UH as a part-time student and take at least one class at a time online. He has enough downtime that he could do it, even if he is racing all over the world. He never even thought about it, but now he has, and I guess his dad agrees with me that he should go for it."

The rest of us looked at each other. "That's nice," Kylee said flatly. "Now where the crap is he?"

Tara was already typing. "I'll ask."

"His dad," Zane echoed thoughtfully. "His parents still live in Waialua. I'm sure of it. He told you before that his mother was on the Big Island taking care of his aunt, but if he's with his father, he could be on the North Shore right now."

"Or his father could be with him in Honolulu," I pointed out.

"True," Zane agreed.

"Baldy!" Kylee screeched.

She pointed to nothing, and Zane's gaze snapped immediately to the same spot. After a moment, they looked at each other. "What's that way?" Kylee asked.

Zane looked back at the highway that ran near the park, seemingly to get his bearings. "Waialua," he murmured.

"What are you seeing?" Tara begged.

"The bald ghost with the surfboard was standing right there, looking at us and pointing," Kylee explained.

"Then Makani is in Waialua?" Tara breathed.

Zane shook his head. "All we know is that he pointed vaguely in the direction of the North Shore. But if he has a gift for timing—" His eyes suddenly shifted to a new location. I looked at Kylee and saw her staring at the same place.

In the next second they both shifted into action.

"Let's get your parents and go, Kali," Zane said.

"Makani must be in Waialua!"

"About time that guy made himself useful," Kylee said as we all set off at a jog.

"Baldy?" I asked.

"No, Jabba!" Kylee answered. "Jerk shows up just long enough to nod his head, and even then, he's got to do it with an attitude. Like we're all stupid to even *need* his help! Where does he get off, anyway? After trying to scare us away, when we're on his side! If you ask me, *he's* the stupid—"

"Kylee!" Tara ordered. "How about we play nicely till we don't need each other anymore?"

Kylee muttered something under her breath and kept moving, and I said nothing, knowing that Tara was right. But secretly my sympathies were with Kylee. I'd had more than enough of bully ghosts with bad attitudes.

My parents sprang into action with us. They got into my dad's car and we piled into Zane's, which I insisted on driving. Zane didn't argue, since we agreed that he should try to zone in on Makani's location while we were en route. Waialua was a mostly residential area right next to Haleiwa, and he wasn't familiar with any of its side streets. But if Makani and his dad were eating out in Haleiwa or walking around on any of the main drags, there was a chance Zane could spot them.

Tara sat in the back seat with her phone in her lap, and every few miles she would let out a frustrated sigh. Unfortunately, Makani's burst of inspiration for communicating via cell phone had come and gone. She had written him back with a simple "That's great!" expecting to engage him in a longer conversation. But instead he had gone quiet. Her later, "So, what are you up to today?" still hung out there unanswered.

Despite our initial enthusiasm, our drive to the North

Shore proved to be as tense and endless as the rest of this accursed day. "Still no sign of Makani?" I asked as Zane pulled his hand off my knee, where it had been resting while he remote viewed as I drove.

He stretched his arms and legs as much as possible in the small car and looked at me with still-bleary eyes. "No," he answered with disappointment. "He's probably just hanging out at his house. But the good news is, he's not too likely to go in the water. The swell they forecast is starting to come in, but so far it's just little stuff. The people out now are only goofing off. Beginners. Stand-up paddlers. A few locals who haven't been able to get to town and are dying to surf on anything. You know."

I didn't know. Not really. But I took his word for it. Still, as glad as I was to think that Makani was in no immediate danger, I couldn't stand the thought of another day like this one. Besides, had the ghosts not sent us here? Now?

Kylee screamed. Zane made a noise and jumped as well, and the car swerved toward the centerline as I startled, allowing my hands to shift on the wheel. *"Don't do that!"* I ordered, trying to calm my racing heart as I plastered my palms in the ten and two o'clock positions and pulled the car back into place again. Thank goodness my parents were ahead of us — I could only hope they weren't looking out the rearview mirror at the time. That kind of grief I didn't need.

"I'm sorry," Kylee squeaked. "But I couldn't help it! The old woman ghost was right in front of the windshield! I mean, what was she thinking? If Zane or I was driving we would have run off the road for sure!"

My teeth gritted, but I said nothing. Kylee had conveniently forgotten that I committed vehicular shadow-cide on a daily basis.

"Well, what did she do?" Tara asked.

"Nothing helpful," Zane answered heavily. "She just looked upset, as always."

"She looked completely beside herself," Kylee elaborated. Then her voice lowered. "I think she was trying to tell us to hurry."

Oh, no. No, no, no...

My foot pressed down on the accelerator. Then I realized what I was doing and eased up again. We could only get to the North Shore so fast. There was only one two-lane road here and when traffic was heavy it went the speed it went. We would get there when we got there, and not a moment sooner. The car felt hot. Beads of sweat began to break out on my forehead.

"I'll take another look around Waialua," Zane said, putting his arm across the seatback and resting his hand on my shoulder this time.

"I'm going to call him," Tara announced. But within seconds I heard her phone plunk down in her lap again. "He's not answering," she reported miserably. "I swear I think he only looks at the thing when he feels like it, and keeps it on silent the rest of the time. Which isn't a bad way to live, really. But—"

She broke off her next thought, leaving the words "to live" hanging awkwardly in the air. I couldn't see her face and was afraid to take my eyes off the road, but I thought I heard her gulp a bit.

All of a sudden Zane straightened and opened his eyes. "I just saw Lacey and Matt!"

"You did?" I thought he was probably mistaken until I remembered Lacey's earlier text. "Oh, right! Where?"

"At Ali'i Beach Park in Haleiwa," he explained. "They were just walking out from the parking lot. Lacey has a surfboard with her! She told me she used to go surfing with her brother and his friends, but that she hadn't been out in a long time."

"Well, good for her," I thought out loud. It seemed she was getting some quality time with Matt after all.

"I know they're not who I'm supposed to be looking for," Zane said more soberly, "but it's nice to find *something*. Now I know why the handlers of those drug-sniffing dogs plant some goods every once in a while, just to keep up morale."

"You so totally deserve a dog biscuit," I said with a smile, trying to encourage him further. His eyes looked weary, drained. He had been stressed enough before, but the appearance of the suicidal old woman had frayed all our nerves even further. And I knew that Zane probably felt at least twice as strung out as he was willing to let on.

I fought the urge to floor the accelerator again. We still had at least ten minutes to drive.

"I'd better do a full sweep again," Zane said determinedly. He settled back in his seat, and only I heard his quiet sigh.

I wondered if what he was doing made his head hurt. I wondered if Makani would ever text Tara back. And I wondered if the old woman ghost would have taken the risk of running us off the road if the famous surfer was doing nothing but sitting on his dad's couch eating burgers and watching television.

Zane jerked upright. His eyes were fixed wide open, staring at the road ahead.

"Makani is at Ali'i Beach Park right now," he announced. "And he's headed for the water."

chapter 22

We piled out of the cars, and Zane raced to unhitch his board from the roof rack.

My heart pounded. "Zane," I pleaded, sounding shrill and panicked and nothing like myself. "Do you have to take the board out? You're practically a zombie right now!"

He shot me a quizzical look, but didn't pause. "I'm all right," he insisted. "I have to stay close to him on the water. It's the only way."

"You don't know that!" I argued. I really wasn't sure what was wrong with me. All I knew was that at that moment, I was more worried about Zane than I was about Makani. "You're not yourself. We don't know what all this remote viewing has done to you!"

He finished untying the board and gave it a tug.

"Which way?" my dad called. The others were already heading out of the parking lot toward the beach. When Zane pointed, they hurried forward without us.

Zane pulled down his board and tucked it under his arm. "Look me in the eyes, Kali," he said as we walked after them. "All day I've had my brain split over two places. But as of now, I'm all here. You can tell that, can't you?"

I looked deeply into his expressive green eyes, and he was correct that they were no longer distant or unfocused. He was fully present and fully engaged. But he still looked exhausted.

"You're tired," I insisted, even as I had to double my pace to keep up with his long strides. "You know that all this psychic stuff has drained you!"

He looked away from me. "Not physically it hasn't," he proclaimed. "And all I need to do is swim."

We reached the crest of the hill and looked out over the sand and across the water. Ali'i Beach was a vast, inviting arc of sand and rock that extended southwest down the coast from the small boat harbor in Haleiwa. Having ample facilities and being located right in town, it was a favorite spot for family picnics, turtle-walks, surfing, diving, fishing, barbecues, community events, and general hanging out — and had been so for generations.

Today, both the beach and the water were hopping with activity. People of all ages milled about on land, while children played in the sand and swimmers waded in the shallows. Farther out from shore, local surfers who had been waiting all summer for something more than a ripple to shred had taken to the small waves with zest, cluttering the ocean with stand-up paddleboards, shortboards, bodyboards, and every hybrid in between. Zane paused only a second to study the water and determine where he should paddle out.

"I don't see Makani," I said, following as Zane set off again.

"Look where your dad and Tara are focusing their binoculars," Zane offered, not slowing down long enough to point. I turned my head to see my friends and my parents standing on the ridge near the lifeguard tower, gazing out over the break. I knew they would watch Makani like a hawk and alert the lifeguards immediately if anything happened to him. The fact that they didn't seem to be panicking yet must mean that he was still okay.

But I wasn't. I was scared to death.

We reached the water's edge and Zane set down his board. He pulled off his shirt and handed it to me, then attached his leash strap to his ankle.

I didn't want him to go. Had he ever even had real lifeguard training? Could any of us be sure that the doom I kept sensing was all for Makani? What if we did manage to change the course of events? What then?

"Zane—"

He reached out and brushed the hair from my face, then slid his hand behind my neck, turning my face up towards his. He stepped closer. "I am coming back," he said slowly, firmly. Then he leaned in and kissed me. Warmly, but quickly. "I love you, Kali."

And with that, he picked up his board, turned his back to me, and paddled out.

I stood on the sand and stared after him. I couldn't say anything. I couldn't move. My whole nervous system was numb. He'd never said those words to me before... I almost couldn't believe he'd said them now, so casually and just like that, when my head was already spinning. I was happy, I was delirious with joy, and at the same time I was paralyzed with terror.

Why did he say those words *now?* Did he really believe he would be okay? Or didn't he?

"Kali! What are you doing out here? I didn't know you were coming!"

I looked over to see Matt striding toward me, shirtless, tanned, and smiling from ear to ear. He seemed not to have a care in the world, and his presence here now felt like an awkward moment in a really bad movie.

"I'm... um," I stammered badly. "Zane's surfing," I finished, pointing.

"Cool!" he replied, looking out to see Zane paddling hard to reach the lineup. "Lacey's out there, too. Do you believe it? She's been trying to get me to take a turn, but it ain't gonna happen."

I drew air into my lungs in deep, long gulps, trying to get a grip. While we were still in the car driving over, Kylee had tried to call both Matt and Lacey from my phone in hopes of putting them on some kind of covert Makani-watch, but neither of them had answered. I always loved seeing Matt, and his help would be welcome, but what he *didn't* know made this incredibly difficult. If only I could act like less of a babbling idiot now, perhaps I could think of a way to enlist him. *Calm down, Kali!*

Lucky for me, Matt wasn't the most observant guy in the world.

"Hey, you'll never guess who else is out there!" he went on excitedly.

I decided to let him tell me.

"Makani Marro!" he announced. "Lacey told me you guys were supposed to meet him yesterday. How'd that go?"

I couldn't do this. I could not, on the fly and purely for Matt's benefit, create some bizarro alternate version of yesterday. I simply didn't have the brain tissue. "It was great," I answered, trying my best to sound perky. "Where is he?"

"Out that way, moving to the right now," Matt said, pointing. "In the middle of that big bunch of guys. His board's white with blue and black on the tip. He's right next to a guy on a red board, see?"

I nodded. My vision wasn't quite good enough to pick out Makani's face in the crowd at this distance, but I could see the front of his board. You could usually only see the boards when a surfer was leaning or paddling, because when they sat flat waiting for waves, the board was underwater and the surfer was only visible from the waist up. The very first time I'd seen surfers way out in the lineup at Sunset Beach, I'd mistaken them for pelicans.

I turned my clearly distressed face away from Matt and headed toward the ridge where the others were keeping watch. "How's Lacey been doing?" I asked, trying hard to keep my voice steady.

"Aw, she's awesome," he said proudly. "I've never seen her surf before. She's pretty good! I am *so* glad the pool pump broke down. And that I don't have practice today." He smiled and shook his head. "Great weather, fun little waves... serendipity, man!"

I faked a smile back and hurried on up to where Tara and Kylee stood trading off one of our two pairs of binoculars. They greeted Matt with acting jobs only marginally better than mine, but still, he seemed not to notice. He treated them like old friends and then, like the diplomat he was, he stepped over to say hello to my parents.

"The ghosts?" I whispered to Kylee.

She bit her lip and nodded. "They're here. They're all around him."

I let out my breath with a whoosh. I wasn't sure if that was good or bad. "Are they doing anything... helpful?"

She frowned. "Not at the moment. They come and go. They hover. Our three regulars are here, and there are a few other fainter ones. Not like at the museum, but there's clearly a... well, there's an energy here, and I'm sure it's because of the people. They love Makani. You can feel it. Can't you?"

I knew what she meant. But all I could feel was an icy clench of terror as my eyes darted constantly between Zane and Makani. Zane was working hard to close the gap, but he was hardly the only surfer with a desire to be near the icon. Makani had drawn a crowd already. Not only in the water but all along the shore, clusters of people pointed excitedly in his direction, smiling, talking loudly, and taking pictures.

"Everyone knows he's here," Kylee confirmed. "Including the water patrol. We heard he got mobbed on the beach and had to stop to sign a bunch of autographs before he even got in the water. He doesn't seem to mind, though. You can tell when you're looking at him up close that he's having a good time."

"I don't think he's even out here to surf. Not really," Tara said with the binoculars pressed to her own glasses. "I think he's just goofing off at his home break with his friends from the neighborhood, you know? He's not even looking at the waves... the whole time I've been watching he's just been sitting out there bobbing around talking to the other guys and laughing."

The sun that shone down on my dark hair was hot. Every image that met my eye — including the current shadows — was happy and bright and positive. There was joy and warmth and a sense of community pride all around me. Nothing that was obvious to the senses held even the slightest hint of sadness, or danger, or fear. The surf conditions today were pure beginner-level. Neither the waves nor the current could be considered perilous, and Makani was a world-renowned surfing expert. There was absolutely, positively not one logical, non-mystical reason why any of us should have any reason to suspect that he — or anyone else here today — was in any sort of danger.

But there was danger. Grave danger. And I knew it.

And that was all that mattered.

"You look, Kali," Tara suggested, handing me the binoculars. "Zane is to the left of Makani's group, now. And way over to the right, there, you can see Lacey. She's kind of gotten pushed out of it, I think."

I looked. The lineup was a total zoo. If Makani himself wanted a wave the others would no doubt melt away to make room for him, but for everyone else, it would be a paddle battle royal. Makani didn't appear to notice Zane, who seemed content to hang out nearby along with a flotilla of other fans. Stand-up paddleboarders were right in the mix with the regular surfers and even a few kayaks crisscrossed the shallow waters closer to shore.

"You watch," I said shortly, handing the binoculars back to Tara. I was so antsy I felt like running somewhere. If I could surf I would have paddled out right next to Zane. Come to think of it, if I'd had a board, I would have paddled out whether I could surf or not.

"Oh," Tara said suddenly, grimly.

"What?" Kylee and I asked together.

"I think they're trying to get Makani to take a wave," she answered in a whisper. "No, I'm sure they are. Listen."

We looked out. A nice set of smallish waves was rolling in on the horizon, and we could hear the chant carried to us over the water as voices were added and the chorus grew. "Makani, Makani, *Makani!*"

Tara drew in a shuddering breath, grabbed for Kylee's hand, and clutched it. "He's going to do it. He's going to take one of these next waves. Oh, my God."

"Mom! Dad!" I called around to the far side of the lifeguard tower. "It looks like Makani's going for it!" A fairly normal thing to say, I told myself. Never mind the tone of horror in my voice.

We all moved down the beach a little toward the base of the rock jetty that extended out into the bay and separated the boat harbor from the edge of the surfing beach. My dad took his binoculars and began walking out onto the jetty. My mom started walking with him, but stopped at the rocks, pulled out her cell phone, and checked to make sure she could get a signal. Tara, Kylee, and I stayed at the highest point with the best view that was also close to the lifeguard tower. My eyes continued to dart from Zane to Makani and back again and my heart could not beat any faster.

The waves rolled into the lineup. The others surfers parted like a curtain, leaving Makani all to himself. They continued to chant as the first wave rumbled by, but Makani wasn't interested. Too flat, too thick, too crumbly... who knew? Whatever the fault, it didn't pass inspection for the pro. But plenty of less picky surfers to either side of him were only too happy to take his leavings.

"Lacey's going!" Kylee cried, pointing to a spot far to the right of Makani's group, where Lacey was just managing to stand up on a mushy mess that barely moved her fifteen feet before flattening out to nothing and leaving her teetering precariously on her bright white, egg-shaped board.

"Woohoo! Way to go, Lace!" Matt screamed at the top of his lungs, deafening us all. I couldn't see her face well, but I'm pretty sure she flashed him a brilliant smile before slipping on her board like it was a banana peel and walking off it backwards, butt-first into the ocean. She popped back up immediately though, still smiling, and threw Matt a hearty wave. "Awesome job!" he praised, moving away from us toward the water's edge.

"Makani's going now!" Tara shouted.

My eyes flew back to Hawaii's favorite son. We all watched helplessly, breath held, as he paddled into the pert little wave and stood up with ease. It was a short left, but he made the most of it, doing a couple nice trick turns and jumping off his board at the finish with a showy flip. My lungs had no oxygen remaining as I waited, every muscle in my body tensed, for his mop of dark hair to resurface by his board. When his head did pop up, just as expected, to a rousing chorus of cheers from his fans, I bit my lip so hard that it bled.

Kylee, Tara, and I all breathed out in unison. "He... he's okay," Tara stammered. "He's smiling." Makani slid back onto his board and turned its nose back toward the lineup. The third wave in the set was coming through now, and tons of surfers had jumped on it. Makani was alert to them and stayed out of their paths. But he did not have eyes in the back of his head. And it was from directly behind him that the missile came. Somewhere out of the chaos of the passing wave a heavy paddleboard, evidently unleashed, shot out from beneath the feet of its unskilled rider and sailed directly into the back of Makani's skull.

The force of the blow knocked him off his board and he slipped into the ocean like a stone.

Kylee screamed. Tara made a moaning sound. I could make no sound at all. We were not the only people who had witnessed what had happened, and Kylee was not the only one screaming. Out of the corner of my eye I could see my mom dialing 911, as was the plan, but there was no need for anyone to alert the lifeguards. They were watching it happen with us.

Both Makani's surfboard and the paddleboard now floated along together without him. But of the mop of shiny black hair, there was no sign.

Every surfer in the area headed full speed for the riderless board. Within a matter of seconds, people started diving.

"He'll be all right," Tara told herself. "They'll pull him up. All they have to do is follow the leash. And the lifeguards are already on it... Right?"

I realized I didn't know where Zane was. I practically hyperventilated as I scanned the surface of the ocean for his blond curls. Where was he? *Yes!* I spotted him and relaxed a bit, but then just as quickly stressed out again. He was nowhere near Makani's empty board. He had been trying to stay as close to the surfer as he could, but the ride had dumped Makani a long way from his starting point, and the board was drifting even further away in the current. But strangely, Zane did not even appear to be moving in that direction. He was fighting the crowd that was moving toward Makani, paddling almost at an angle to them. He seemed confused, possibly disoriented, and he kept lifting his head to look above the surface of the water.

An icy fear crept up my veins. *What was wrong with him?*

The amateur divers popped back up, one after another. None of them had Makani. They shouted to each other. They went back down again. The lifeguards were in the water now and swimming hard with their rescue gear.

"Something's wrong," Tara whimpered as she continued to look through the binoculars. "They're not finding him!"

"No," Kylee murmured to herself. Then she shouted out loud. "He can't see you! Let me see you!"

Both Tara and I turned to stare at her. Her face was red with fright and anger and her lower lip trembled. "Go higher!" she screamed into the air, not caring who overheard her.

I looked out toward Zane again and saw him surge forward, pumping his arms hard, paddling with everything he was worth.

Footsteps thundered on the sand. My dad was suddenly beside us. "Makani's got no leash," he said breathlessly. "Damn log probably snapped it clean off." He handed my mother the binoculars and took off his shirt.

"Mitch—" my mother began.

"They don't know where he is, Diane!" my dad shot back. "If he's unconscious and drifting down there deep…

The way these currents move... Like a damn needle in a haystack! There isn't time." He shucked off his sandals.

"The ghosts know where he is," Kylee declared, staring out over the ocean. "They're leading Zane to him right now. But..."

"But what?" Tara cried frantically, kicking off her own sandals.

"Don't even think about it, unless you've got lifeguard training yourself!" my dad barked. "Ocean diving isn't child's play. The lifeguards don't need extra people to rescue!"

Tara froze.

"It's just... oh, my God, Zane's too far away!" Kylee wailed. "Makani keeps drifting farther and—"

"Show me where he is!" my dad ordered.

Kylee moved to where she could point directly for my dad's line of sight. "You see how that column of water there is moving that way? She says he's down under the tip of my finger now, and moving that way, towards *holy crap!*"

Kylee started running. She ran down to the base of the rock jetty. Then she started scrambling out onto it. The rest of us followed. I heard a splash as my dad peeled off and waded into the water. Kylee cupped her hands around her mouth and shouted as loud as she could over the din of voices already surrounding us.

"LACEY!"

I looked up to see Lacey, whom we had all forgotten, bobbing on her board watching the commotion from a distance. Although it seemed like an eternity since her inglorious ride, scarcely a minute had passed. She had probably just started to paddle in when it happened. She heard Kylee's scream and looked over.

"Makani!" Kylee shouted, pointed forcefully downward. "He's floating right underneath you! Dive down deep now! *Do it NOW!"*

Lacey stared back at Kylee, then down into the water, and then back at Kylee again, for all of about three seconds. There's no telling what she was thinking, but it must have occurred to her to wonder how Kylee could possibly know such a thing, when the ocean water was so dense and frothy that Lacey herself could barely see down six feet.

But God love her, Lacey didn't ask. What she did was reach down, unstrap her board from her ankle, and dive.

No argument. No clarification required. The girl just freakin' *dived.*

When her small pink feet disappeared under the water, I couldn't seem to breathe myself. I checked on Zane again and could see him still paddling over. He was heading right towards Lacey, as he had been all along, and he seemed to be in fine form. But he had a long way to go, and he was fighting not only the ocean currents but the hoard of good Samaritans who continued streaming into the water toward the place where Makani went under. My dad was also swimming hard now, heading for where Lacey had just gone down. But he had a ways to go, too.

How long had Makani been under?

Blood in the water. Sinking down...

I was beginning to feel light-headed. I remembered to breathe.

The seconds ticked by.

How long had Lacey been under?

"She's back!" Tara cried.

The four of us — Kylee, Tara, my mom, and me, all clutched each other's hands as Lacey's small blond head popped up out of the water. But her head was all by itself. She treaded water for only a moment, during which she took several deep breaths. Then her head disappeared under the surface.

"She's found him," Kylee said confidently. "I know she has. I'm just not sure she can get him up."

"But at least everyone else will believe us now!" Tara cried. She took a step forward, cupped her hands around her own mouth, and shouted to whomever would listen. "Here! Makani is over here!"

But no one did listen. There was too much chaos, and none of it was focused where we were. My mom and I joined in the shouting and pointing, and some people glanced our way, but when they saw nothing floating in the water where we were pointing, they simply dismissed us.

Lacey! Where are you?

Zane and my dad were getting closer. They were working with all their might.

Had we asked her to do the impossible?

Ocean diving isn't child's play.

"Oh my God, why won't anybody believe us!" Tara wailed.

"She's... in the right place," Kylee whispered softly. "The ghosts are... wait... oh, wait..."

A splash and a gasp.

"Lacey!" we all cried out as the bedraggled little head surfaced, not fully even, but just enough to draw a breath. It went under again, for a long moment, but then popped back up, with another head beside it.

"Makani!" my mom yelled, in the loudest voice I could ever remember hearing her use. "He's here! He's here! She's found him!"

This time when people looked over, they saw something. And this time the word began to spread. My dad was a few strokes away now. Zane was closing in.

Lacey struggled to keep Makani's head out of the

water. Her board had drifted away, she had nothing to cling to, and she was out of breath. Several times, while holding Makani up, her nose and mouth sank beneath the surface.

"She's in trouble!" I cried.

"Take him, Mitch!" my mom shouted. In the next instant, my dad was there. He lifted Makani's dead weight from Lacey's arms and secured his limp form in a rescue hold. Lacey treaded water for a moment, gasping for air and coughing.

Then her whole head slipped under the water.

chapter 23

"Zane!"

I didn't need to yell. He was already there. In one motion Zane rolled off his surfboard, gave it a push toward my dad, and dove towards Lacey. In a flash, her head and shoulders were back above the surface, supported by his strong, tanned arm.

"Oh, wow," Kylee breathed, beside me.

Lacey sputtered and coughed some more, but once she had Zane's board to cling to, she appeared to be all right.

Makani was another matter. His wavy black hair was streaming with blood and his body was still and lifeless. My dad and Zane loaded him carefully onto the board and the whole group immediately began moving towards the rescue team that was already wading out from shore. Even Lacey was obviously kicking her heart out to keep the board moving as fast as possible while she clung to its tail.

Things started happening fast. Swimmers and surfers already in the ocean converged upon the small convoy from all sides. The rescue team reached Makani and went right to work, starting CPR even as they brought him in. A crowd formed instantly on the beach, cutting us off from where the team came ashore. Sirens blared on the streets. Multiple jet skis approached on the water. An ambulance pulled up on the grass.

"Zane!" I called out. But I couldn't see him anymore, much less reach him. We couldn't reach any of them. The crowd had become a mob.

My mom, Kylee, Tara and I stuck close together, pressing forward toward the ambulance. "The paramedics will probably want to check Lacey out too," my mom reasoned. "I'm sure they'll all stay together."

"Do you know—" I asked Kylee, but she shook her head.

"The ghosts were happy when Lacey got him up," she reported, practically needing to yell, even though we were moving shoulder to shoulder in the jostling crowd. "They were even happy when Zane got Lacey up. They practically had a party. But then it was like their energy was spent. They faded and I couldn't see them anymore."

"Doesn't that mean—" Tara said hopefully.

"I don't know what it means," Kylee interrupted, her usually chipper voice choking up a little. "All I know is how awful Makani looked, and the way he was—"

"He wasn't underwater as long as it seemed," my mother shouted back. "And his head was still bleeding. Did you see that? He must have had a pulse."

A ray of hope shot through me. *Yes.* He *was* still bleeding!

"Everyone stay back!" a forceful voice ordered through a megaphone. "We need space to work here, do you understand? I need everyone to back up at least ten feet!"

The crowd grumbled with complaint, but complied. We began to lose ground, but my mom was having none of it. "My husband is at the ambulance," she kept telling people as she elbowed them aside. "Excuse me, my husband is with EMS!"

A little literary license, I suppose, but I wasn't going to argue with her, because it worked. The rest of us stuck to her like a conga line and slowly but surely, we all worked our way forward. "Aw, look," a man near the front said sadly. "More than one of them's drowned. That's a shame."

My heart went spastic again. Had Lacey swallowed more water than I knew? What about my dad? The Colonel had been solid as a rock in his day but the man was no spring chicken and his cholesterol was high. And God only knew what havoc the remote viewing had wreaked on Zane before he decided to paddle himself to exhaustion... before he had fully recovered from his own near-death experience!

Five more seconds, and I swear I would have lost it. Lucky for me, I caught sight of those wonderful, beautiful, fantastically gorgeous dripping-wet dark blond curls in three. *"Zane!!!"* He was standing to the side of the ambulance with my dad.

"Mitch!" I heard my mom yell in front of me. It was all I could do not to make a beeline for Zane by running straight through the clear zone in which Makani was being treated, but I had to fight my way around through the crowd instead. I wasn't sure whether our cries were heard, but the second Zane saw me, his green eyes lit up with a tired, but brilliant smile.

His arms opened wide and I flung myself into them. His chest was wet, and the water was cold. But the arms around me were strong, and the beat of his heart was the most amazingly fabulously glorious thing *ever.*

Bliss.

For a moment, no one else existed. "You're all right," I stretched up to whisper in his ear, needing to confirm the fact. "You came back."

"I told you I would," he said with a hint of amusement, still hugging me tight.

I wanted to say, "Then why did you wait till *that* moment to tell me you loved me? Were you trying to rip my heart out? Were you trying to give me a heart attack?"

But I didn't say any of that. I knew that he loved me. I

knew because he acted like it, even if he hadn't said it before. And I could hardly fault him for withholding the words when I'd done the very same thing. I'd loved him for ages, and I'd confessed it ages ago too, but I'd never been quite sure if he'd heard me or not, seeing as how he was in a coma at the time. More recently, I'd just been scared. I didn't want him to feel like I was pushing him. But I had liked it when he said it.

"I love you, too," I whispered back.

A roar arose from the crowd. At first it was a general increase in chatter, but then it escalated to cheers and whoops of joy. I rotated in Zane's arms and looked over to see the paramedics loading the stretcher onto the ambulance. The stretcher's occupant was coughing.

Coughing!

Makani was curled up on his side, his face and hair still bathed with blood. He gasped, spewed, and spit.

The crowd had never seen anything more marvelous.

Tara and Kylee collapsed into each other's arms. "He's going to be okay," Tara announced, her voice choking up. "He really is."

"We did it!" Kylee agreed with a nervous laugh. "All of us!"

"Mitch," I heard my mother say worriedly, "are you sure you're all right?"

"Diane," my dad replied with a growl, "if you ask me that one more time—"

"All right, all right!" she conceded.

I looked up at Zane with a smile, but said nothing. He smiled back. He knew that I had freaked out earlier because I was worried about him. And that I was worried about him because I loved him. Apparently, he was okay with that.

Which was good, because it looked like he'd have to

get used to it.

The paramedics finished loading the stretcher into the ambulance. Only then, to my shame, did I remember Lacey. She hopped out of the back of the ambulance with the aid of an EMT with whom, oddly enough, she appeared to be arguing.

"I swear to God, I *will* go to the ER," she insisted. "But I don't need an ambulance. I've got to find my friend, first. He can take me."

"We'll take care of her," my dad spoke up. "We'll take her straight to Honolulu. Her parents can meet us there."

They haggled a few more moments while the medical crew finished loading up, but ultimately Lacey prevailed, and the ambulance screamed off with its siren wailing. The crowd remained a mob scene, with everyone still nervous and distressed despite Makani's rally. Every second another newcomer raced up to find what was going on and three witnesses were eager to tell their stories. The police had arrived on the beach as well, which was fortunate, since the stand-up paddleboarder who had used no leash was less than popular at the moment. The crowd became so thick that even after the ambulance pulled out we could no longer see either the ocean or the parking lot for the mass of humanity around us.

"Lacey, you were amazing," I said gratefully, giving her a heartfelt hug. I made sure it was a gentle one, however, because she truly did look terrible. Her eyes were bloodshot, her complexion was pale, and her usually springy blond locks were plastered to her neck and dulled brown with murky seawater.

Her only response was a cough.

"Lacey! Where are you? *Lace!!!*" We could hear the voice, but we couldn't see the speaker. Matt was somewhere out there, lost in the crowd. His tone was hoarse and he sounded just short of panicked.

"Can someone else answer him?" Lacey rasped faintly. "I'm not sure—"

Six other voices shouted back at full volume. After a good thirty seconds of Marco Polo, we at last caught sight of Matt hustling toward us. He was still shirtless and now dripping wet and barefoot besides. Given when he had disappeared and how long he'd been absent, I was sure that he'd swum out with all the others when it looked like the only way to save Makani would be a random dive-a-thon. He might not be a surfer, but his favorite sport next to football was water polo, and I knew he was a powerful swimmer. Still, right now, he looked as exhausted and pale as I'd ever seen him.

I watched his expression as he recognized each of us in turn, and I could tell the exact second he located Lacey. The alert, determined look in his eyes melted to puppy-dog joy right in front of me. He barreled through the remainder of the crowd like it didn't exist, swept her up in his arms and held her there, her feet dangling well above the ground.

"Matt!" Lacey laughed, beating on his broad back. "Put me down! I can't breathe!"

He dropped her quickly, but did not let go. His blue eyes bore into hers. "It was you, wasn't it? I heard that a girl pulled him up. They said she almost drowned. Somebody said she *did* drown. And then I couldn't find you anywhere." His voice roughened. "I couldn't find any of you."

"Sorry about that." Lacey smiled at him apologetically. "But I *am* a trained lifeguard, you know. I'd be pretty proud of myself if it weren't for the small fact that I *would* have drowned if Zane and Colonel Mitchell hadn't gotten to us when they did."

"Don't say that," Zane protested. "What you did was incredible!"

"It was a team effort," my dad proclaimed. Then he winked at Lacey. "But you were definitely our MVP."

Matt's face beamed down at her. He still hadn't let her loose. "I'm not surprised."

"Hey!" A skinny boy of eleven or twelve fought his way over to us. He smiled broadly at Lacey and pointed behind him. "This your board?"

We looked to see a half dozen other boys crowding behind him, one of whom held Lacey's lost egg board. Her face broke into a grin. "Oh, you found it for me! Thank you! My brother would have killed me if I'd lost it."

The boys handed the board back toward Lacey, but since Matt still wouldn't let her go, Zane took hold of it for her. The boys beamed at her as if she were a rock star and peppered her with questions.

"How'd you know to look way over there?"

"How'd you get Makani up? "

"How'd you see him?"

Lacey looked a little uncomfortable. She shot the briefest of looks at Kylee before smiling back at the boys. "My friends on shore thought he might be drifting my way," she answered. "So I decided to take a look. I saw him because of all that beautiful dark hair of his. It made him easier to spot. But he was pretty deep, and he was heavier than I thought. I got him halfway up once and then ran out of breath. I had to let him go and come up for air. But then I caught him again and the second time I didn't have so far to pull him. When I got him to the surface my friends were there to help me, which was good because I couldn't swim much longer. I was beat."

The boys chattered excitedly among themselves a moment, chorused a round of thanks to Lacey for helping

Makani, and scampered off.

"We need to get you to the ER, Lacey," I reminded.

"What?" Matt demanded.

"That's what the paramedics said," I explained.

"I'm all right," Lacey protested, coughing again. "It's just that as a precaution, they—"

Lacey's feet were off the sand again. This time, Matt swept her up sideways, carrying her in both arms against his bare chest. Interestingly, he did not look tired anymore. "What hospital do you think?" he asked my dad.

The decision was made, and we all headed for the parking lot.

"Let me," I insisted, watching Zane attempt to carry both surfboards. I took Lacey's egg board away from him and tucked it under my own arm, and he didn't protest. We stepped a little bit apart from the others and I spoke where he alone could hear me. I couldn't help it. I was still worried about him. "When Makani first went under, you looked confused. What was going on?"

To my surprise, he huffed out a breath with a smile. "Um... let's just say we owe it all to Baldy."

"Baldy?"

Zane chuckled under his breath. "The ghosts were all trying their best to help. But, well, it's not like dying made them any smarter than when they were alive, if you know what I mean. The old woman kept gesturing to me, but then she would disappear. I don't mean fade out, either — I mean she'd drop really low behind a swell, where I couldn't see her. A couple times she even went underwater. And the other two seemed to be giving me different directions. I finally figured out that Jabba wasn't giving me directions at all and that I just needed to follow Baldy. He was great. He had a surfer's instincts. He kept an eye on the crowd and he helped me navigate through the people as well as the currents."

"Well, what was Jabba doing if he wasn't guiding you to Makani?" I asked, amazed.

Zane's green eyes sparkled at me. The color had returned to his cheeks and he seemed, finally, to look more like his old self. "Beating up all the people who were in my way, of course. How else do you think he'd contribute?"

I laughed out loud. "Well, hey," I pointed out, "at least he was on our side!"

I wondered if I should feel as happy and as relieved as I did, knowing that Makani was still being rushed to the hospital. But deep inside I knew that not only would he be okay, he would eventually make a complete recovery. I knew it in my bones.

Kylee hustled up to my side. "Kali, what are we going to do?" she asked in a hushed tone. "What am I supposed to tell Lacey when she asks me how I knew where Makani was? I don't think it's possible to see that far down from where we were. Is it?"

"Probably not," Zane answered. "But she can't know that he wasn't closer to the surface when you saw him."

"*If* you saw him," I reminded, feeling too good to be dragged down by technicalities. "Does it really matter, Kylee? If you don't want to lie, all you have to do is be vague and avoid the question while you're here. But I think that at some point, I can tell Lacey at least part of the truth. Like, 'Kylee just had a feeling he was there. Sometimes she does that.' Then we'll see how it goes."

Kylee studied me with admiration. "You know, Kali, when it comes to the supernatural, you've come a long way from 'I'm a freak and no one will ever understand and it's worthless so I'm just going to ignore it.'"

"Well, I do still feel like a freak sometimes. But real

friends understand," I answered, smiling at her. Then I shot a smug look at Zane. "And I was definitely wrong about the worthless part."

"Matt, please!" Lacey fussed at full volume now, kicking her feet in the air. "I am perfectly capable of walking!"

"I'm sure you are," he replied. "Now be quiet and hold still."

Lacey growled. "Since when do I take orders from you?"

"Since never." Matt continued to plod along over the uneven ground, carrying her as if she weighed nothing at all.

"So who do you think you are?" she demanded.

"Good question," he snapped back. "Hey, Lace. You want to go out with me Saturday night? Like, on a date?"

Kylee, Tara and I all whipped our heads around. Lacey's pale cheeks blossomed with crimson. Her feet stopped kicking and she went a little limp.

"Yeah," she said after the briefest of pauses. Her voice still sounded angry. "*Yeah*. As a matter of fact, I do!"

"Well, *good!*" he answered in a voice that was equally cross, although it was obvious he was fighting hard not to smile. "It's about time you dated a real man."

epilogue

"I mean it, Kali. You don't have to go through with this if you're not feeling it. Only do it if you really want to," Zane said seriously. He was looking deep into my eyes with that mesmerizing gaze of his, the one that could melt my every defense into a puddle. I wasn't sure if he knew how much power that gaze had over me, but if he didn't, I had no intention of telling him. Not that I feared he would ever use it against me. Right now, for instance, I knew he felt pretty guilty about all the pressure he'd laid on me the last twenty-four hours.

"I didn't say I didn't want to," I answered, a little more sharply than intended.

"You don't exactly look happy about it, either," he replied.

I took a deep breath and looked up at the sky. It was a gorgeous day in Hawaii, as usual. Azure sky, spotty clouds, warm sun, light winds. Somewhere nearby, palm trees were rustling and roosters were crowing and feral cats were prowling and children were playing in the sand. But I wasn't there. I was out in the middle of a friggin' cold ocean bobbing around on a piece of fiberglass.

A rousing chorus of cheers met my ears, and I looked to see Tara standing nearly erect on her board, arms stretched out to either side, riding a nice, cooperative little wave practically all the way into the shallows. I tried hard to be happy for her while the figure on the beach with the megaphone pumped a fist with excitement. I *was* genuinely happy for her the first time she managed to stand up on her board. The fifth time was a little much.

"That was *so* awesome, Tara! You are a natural, girl!" Makani gushed into the megaphone. She could probably hear him shouting without it, but since his doctors had strictly forbidden his getting in the water yet — and we suspected he probably wasn't even supposed to be out of bed — he had gotten used to calling out instructions from the comfort of his beach chair.

"She does have an amazing sense of balance," Zane commented, floating on his board beside me.

"*Et tu, Brute?*" I said uncharitably. My English Lit teacher would be proud.

But Zane only looked at me curiously. "This isn't a competition."

He was right, of course. "I know. I'm sorry," I apologized, feeling petty. I should be enjoying myself right now. Everyone else certainly was.

Tara had been floating around in her own personal paradise ever since Makani had called her cell phone from his hospital bed. He had no idea at that point that Tara even knew the mysterious female surfer who had pulled him from the water. But he remembered that Tara was only in town until Saturday and had wanted to watch him surf, and he was calling — so he said — to let her know that wasn't going to happen. After Tara told him the whole story (well, the non-supernatural version, anyway), he had insisted on taking the whole group of us out on the waves as soon as he was released.

Personally, I thought maybe getting to meet his parents on dry land over a slice of lilikoi cheesecake would be more than adequate for a thank you, but Makani seemed to have a thing about getting everybody involved in his rescue "back on the horse," so to speak, so that his misadventure wouldn't color their view of Hawaii in general or surfing in particular. And who was going to argue with him?

Since the accident had left him with dozens of stitches in his head and who knew what kind of grief to his lungs, we really didn't think it would actually happen. But Makani had been true to his word. Bright and early on Saturday morning, Tara and Kylee's last day in Hawaii, he had rounded up a bunch of his friends and led us all to one of his favorite "secret" surfing spots on the South Shore. The break was somewhere off the beaten track past Ewa Beach, so it wasn't easy to see or to get to, and if it had an official name, Zane had never heard it. But it was uncrowded and the conditions this morning were, according to Makani himself, "beginner perfect."

Kylee screeched. I noticed that over the last week Zane had become so used to the sound that he no longer flinched. "Ahhh!!!" she bellowed, cartwheeling her arms to either side. "I'm gonna fall!!!"

"Nah, you're good!" the bronzed hottie surfing along on her right encouraged.

"Stay low!" called the grinning guy to her left. He was even cuter.

Kylee laughed, then screamed, then toppled sideways off her board and splashed awkwardly into the water. The two guys chuckled as they effortlessly turned their boards and then jumped off into the ocean beside her.

"She is eating this up," I murmured. "I swear she keeps falling off on purpose. And I *know* she could get back on that board all by herself if she wanted to!"

"I'm pretty sure they know that, too," Zane said with a grin.

"Coming through!" This time both Zane and I flinched as Matt's thunderous voice carried to us over the water. He was nowhere near us, really, but it never hurt to check. The guy was a one-man disaster zone.

Matt stood up on his extra-wide beginner board for all of about two seconds, standing on one foot while the other foot stuck straight out sideways. He flailed his arms like he was trying to fly, then kicked the board out and flew off of it. He landed on his back like a turtle, creating a giant splash that was almost more impressive than the wave he had tried to take off on.

Everyone cracked up laughing, and the loudest of all was Lacey. "That was the best move you've had all day!" she praised when he resurfaced. Lacey had been correct when she insisted that she was fine, in that she hadn't taken any significant water into her lungs. But ever since the ordeal, she'd been more than fine. She'd been looking as happy and healthy and as radiant as I'd ever seen her. And far from being afraid to get back out on the water, for the last hour she and her egg board had been doing some serious shredding.

Matt smiled back at her, shook the water from his hair, and gave her a big thumbs-up sign. "I aim to please!" Tonight, I reminded myself, would be their first real date. Unless, of course, they'd managed to sneak in a bonus outing since the last time I saw them. Judging from the looks they'd been giving each other all day, that seemed a distinct possibility.

"Hey, Kali," he yelled back at me. "You scared you can't look worse than me? I got the bar set pretty low over here!"

"Oh, I can look stupider than you!" I said with a laugh, unable to resist his bait.

"Can *not!*" he taunted.

"Come on, Kalia!" my grandfather Milo cajoled.

He and my dad both smiled with encouragement. They had both been hovering expectantly for the last hour, surfing a little here and there, trying to pretend they weren't watching me. But I knew they were. I also knew that my mother was standing on the beach by Makani holding about six different cameras.

Three generations of Lam-Thompsons surfing together.

No pressure or anything.

"I'm not sure she's feeling it today, Milo," Zane defended mildly.

I wanted to jump off my board and hug him. I really did love the guy. So much. But he didn't understand why I hesitated. I wasn't afraid of drowning anymore, not even after everything that had happened this week. I was over that. And I certainly wasn't afraid of looking stupid. I'd felt like a freak all my life! It wasn't even the pressure of the whole "three generations" thing. I knew that I probably *could* surf. At least long enough for my mom to take one picture.

I just didn't think I would like it.

Zane's expression of concern nearly melted me. He wanted this so very badly. We'd been working up to it all summer long. My eyes got moist.

He reached out and grabbed my board and pulled it right alongside his. "Enough," he said quietly, where only I could hear. "Tell me the truth right now. What is it? What's wrong?"

Honesty, Kali.

"Nothing's wrong, exactly. I'm not scared, if that's what you think," I attempted to explain. "Well... no, that's not true. I am scared. But what I'm scared of is..."

He waited.

Crap, this was hard.

"I'm afraid I'll disappoint you," I forced out. As expected, he opened his mouth to argue, but I interrupted him. "*Not* because I won't be good at it, Zane! I know you'd be a patient teacher. But because I know myself well enough to know that there's no way I'm going to love it like you do. I may not even like it. And I know you have this whole fantasy in your head of us surfing off into the sunset together!"

His face registered a stunned sort of shock. "I..." he began.

"Don't deny it," I said sadly. "I like to fantasize about your dancing ballet with me, too. A *pas de deux*. And we both know that's never going to happen."

He shut his open mouth. "I'd give it a try," he said weakly.

I smiled at him. "That's sweet. I may take you up on that someday. But you don't have to do everything I do. We both like other kinds of dancing."

His green eyes studied me for a long moment. "I'm sorry, Kali," he said softly. "I didn't mean to pressure you into anything. If you like surfing, great. But if you don't, you can always admire my moves from the beach."

I smirked at him. "See, you're making a joke. But it's not. I *love* admiring your moves from the beach."

His distressed look at last gave way to a smile. "Really?"

"Really," I assured.

"Well, that's a coincidence," he replied, his eyes twinkling mischievously. "Because I love admiring your ballet moves in the studio. From the other side of the waiting room window, that is."

I chuckled. Zane's occasional presence at the dance studio caused more of a stir than he knew, even — embarrassingly enough — among the dance moms. I was so amazingly lucky.

"Just give it a try, honey!" my dad called out impatiently. "You have great balance!"

"You never know how much longer I'm going to live!" Milo teased.

"It's not that hard, Kali, I swear," Tara called, paddling her way back out toward me. "I never thought I could do it!"

I huffed out a breath. I *could* do this. Zane had taught me the various stages of how to get up on the board, and I could do them all with no problem — as long as the board was flat on the ground and not moving. We had practiced them multiple times on multiple days, in fact, as opposed to Tara and Kylee, who had run through them on the beach with Makani and his buds for all of about five minutes.

So seriously, how hard could it be?

"I'm ready now," I announced to Zane.

He flashed me a brilliant smile. "Well, all right!" He helped me get my board oriented, and we waited for just the right wave. My dad and Milo waited off to the side, hoping to catch the same wave a little farther down. We did not have to wait all that long.

"Okay, this one's perfect. Get ready," Zane coached excitedly as a nice little baby wave rolled up behind us. "Okay, paddle now!" And with that, he gave the tail of my board a push.

I felt the rush of the water around me and paddled hard with my arms until I could feel the wave itself moving my board. Then I grabbed the sides of the board (Zane called them "the rails") and pulled my chest and head up into a cobra-like position.

So far, so good!

Quick as I could, I pulled my knees to my chest, then moved my left foot up and to the center. *To the center!* I wobbled just a little, but then got it right. I couldn't believe how weird it felt... When you watched a surfer it seemed like they were driving the board, but this board was running away from me!

Next step, swivel to side. I braced my feet as well as I could and did a swivel. It was an awkward crouching position, but my dancer's muscles served me well.

Now let go of the rail.

"Are you freakin' kidding me?" I yelled out loud to no one. It seemed impossible. There was no way to balance on this thing. It was moving! Dancers had good balance, yes, but a dance floor didn't move!

"Awesome! Yes! Kali, you're doing great!" That was Zane.

"Yay, Kali!" Tara.

"You can do it!" Kylee.

"That's my girl!" The Colonel.

"You got it!" Milo.

"Smokin'!" Matt.

"Woohoo!" Lacey.

I let go of the rail. The board under my feet felt like a runaway train. It rumbled and shook beneath my feet, but to my amazement, I stayed on. Two seconds, three, four. I wasn't standing straight up but I wasn't doubled over either — I was kind of crouching awkwardly and I probably looked ridiculous, but who cared? The fast, deep water was moving beneath me carrying the board, and that board was carrying me, and we were all out moving together on top of the wide and wonderful Pacific.

"Don't look now!" I heard my grandfather call gaily.

"Three generations!" my dad shouted.

I probably shouldn't have looked. But of course I did. I looked up just long enough to see the other two generations of Lam-Thompsons surfing to the near side of me. And not only did I see their proud faces beaming, I'm pretty sure I saw my mom smiling from the beach beyond.

Then I fell butt-first into the water.

It wasn't bad. It was even kind of fun. But I'd been right about myself... surfing would never be my passion. Thank goodness Zane loved me for *me*.

He paddled his surfboard up next to mine and then rolled into the ocean. I had already gotten back on my board, all by myself, and so was pretty surprised when he pulled me back off of it.

"What was that for?" I sputtered, hanging onto the rail.

"I can't kiss you up there," he explained, grabbing onto my board with one arm while sweeping me up against him under the water with the other. "And I've always wanted to kiss a surfer chick."

I grinned at him. "What if we cause another tsunami?"

His green eyes sparkled. "I have the feeling that our being together may cause all kinds of scary surprises down the road."

"Looks that way," I agreed. "You sure you're okay with that? The road, I mean. Not knowing where it leads?"

He smiled that incredibly irresistible, sexy smile of his. Then he leaned in for a kiss right in front of my whole family, all our friends, an ocean full of fish, and everybody.

"I like long drives," he answered.

about the author

USA-Today bestselling novelist and playwright Edie Claire was first published in mystery in 1999 by the New American Library division of Penguin Putnam. In 2002 she began publishing award-winning contemporary romances with Warner Books, and in 2008 two of her comedies for the stage were published by Baker's Plays (now Samuel French). In 2009 she began publishing independently, continuing her original Leigh Koslow Mystery series and adding new works of romantic women's fiction, young adult fiction, and humor.

Under the banner of Stackhouse Press, Edie has now published over 25 titles including digital, print, audio, and foreign translations. Her works are distributed worldwide, with her first contemporary romance, *Long Time Coming*, exceeding two million downloads. She has received multiple "Top Pick" designations from *Romantic Times Magazine* and received both the "Reader's Choice Award" from *Road To Romance* and the "Perfect 10 Award" from *Romance Reviews Today*.

A former veterinarian and childbirth educator, Edie is a happily married mother of three who currently resides in Pennsylvania. She enjoys gardening and wildlife-watching and dreams of becoming a snowbird.

Books & Plays by Edie Claire

Romantic Fiction

Pacific Horizons

Alaskan Dawn
Leaving Lana'i
Maui Winds
Glacier Blooming
Tofino Storm

Fated Loves

Long Time Coming
Meant To Be
Borrowed Time

Hawaiian Shadows

Wraith
Empath
Lokahi
The Warning

Leigh Koslow Mysteries

Never Buried
Never Sorry
Never Preach Past Noon
Never Kissed Goodnight
Never Tease a Siamese
Never Con a Corgi

Never Haunt a Historian
Never Thwart a Thespian
Never Steal a Cockatiel
Never Mess With Mistletoe
Never Murder a Birder
Never Nag Your Neighbor

Women's Fiction

The Mud Sisters
Soccer Mom in Galilee (as Rachel Stackhouse)

Humor

Corporately Blonde

Comedic Stage Plays

Scary Drama I
See You in Bells